PRAISE F(
Bottom of the B

T0418130

"Mills effectively examines the self-destructive thought patterns women often fall into in their quest for happiness. . . . Readers will savor Cyd's intense journey, rooting for her to navigate her trauma and emerge on the other side, ready to become a woman who 'believed she would find her way.'"

—BookLife Reviews

"*Bottom of the Breath* is an uplifting, well-paced story with a touch of humor—a great read."

—J. A. Wright, author of *Eat and Get Gas*

"Set against the grandeur of the American Southwest, this is a story of seeking—not only for answers but the physical strength and spiritual clarity needed to recover from a profound emotional blow. Populated by an eclectic cast of characters, this inspiring journey takes us to the depths of the Grand Canyon and reveals the resilience of the human heart."

—Kerry Sanders, former *Today Show* correspondent

"Are you on the hunt for a read that hits that sweet spot between heartfelt and engrossing? You've found it."

—*Los Angeles Wire*, "4 Beach Reads for Your 2025"

"I was drawn into this delightful debut novel by the promise of secrets revealed and pulled along by Jayne Mills's sprightly and approachable prose, vibrant characters, and satisfying plot surprises. Readers who enjoy multigenerational family secrets and stories of women triumphing over whatever life throws at them will devour this book."

—Alice C. Early, author of *The Moon Always Rising*

"Jayne Mills's vivid storytelling pulled me straight into Cyd's journey through the Grand Canyon and beyond, and I couldn't help but feel the magic of the place myself. With humor, heart, and deep insight, this story beautifully explores how nature, friendship, and self-discovery lead us back to what truly matters. If *Eat, Pray, Love* and *The Celestine Prophecy* had a love child, *Bottom of the Breath* would be it—in the best way possible."

—Megan Walrod, author of *It's Always Been Me*

"Using the breath as a yogic metaphor for going deeper, Jayne Mills's novel guides readers on a vision quest that starts with the trauma of divorce, runs through the Grand Canyon, and uncovers pathways to healing. A lively read that, like the breath, will hold your attention and sustain you."

—Jude Berman, author of *The Vow*,
a 2024 *Kirkus* Best Indie Book

Bottom of the Breath

Bottom
of the
Breath

A Novel

Jayne Mills

swp

SHE WRITES PRESS

Published 2025
Printed in the United States of America
Print ISBN: 978-1-64742-926-3
E-ISBN: 978-1-64742-927-0
Library of Congress Control Number: 2025905818

For information, address:
She Writes Press
1569 Solano Ave #546
Berkeley, CA 94707

Interior design by Stacey Aaronson

She Writes Press is a division of SparkPoint Studio, LLC.

For Valerie

*It seems a gigantic statement for even Nature to make all
in one mighty stone word, apprehended at once like a
burst of light—a new revelation in the life of every soul to
whom it is shown.*

—JOHN MUIR

*Your task is not to seek for love,
but merely to seek and find all the barriers within
yourself that you have built against it.*

—RUMI

Part One

Inhale

1

Tuesday, June 1, 2019
Phoenix, Arizona

Cyd Carr sits across the large desk in a leather chair. She hasn't given much thought to what might happen, which she realizes now is odd, almost irresponsible. She had been too concerned about the flight, preoccupied with the storm, to think of what questions she should be prepared to ask.

Mr. Walker, the lawyer, is younger than she surmised from their brief conversation—early fifties maybe, about her age. When she called to make the appointment, he hadn't been surprised to hear she planned to leave immediately and drive all the way from Florida. That *they* planned to drive. Maybe it was simple politeness that stopped him from asking for more information. But she was relieved that he let her off the hook as if it were a perfectly rational decision. The one to drive such a long distance. The one to outrun a hurricane.

As it turns out, she flew. Or, more accurately, they drove as far as Texas together, and then she flew on alone. She had looked for a sign, any sign, that it would be all right. Millions of people flew every day—*was it millions?* She didn't really know, but that's what she told herself as she boarded the plane, something she hadn't done in a very long time. Before the disgrace of removing your shoes. Back when people could walk you to your gate and wave goodbye as you stepped onto the jet bridge.

In the end, she resorted to half a Valium and a scolding. She told herself to get on with it already, and she had. More as a result of sheer determination and less from actual bravery. She simply had no other choice.

Mr. Walker offers her a bottle of water and looks concerned. Most of what he has said should not be upsetting to her. Certainly not the part about the money or the house—the cabin, her aunt liked to call it—but the rest of it feels almost devastating. So unexpected. As if she's just been made a fool.

The wooden box looks like the gift it is intended to be— obviously old and quite pretty with a brass lock and hinges. But what about the rest of it? What is she to think about this *news*?

He asks if she has any questions.

She simply doesn't have the mental bandwidth at the moment to think much of anything. What she really wants to do is plop her head down on the big mahogany desk. *Are you kidding me right now?* is the only question that comes to mind.

Instead, she says no, she doesn't have questions and tries to look as if she understands, though she does not. She supposes she needs time to get used to the idea. She needs time to get used to a lot of things. The list seems to be growing by the hour.

Cyd takes the box from Mr. Walker and thanks him. It is surprisingly heavy for something the size of a shoebox. The house key he has given her is tucked in the side zipper of her purse. She calls for a ride and it is already waiting by the time she takes the elevator to the first floor and uses the restroom. No sooner has the driver pulled out of the parking lot than she's decided. She doesn't even bother to ask what the fare will be. It makes no difference. She simply asks, "When we get to the hotel, will you wait while I get my things and then drive me to Sedona?"

The man's eyes meet hers in the rearview mirror.

"Sedona's over two hours away on the best day, and with this road construction—"

Cyd cuts him off. "I'll pay you for the round trip. Please."

"All right then," he mumbles, turning up the ramp and onto the highway, merging into heavy traffic. "It would be quicker later tonight. Or early tomorrow."

Cyd looks out the window at the parched landscape, so different from what she is used to. Almost alien.

"I'm in no hurry," she replies, resting her head back. She closes her eyes against the biting midday sun and adds softly, "Besides, tomorrow is guaranteed no one."

2

Four Days Earlier
Friday, May 28, 2019
Lola, Florida

Cyd walks along Water Street as the first sunlight reflects soft pink off the bay. Her stride is rhythmic and naturally long, and she is aware of the ease with which she moves, having already escaped her usual morning stiffness. She focuses on her posture as she does whenever it occurs to her. She appreciates good posture even if it can be intimidating or mistaken for snootiness—her pulled-up spine, her leveled chin. Her mother, who stood a half foot shorter, always told her tall girls should never slouch. But Cyd's good looks are her father's, and he was born as straight and regal as a royal palm.

The morning is pleasantly cool for this time of year. The day is expected to be near perfect, in fact, which is not unusual before a big storm. What *is* unusual is that this storm may hit in three days, one day prior to the actual start of hurricane season on June 1. It is called Abigail and is being compared to an unnamed storm that struck the Florida panhandle just west of this very spot on May 28, 1863. The knowledge of this even earlier hurricane gives Cyd some reassurance, though she's not sure why.

She breathes deeply, deliberately. The fresh air is mingled with a slight, fishy tartness. Several well-worn shrimp boats bob along the water's edge, their nets drooping like wilted lettuce, their crews milling about on deck with unusual seriousness. They are preparing for the journey out of Apalachicola Bay, north to the Chattahoochee or south out of St. George Sound toward Ten Thousand Islands and away from the storm's most likely path. Smaller boats have already been pulled out of the water and moved to higher ground. A few may remain moored in the bay for one more day, hoping this is another false alarm, as is often the case with hurricane forecasting along the Gulf Coast.

Turning left, she heads inland toward the small downtown and the white two-story structure with its wraparound balcony and gabled roof. The Osprey Cafe looks much as it has for the past 170 years, unpretentious and welcoming. She enters the restaurant's kitchen through the back door next to the loading docks, where crates of fresh oysters, glossy and musty-smelling, have just arrived. Boxes piled with tomatoes, sweet onions, and collards are being unloaded from the back of a local farm truck.

Nick is in his usual spot behind the long stainless-steel counter when Cyd enters. The glistening blade of his chef's knife moves with mechanical precision along the length of a carrot. A large dented pot simmers behind him—fish stew, she suspects. The clock on the shelf above his head reads 5:55 in large red numbers. Five is the number associated with freedom— if one believes in such things as numerology, which Cyd does— and five is one of her favorite numbers. Numbers are reliable truth-tellers, deliverers of order, momentary reminders that all is not random chaos. Simple little numerical oddities that pop up during the day and bigger mathematical miracles at work throughout the natural world—all of it, right there. You just had to pay attention.

"Hey, Nicky. Look at that: five fifty-five. It's going to be a good day," Cyd says, tossing her small backpack into a locker alongside the door.

"If you say so," he says flatly, glancing up as he spins to drop the carrot chunks into the pot, his biceps straining against the rolled-up sleeves of his white chef's jacket. "Why so early?"

"I woke up early, and it's a beautiful morning," Cyd answers, amping up her cheerfulness. "I slept last night for a change. These hot flashes are going to be the death of me."

"Spare me the womanly details if you don't mind. But I'm glad you're here. We have a hell of a lot of work to do. Helen's cracking the whip. She wants us to start boarding up tomorrow."

"Good morning to you, too," she says as she walks around the counter and kisses his cheek above the balmed, V-shaped beard. "We'll get it done. We always do."

Cyd pushes through the swinging door and walks into the dining room. Across the expanse of the wide-planked floor, Nick's sister, Helen, turns the bolt on the front door until it clunks. Several men are waiting outside. "Good morning," Cyd calls, grabbing a freshly pressed apron from the antique sideboard.

"Hi," Helen says, holding the door open as the men shuffle in, mumbling their greetings. "I didn't expect to see you for another hour."

"You know I can't stay away for long, and I know we have a lot to do today. Besides, Loren decided to put up our shutters at five this morning. I love my husband, but one thing he is not is quiet in the morning."

Cyd has always liked this time of morning at The O. Nearly every one of her childhood memories is intertwined with the restaurant and its owners. She practically grew up in this building, its history captured in the old black-and-white photographs that line the walls: fishermen on docks with giant hooked fish hanging in the background; horse-drawn carriages parked along Main Street; The Osprey Cafe before the Kondilis family bought it, surrounded by dirt streets and a few brick buildings. One shows the building with a line of men on the old wood porch, a few feet from where Cyd now stands, the hand-painted signage boldly advertising *MEALS at all HOURS* on one side of the front door and, on the other, *OYSTERS and COLD DRINKS*.

The upstairs balcony off the more formal dining room was one of her favorite childhood hideaways. When the restaurant was quiet, Cyd and Helen would crawl under the corner table, peering out to the water and the street below, and pretend to be princesses locked away by an evil stepmother, planning their escape. She still likes the feel of the old floorboards under her feet, worn but sturdy. Dependable. Uncomplicated.

"Let's turn on the weather forecast in Nick's office. Is Holly on this morning?" Helen asks, referring to Cyd's daughter, a meteorologist now living in Savannah.

"She is. We spoke to her last night. It looks like we'll get a ton of wind and rain even if it's not a direct hit."

"I love getting our personalized weather forecast," Helen says as she angles the wood shutters on the large east-facing windows.

The kitchen falls under Nick's domain, but the front of the house is all Helen, a role in which her calm pragmatism serves her perfectly. Nick had always planned to follow in his father's footsteps, who followed in his father's, but Helen's life plans were hijacked after their father's sudden heart attack. She had wanted to live in Greece for a year, maybe longer, after college.

Stay with family in Athens. See the world. "There has to be more," Helen had said, practically bouncing out of her flip-flops as she counted out the ticket price in cash at the travel agency.

They—Cyd and Helen—had spent four reckless, impetuous years sharing an apartment while attending Florida State University. (They both majored in hospitality, a field of study they chose almost as a joke. "Does schlepping plates of eggs count as hospitality?" they often asked each other.) Their adult lives had just begun to take shape, and they were embarking on their separate paths for the first time since childhood when Helen was suddenly called back.

While in Greece, Helen had fallen in love with a woman—fallen hard—though only Cyd was privy to that detail. "We're going to talk about this one time, sister," she had said when Cyd retrieved her from the Tallahassee airport. "It's over. That life is for someone else to live." Cyd then watched as Helen took up her family responsibilities without complaint despite the dual grief of her father's death and the loss of her first true love. Cyd herself was in love by then, too, and would return to Lola soon after, though voluntarily, with her new husband and their daughter on the way.

Within three years of returning, Helen had married Frank—sweet, reliable Frank, who had been waiting and hoping all along. And they are married still, lovingly, contentedly, as if they were always meant to be. Helen's recipe for a happy life, then and now: *Stop wanting something other than what is.* Whenever Cyd needs reminding, Helen will rattle off this versatile piece of advice with a wave of her pretty hand and, on those more serious occasions, sit her down with a platter of food, a box of tissues, and a jug of Greek table wine.

At times, like now, seeing her friend backlit by the morning light, Cyd is reminded how differently things might have turned out, and that realization always feels like she's walked through a pane of glass miraculously unscathed.

3

WEATHER REPORT:
WSVA Channel 6,
Savannah's First Alert Weather
Friday, May 28, 7:32 a.m.

ANCHOR: "Meteorologist Holly Carr is here to update us on the system that's been developing in the Caribbean. How are things shaping up at this hour, Holly?"

HOLLY: "Good morning, Bill and Natalie. We are four days out from the official start of hurricane season, but as of this morning, we are tracking the first hurricane of the season. The National Hurricane Center upgraded Abigail from a tropical storm last night, and it quickly strengthened into a Category 1 hurricane."

"We are watching a dangerous situation unfold for the Windward Islands with wind gusts up to ninety miles per hour. This satellite image shows a defined eye wall and organized convection around the center as the storm moves toward the southern coast of the Dominican Republic and Jamaica. It is expected to track north into the Gulf of Mexico. The threat to the Florida coastline is unclear, but we need to take this storm seriously. Now is the time to pull out your hurricane preparedness checklist. As we always say, don't wait until the last minute to prepare."

4

"Yo, C! Come here a minute."

Cyd traces Nick's deep voice to the walk-in refrigerator. It is late morning. The breakfast rush is over, and the staff has started prepping for lunch.

"What's up?" she asks, peering into the cavernous opening.

Nick emerges, cradling quarts of cream and bricks of butter in the crook of his sculpted arm, much as he might have held an opponent's head in one of his championship-winning wrestling moves. He still looks and moves like the wrestler he was in high school—"built like a brick shithouse," Helen says—but agile, almost graceful, like a good dancer.

"The damn dairy shipment didn't come today from McMurray's. I'll barely make it through lunch, much less dinner, on what's here. They said we can pick it up today, but we need to go to their Gulf Shores warehouse. Do you mind making a run down there?"

"Really, Nicky? Traffic will be a bitch with all the storm prep, and you know I hate driving Helen's car." Cyd realizes she is whining, but seriously, who other than Helen has a manual transmission these days?

"It's either that or my motorcycle. Take your pick," he says, walking past her to the counter.

"Are you sure there's no one else?"

She knows the answer as she asks the question. Of course, he wouldn't ask unless he really needed her help. Nick is the one person she can count on not to hassle her about her reluctance to drive, about her choice to give her car to her son, Bo, and not replace it. Two years have passed since Bo graduated and moved to Miami. It was a perfectly reasonable thing to do. Parents pass along used cars to their children all the time. So what if she never bought another one? She prefers riding her bike or walking. It's a small town. It doesn't need to *mean* anything.

"We're understaffed and have a shit ton of extra work. You're the only one I can spare, unless I let Marco go instead, and you lug shutters up to the second-floor windows." Nick's head is tilted for emphasis, his brown eyes endearingly downturned at the corners. "Come on, C. If you leave now, you'll be back in less than three hours. You're the one who told me it would be a good day. Have a nice drive along the coast. Enjoy the view. It will be your last chance to relax for the next few days."

Once she's fished the car keys from Helen's bag and traded the apron for her backpack, Cyd heads out the back door. A wind whips at her hair, and she looks up. Overhead, the sky is clear, but to the south, dark clouds are forming an ominous, distinctive ledge. Cyd walks toward the small parking lot across the back alley just as a Jeep Wrangler turns into the alleyway. The windows are down, the music is up, and a long-fingered hand taps to the beat on the side of the door.

The vehicle pulls up next to her. "Hey there, Sunshine. Where you off to so early?"

Cyd stops. Bobby smiles his signature smile, all dimples and perfect teeth, peering at her from above mirrored sunglasses. His dirty-blond hair is pushed back off his tan forehead. Cyd is certain there's not a woman in Lola who can resist going weak in the knees under the dual spotlight of his baby blues and inescapable charm. Well, maybe Helen can, but few others.

"Hey, Swanson. I'm running an errand for Nicky up to Gulf Shores. There's no one else to do it with everything going on today."

"You? Driving to Gulf Shores? Not a good idea. The roads are crazy. I'll drive you. I can get someone to make sure the bar is set up for lunch."

Bobby is arriving for his shift behind the bar in the upstairs dining room when it opens for lunch. He was an unlikely addition to The O's staff when he arrived in town five years ago on his 1956 Rybovich—a one-of-a-kind thirty-one-foot Sportfisherman—a boat that Cyd knows is revered within Lola's boating community and beyond. Bobby claims his bartending earns him "extra drinking money" and supplements the income he makes running fishing charters for tourists, but Cyd suspects Bobby likes the social aspect of being behind the bar far more than he needs the money. He says he didn't intend to stay in Lola, yet here he is, living on his boat, holding court behind the bar a few times a week, entertaining the men and charming the women with his laid-back demeanor and animated fish tales.

Cyd laughs as Bobby's captivating smile turns to concern. It is just like Bobby to think of her at a time like this. She knows full well he has his own long and essential to-do list in light of the impending storm. He needs to take extra measures to keep his boat safe. Not only is it his home but a nautical treasure. Unless something changes, he will need to move it out of harm's way very soon.

"I'll be fine. It's not like I can't drive; I just prefer not to. Besides, Nicky needs you here, and you have plenty of other stuff on your plate. I'll fill you in on all the exciting details when I get back." Cyd knows she will do precisely that. Her shifts seem half as long and twice as fun when Bobby is behind the bar, and she never tires of his company.

"Okay then. But be careful. All the crazies are out today."

Bobby pulls away slowly, and Cyd continues to Helen's car. When she turns to look over her shoulder, she sees him watching her in his side mirror, no longer tapping to the beat of the music.

Cyd jumps to turn off the heavy metal that blares when she starts the car—*Really, Helen?*—and tunes in NPR. The most direct route from Lola to the town of Gulf Shores is Highway 98, a mostly two-lane highway that covers the entire stretch of the panhandle from Alligator Point to Pensacola.

As expected, traffic is heavy, with a steady stream of vehicles going in both directions. Cyd knows it will only get worse if the storm continues its expected march toward the Gulf of Mexico. Holly's morning report had confirmed her fears. They may be in the direct path of a major hurricane.

Once in Gulf Shores, Cyd lets the warehouse workers load several boxes into the back of Helen's car, signs the receipt, then considers any personal shopping she might want to do while she's here. She considers a list of necessary supplies, though she and Loren keep a well-stocked pantry for this very purpose. While Lola is lively enough for a small town, with two decent hotels and several streets of shops and restaurants, any real shopping has to be done in Pensacola or Tallahassee. Even Gulf Shores, not much bigger than Lola, has a few chain stores that

Lola does not. *Now is the time*, she thinks, running down a mental checklist.

When she pulls up to the stop sign at Highway 98, she debates whether to turn right and go to Target or turn left and head back east to Lola. She looks down at the dashboard and checks the time: 11:11. She smiles instinctively. Catching 11:11 always brings a ping of happiness, a little flip of optimism no matter her mood. It is too perfect not to be a sign of good things to come.

A light rain starts just then, and the sky turns suddenly dark. It is too early for the outer bands of Abigail, and yet something has been stirred up, perhaps nothing more than a typical summer shower.

The last thing she will remember is cursing the stick shift as she struggles to find first gear, cringing at the grinding noise as she lets up on the clutch. She looks down at the console and up again, then pops out onto the highway, never seeing the grey BMW that blends so seamlessly with the pavement, the sky, and the dark slate water of the Gulf of Mexico.

5

Friday, May 28, 2019
Panama City, Florida

The room is cold. The shades are pulled tight, creating a false dimness. Cyd sees Helen's face floating above her, then slowly coming closer. It is the sensation of emerging from the bottom of a pool, eyes wide, vision blurred, rising. When she bursts through the surface into clarity, Helen's face is too close. Her first reaction is to raise her hand as a barrier. Why is Helen leaning over her so intently? She can't make it out.

"Hey," Helen says with uncharacteristic gentleness.

"What?" Cyd asks. This one word is all she can think to say. Her brain is sluggish. There is a pounding across her forehead. Her throat is dry, and her voice comes out hoarse.

Helen squeezes her hand, drawing Cyd's attention to a tube taped to the top of her forearm. A tremor of panic rises from deep in her belly.

"Please tell me why I'm in a hospital room."

"You don't remember anything?" Helen asks.

"No, actually, I don't." Cyd blinks, trying to relieve the pressure behind her eyes. "My head hurts."

"I'll call the doctor."

Helen reaches across Cyd's torso for the control box draped over the bed rail.

"Wait!" Cyd says sharply. "Tell me what happened."

"You were in a car accident. You have a concussion. Here, drink." Helen holds a straw to her lips.

Cyd sips. Her neck twinges. "An accident?"

"Yes, when you were pulling out onto 98 from the warehouse. You were T-boned. You're very lucky it was on the passenger side, not the driver's side. I'm sure all the numbers and stars and voodoo magic aligned in your favor, but you can analyze it later. For now, you need to rest. Let me ring for the nurse and let her know you're awake."

Cyd is used to Helen taking charge, but there is something odd in the way she rushes her words. Cyd struggles to keep up.

"Where's Loren? Is Loren here?" Cyd is certain her husband would have come immediately. She wants to see him. She wants him to know that she is all right.

"It's a miracle it wasn't worse. Someone could have been killed."

Helen's fine-boned features look strangely distorted, too large somehow. Cyd raises her head, looking down at the length of her body on the bed.

"You're okay," Helen says. "The doctor says you really are okay, but you scared the piss out of all of us."

Cyd struggles to make her brain work. "Where's Loren? Did you talk to Loren?" Was she repeating herself?

"Loren knows." Helen's hand remains on Cyd's arm, but she breaks eye contact.

"Where is he? He was staying home today. He was going to start putting up the shutters. Did you call him? What time is it?" Her thoughts come in fits and starts.

"It's four o'clock. We really should talk to the doctor. He'll want to know you're awake."

Helen starts to move, but Cyd clamps her hand over Helen's.

"What the hell does that mean?" Cyd asks, irritated by her confusion.

"It means let's wait until the doctor gets here, okay? I know patience is not your strong suit, but I really think you need to relax right now."

Cyd feels a sudden clarity. "*Have* you talked to Loren?"

"Cyd, you need to listen to me," Helen begins.

"Where's my phone?" Cyd says, leaning forward, suddenly certain about what to do, scanning the room for her backpack. The movement brings a roil to her stomach, and she lies back. "I'll call him. I don't want him to worry."

"Look, Cyd, this is going to sound . . ." She stops mid-sentence. Helen, typically as direct and succinct as a well-aimed arrow, seems to be at a genuine loss. Her eyes are locked on Cyd's as she continues. "This is not as bad as it may seem right now."

This one moment of hesitation tells Cyd everything. "What the fuck is going on, Helen?"

There is stillness then. A background hum fills the void. Muffled noises fade in and out on the other side of the door.

"Loren was not putting up the shutters." The bland words do not match the seriousness with which they are spoken. "He was a passenger in the car that hit you. He wasn't hurt, thank God for that, but the thing is, apparently, a woman was driving the car."

Cyd's brain thumps against the inside of her skull. "What? What does that mean?"

"They were . . ." Helen begins again, speaking softly. She is stroking Cyd's arm. "They were together. Loren was with a woman."

Cyd tries to focus as the room tilts. She struggles to find a thread of sense in what she has just heard. The pressure behind her eyes is blinding. A wave of nausea forms. She tries to swallow the sensation. "Who? What woman? What are you talking about?"

"I have questions, too. We all do. We're just relieved no one was seriously hurt. That's what's important, Cyd. You're going to be okay."

Cyd examines a thick strand of dark hair that has fallen over Helen's high-set cheekbone. It is black and silky and lying across the smooth skin. It is a dark slash across the lovely face that Cyd has looked at nearly every day of her life. Her vision begins to narrow. She searches the familiar onyx eyes. A ringing takes hold in her ears.

"Loren was with a woman? Today? I don't understand."

The room is spinning now. Her focus blurs. She closes her eyes as a sickly whirl twists her insides.

Loren was in the other car? In Gulf Shores? How? Why?

She wants to speak but feels as if she is sinking into a cool, dark pool. No words come. Her thoughts surface in confusing snippets, and she can no longer muster the effort to open her eyes.

She hears Helen speaking authoritatively from the doorway. Then, a nurse is there. She is asking Cyd to open her mouth. She is taking her temperature.

There must be some mistake. I need to talk to Loren.

The whirling takes over.

Now, there is a doctor. He tells her that her scans are clear. He asks questions, and she answers. He shines a light in one eye and then the other. There is talk of fluids and commotion around the bags hanging from the pole beside her bed. She is so tired. She closes her eyes.

When she opens them again, the room is quiet. The doctor and the nurse are gone.

"Helen?" She blinks, unsure how much time has passed.

"I'm here, sister. I'm right here."

"Helen? I don't understand. I thought we were . . . I thought he was . . ." She wants to say more, but the words escape her.

"It's going to be okay. I promise. I'm staying right here, and it's all going to be okay."

Cyd struggles to push against the oncoming darkness, but she has no strength. Helen is whispering close to her ear. The words are soothing but distant and nonsensical. Cyd is slipping into the darkness, falling into a beautiful, merciful darkness.

6

The voices coming from near the door are hushed. She can see Helen's back blocking the doorway.

"You were supposed to be preparing for a hurricane," Helen hisses. "How could you do this? What the hell is wrong with you?"

"I'm not going to upset her, Helen. I need to see her. I just want to see her."

"You are a despicable piece of—"

"I can hear you guys," Cyd interrupts.

Both Helen and Loren are at her side in an instant. Loren's T-shirt is wrinkled, and there is a smear of red-brown across the front. It is not the shirt he had on when she kissed him goodbye that morning. A small bandage is angled just above his right eyebrow.

"Hi," he says. His smile is meek and frantic. He appears taller than usual or somehow stretched out. Cyd tilts her head as if looking at a distorted television screen. He starts to reach for her but instead grips the guardrail.

"How do you feel?" Helen holds up the big pink cup and presses the button to raise the back of the bed. "Here, drink."

"I feel better," Cyd answers. The pounding headache is almost gone. The ringing has stopped. "You can leave us, Helen. It's okay."

"I'll be right outside the door." Helen glares at Loren. "I'll let the nurse know you're awake."

"Cyd, thank God you're all right. Thank God," Loren stammers as soon as the door closes.

He pulls up a hard plastic chair. His face is close. She can smell stale sweat.

"Have you called Holly? Have you spoken to Bo?" Cyd tries to pull herself upright with an awkward effort. Her neck twangs. "I don't want them to worry. Maybe they don't even need to know. Maybe it's better if they don't know anything."

"Take it easy, please. I spoke to both of them. I told them some. Not everything. Listen, Cyd, I want to explain. I want to try—" His voice breaks. He looks down at clasped hands.

Cyd wants to reach for him but stops herself. This version of Loren is confusing to her: disheveled, pleading, off-balance. She wants him to stop this. She wants him to straighten himself and fix his hair and take her home.

Helen's voice reverberates in her head. *Loren was with a woman.*

"All right, Loren," she says with unplanned coolness as if reading from a script. "Explain."

Loren begins speaking. His voice is tentative, absent his usual authority and self-confidence. Cyd often thought Loren could have played a mobster in *The Godfather* movies with all his handsome Italian machismo. Carrato was the true family surname, shortened and Americanized by his grandfather. It was one of the things she and Loren had in common—their Italian ancestry—though Cyd's came from only her mother's side. As he speaks, Cyd feels an acute bodily separation, as if watching the scene unfold from afar. She studies her husband as if he were a zoo animal and she is wondering what he will do next, what sound will come out next.

What comes out is something *less than*—less than what she would have expected had someone told her in advance that her carefully polished husband would confess the messy circumstances surrounding his being in a car with another woman. The Loren she knows—or thought she knew—would have been tending to his home and his property, checking on his beloved boat that sits on the lift alongside the dock, the very dock they had built over twenty-five years ago when they first bought the charming little cottage on the bay. These are things he wants to protect, things he has worked hard for—that *they* have worked hard for. These are the things that are important to him.

But he was not at home doing any of that; he is telling her as much. She is listening and watching, mesmerized by his performance. As he speaks, she realizes she is expecting more from him on the most basic level. She is expecting a minimal level of respect for her intelligence. He usually doesn't underestimate her *this* badly. The story he is telling is one of recklessness, but her husband is not reckless. He's a CPA, for Chrissake. Planning and execution are part of his DNA. It's as if he couldn't be bothered to make more of an effort, and that is not like him. Loren does not half-ass things. Who *is* this man?

The story that emerges is haphazard, disorganized, and confusing. Cyd cannot tell if it's her fog-filled head or if he's really not making any sense. Today is the day in which every other resident of Lola has begun bracing for a historic hurricane, and this is the day her husband chooses to meet *who?* To get into her car and go *where?* And cover it up *how?* What had he intended to say when Cyd came home and saw that nothing had been done because he had been off doing *what* exactly? What had he planned to say then?

It was just something that happened, he tells her by way of a general explanation. He knows it sounds cliché, he pleads oh-so-sincerely, but he didn't plan it. "It just happened," he repeats. It hadn't been going on for long, only a few weeks, he swears. He was going to break it off. That very morning, he had gone to break things off. He was ending it. He loves his wife. "You know I love you." He will make it up to her. "I will spend the rest of my life making it up to you." Tears pool inside the lower edge of his eyes. He leans in close. She has to believe him. He loves her. He loves their children. He would never do anything to hurt them. It's over. "I swear it's over." She has to forgive him. She has to.

He drops his face into his palms.

She waits. Is he finished? Is that it? That can't be it.

He looks up expectantly. He watches her as if waiting for her to swallow what he has dished out. She is used to his force-feeding her. He is always the one who knows better. He is willing his words to travel the few inches between them and take hold of her, to shake her into compliance. She knows this about him. She has heard this story before.

His knee bounces up and down frantically as if it has gone haywire. He rubs the length of his thighs. Cyd feels strangely unmoved but also enlightened, as if a fog is lifting and she can see clearly for the first time what is right in front of her.

He has stopped talking, she realizes. He lifts his head and looks at her. She has listened to him. She has heard what he came to say. It is dizzying. Her entire head throbs.

Just then, the door opens. A tray is set in front of her. Helen is back, adjusting the bed and telling her to eat. Loren leans over, kisses the top of her head, and then he is gone.

Cyd looks down at the tray and up at Helen and vomits all over the meatloaf.

7

Helen has things cleaned up with her usual efficiency and is talking as she moves around the small room, out to the hallway, and back.

"I asked Annie to go to your house and pick up some things for tonight," Helen says. Apparently, their good friend, Annie, had called more than once, checking on Cyd, wanting to help. "You were sleeping when she was here, and we didn't want to wake you. They're on their way to the airport. She and Tony are catching a flight out tonight."

Lola is a second home to Annie and her husband, Tony. They decided to ride out the storm from the safety of their house in Pittsburgh. They must have gotten the last seats out of town, Helen explains.

"She left this." Helen hands Cyd an envelope. "Annie took in your mail while she was at the house. It's addressed to you and it looks important, so she brought it with her."

Cyd takes the letter and reads the return address: *Ackerman and Walker, Attorneys at Law*, and an address in Phoenix.

"I have no idea," Cyd comments.

She unfolds the letter and reads to herself:

Dear Mrs. Carr,

I am writing as Executor for the Estate of Mary Jane
Williams-Grant. You are a named beneficiary in Mrs.
Grant's estate plan. Her trust was structured so that
should you survive her children and any issue, you would
inherit a portion of the remainder estate. With the recent
death of her last issue, I am now distributing the estate
assets in accordance with the terms of Mrs. Grant's trust.

Mrs. Grant left a letter that I have been instructed to give
to you in person, along with items of a personal and con-
fidential nature.

I understand that traveling to Phoenix may be burden-
some. However, your aunt was clear in her instructions
that I see you in person. If you are physically unable to
travel, other arrangements may be made upon receipt of
proof of such incapacity.

Please contact my office at your earliest convenience to
discuss your options in this matter. I look forward to
speaking with you soon.

Sincerely,
Jonathon Walker, Esq.

"Well?" Helen is watching her.

Cyd holds the letter out and waits as Helen reads. She
hasn't thought about Aunt Mae in years. Mae was her father's
younger sister, his favorite sibling. When Cyd was in grade
school, Mae lived outside Atlanta with her husband, Peter, and
their only son, Andrew, who was slightly older than Cyd. Her

parents took Cyd and her older brother, Baker, to visit Mae occasionally. The details of these visits are vague, but the impression they left are as tangible as a scar. The house was a modern ranch with a screened pool and hot tub. There were no such houses in Lola. Cyd and Baker played in the pool for hours. Their cousin must have been there, too, but Cyd can't picture him. Her parents—Jesse and Iris—along with Mae and Peter, and often neighbors, too, would sit poolside, drinking out of pretty glasses—they called the drinks "highballs," which struck Cyd and Baker as hilarious. Memories of Mae herself are clearer: flowing, sleeveless dresses, stylishly short hair; Mae telling jokes, everyone laughing in response; Mae smoking cigarettes smudged red from lipstick, crushing them into full ashtrays. As the memories surface, Cyd hears Mae's slight Southern accent, her voice laced with an elegant musicality.

"Well, look at you." Mae would hold Cyd by the shoulders and study her. "Aren't you the prettiest thing?" It sounded like *thang* and made Cyd beam.

Once, when she was twelve, Cyd spent the weekend at Mae's without her parents. That first night, Mae led Cyd into her bedroom and sat her at a small desk with a mirror—a dressing table, Mae called it. She let Cyd sit on the cushioned bench and sniff perfume bottles while she spoke from the recesses of her room-sized closet. Cyd had never seen such a closet. Mae let her try clip-on earrings. "Here you go, darlin'. Try these. Oh, yes. Those look real pretty on you." She brushed Cyd's hair and pinned it with a dozen bobby pins. "It's called a French twist," Mae said, handing Cyd a mirror so she could see the neat blond roll. Mae's house and everything in it seemed as elegant and exotic as she was, so unlike their little house in Lola with its homemade kitchen curtains and worn furniture.

When Cyd's parents picked her up that Sunday night, Cyd waited for Mae to invite her to come again. Mae hugged her and took her face in her hands. She told her she loved having her and that she was a beautiful young lady. She hugged Cyd's parents in turn, first Jesse, tightly and for several beats, then Iris. Cyd saw her mother stiffen slightly as she returned Mae's brief embrace. Then Mae stepped back and took her place next to her husband who held the door open, smiling. Mae said nothing more.

Cyd saw Mae one last time, a few months after that visit to Atlanta, at her father's funeral. Mae was nearly unrecognizable, dressed entirely in black with dark glasses and hair pulled back so tightly it must have hurt. She let Cyd sit close to her on the sofa as the crowd from the cemetery clustered around the food-laden table. Mae's posture was rigid, and she looked straight ahead as if moving might cause her to crack.

A few years after Jesse's death, her mother mentioned in passing that Aunt Mae and Uncle Peter had moved to Arizona. Andrew was in a facility of some sort, she said. Drugs, apparently. It seems strange to Cyd in retrospect that she never questioned why Mae had disappeared from their lives. After her father died, Cyd's world had changed so completely that Mae's disappearance from it went almost unnoticed.

It was many years later, while Cyd was helping her mother with her mail, that a letter arrived from Jesse's older sister, Lucy. Mae had been sick for some time, the letter informed them, but in the end, she died quite suddenly. It seemed to Cyd a sad, almost dreadful end to such a vibrant woman. The thought depresses her even now, as she leans against the upright hospital bed.

"Well!" Helen repeats with enthusiasm. "This has to be good

news. She's left you something in her will. It's all that good karma you're always talking about."

"I don't know about that. I don't feel particularly lucky right now." Cyd gestures to the hospital room. "And it's strange, the timing. Why now? Mae's been dead for years. I guess this means Andrew died. What else could it mean?"

Helen's eyes are lit with excitement. "I think you're getting some money. This is great. I mean, it's not great that your cousin died, but otherwise, it is. Andrew always was a weird kid. Baker could engage him. I mean, Baker was so much fun he could engage a rock. But Andrew always seemed off to me. He had shifty eyes."

Cyd looks again at the letter. "Did you notice it says 'children' not 'child' and 'the last issue'? It sounds like there was more than one child, but as far as I know, there were no grandkids. Andrew never married."

"Mae stopped coming around after your dad died, didn't she?" Helen asks.

Helen's memory of their childhood days was legendary. Apparently, all the pot they smoked in college did not affect Helen the same way it did Cyd, for whom entire years were a bit hazy. Even Cyd's early childhood memories often needed prodding to come into focus. *Remember when*, Helen would prompt at the start of a story as Cyd shook her head, *No, I don't remember that.* Only after a persistent stream of Helen's descriptives would the scene come into focus. Cyd has always relied on Helen to be the official recordkeeper of their shared memories. Loren, too, would get exasperated with Cyd. *You need to get your head out of the clouds*, he would tell her. Maybe she was too busy looking up all the time, watching for signs from the heavens. Look where *that* habit had landed her: in a hospital bed with a concussion and a cheating husband. She certainly didn't see *this* coming.

Helen continues, "We could never figure out why your mom was so weird about Mae. We thought she was so cool, like a movie star."

"I never knew why, but my mom didn't like her. Something was off between them. Mom was always kind of bitchy-acting toward her."

"Imagine that!" Helen laughs. "Iris being bitchy!"

Cyd's mother was many things, but warm and fuzzy was not in the mix.

"I asked my mom once, after we heard that Mae had died, why she hadn't kept in touch with her. Mom said, 'Your aunt lived a very interesting life. She and I were different. We lost touch, that's all.' She was very vague about it."

Helen adds, "You were never in touch with any of your dad's family."

"My dad told me that of the six kids, only he and Mae wanted to leave the farm where they grew up. They wanted out of the country, away from that type of life. They were the adventurous ones. All the rest stayed in Virginia. I don't think my mom had anything in common with them. She was more of a city girl. She never made an effort."

"I wonder why you have to go all the way out to Arizona," Helen ponders. "I don't think that's very typical. What could the guy have to give you? I wonder if this means it's a lot of money. Wouldn't that be something? You might be rich!"

"Let's not get ahead of ourselves. I need to get out of here first." Cyd motions again to the bed and the room. "Let's not forget that small detail."

Helen ignores her. "What are you going to do differently?

Are you going to be like one of those people you see on TV who wins the lottery and the first thing they do is tell their boss to kiss off?!"

"For sure," Cyd says. "Kiss off, Helen."

From their first day of kindergarten—when Cyd spotted the mysterious-looking girl with dark, delicate features so unlike her own—she was infatuated. Many of the other children were crying or clinging to their mother's legs, and Cyd wasn't sure what to make of the scene. Then she saw Helen sitting against the wall on the far side of the room, calm, uninterested in the commotion. Cyd left her mother, plopped down on the floor, and picked up Helen's hand. They like to say they've gone through life side-by-side ever since.

"Seriously, Helen. What the hell am I going to do?"

Helen narrows her eyes as if considering something. "You've always wanted to go to the Grand Canyon. It's not far from Phoenix. You could plan a vacation, stay out West for a while, do some sightseeing. You've been staring at that old picture of your dad for, what, like forever? How many times have you said you wanted to go there because you know he loved it? This is your chance. It could be fun." Helen is clearly straining for optimism.

It's true. Cyd has kept an old photograph of her dad taken somewhere in the Grand Canyon, and she did intend to go someday. But now? Under these circumstances? Cyd searches her friend's face as the gravity of the situation settles around them.

"You're going to be okay," Helen says, squeezing Cyd's hand. "We're going to get you feeling better. The doctor says you can go tomorrow." She hesitates. "Unless you want to stay. Do you want to stay and hide out for a few days? I can probably get them to approve that."

Cyd cuts her off. "No. I don't want to stay. I mean, I don't want to go, but I don't want to stay either. I can't fucking believe this is happening, Helen! Can you? Seriously? Can you believe this fucking bullshit?"

Both women know Cyd tends to cuss when she's angry or upset, *like a drunken sailor,* as Helen puts it. Cyd stops herself and looks at Helen again, and they both let out a little burst of laughter.

"Do you want to keep going?" Helen asks, sitting back and crossing her arms. "Feel free. I have time."

Cyd sighs. "Thanks, but no. I'm good."

They fall silent, looking out the window at a squirrel on a palm tree.

"I really believed we had put this kind of thing behind us. I trusted him, Helen. I *needed* to trust him."

"Stop it. Stop it right now. I will not allow you to second-guess yourself. You did nothing wrong. Loren is an asshole, that's all."

"So let's just say I want to get to Phoenix sooner rather than later," Cyd begins, thinking aloud. "I don't suppose you'll drop everything and drive me. It looks like I'll have to wait until the storm passes . . . just go home with Loren and wait. The thought of it makes me sick."

"What is it you like to say—where there's a will, there's a way? The doctor says you can leave tomorrow. We'll figure out a way to get you to Phoenix. I have every confidence. We always figure things out."

"More like you always figure things out, and I tag along," Cyd adds, suddenly tired again.

8

Baker and Cyd were in the back of the big Buick sedan. Their mother sat with a map outstretched on her lap, Cyd knew, because she heard the paper rustling and her mom talking about turn-offs and mileage. Her father wore sunglasses that made him look like Cary Grant. Cyd liked to watch Cary Grant movies. They came on late, after the news, and on the weekends she was allowed to stay up. She usually fell asleep before the end and woke when her mom clicked off the television, but she saw enough to know what Cary Grant looked like in dark glasses. Very cool and very handsome, much like her father.

Baker was stretched across the entire back seat with his head propped on his bed pillow. He, too, looked like something out of a movie—Frankie Avalon on a beach chair, maybe. Sunlight filled the car, and everyone was in a good mood.

Cyd had made up her spot on the floor between the front and back seats like a bed. This was her special space whenever they went on a family road trip. Her father's car, like everything he possessed, was impeccably cared for. His children were taught early to respect their father's things, especially his car—always bought new, always paid for in cash. It was the ultimate luxury, a luxury he had only dreamed of as a child.

Cyd had spread a blanket on the floor behind the passenger seat and situated her pillow opposite Baker's. She arranged herself perfectly with her knees bent over the hump in the middle of the floor. She didn't mind that her only view was that of the blue sky through the side window, part of her brother's face behind his comic book, and her father's neatly combed hair under the temple of the dark glasses.

Baker ignored her, but her father turned momentarily and looked over the low seat into her eager face. He smiled and gave her a little wink. It was the last thing she saw before she heard the screech of tires. Her father's sunglasses flew from his head as his neck snapped forward and he was hurled toward the windshield.

She jerks awake, gasping for air. The room is empty. There is a tapping. She wonders how long she's been sleeping. The tapping sounds again.

"Come in," Cyd says, pushing down the dream, grateful for the distraction.

"Hey, Sunshine."

Bobby's face peers tentatively around the corner. He is holding a huge bouquet of flowers wrapped in paper.

"Swanson! You didn't need to come all the way out here. I know you're up to your eyeballs with hurricane prep."

Bobby looks around the room as if to assess the situation. His eyes find hers, and relief smooths his features. His presence settles her immediately.

"I'm okay. Really, I am," she says, almost laughing, feeling the need to convince him.

"I wasn't going to come, but I had to save these flowers."

"Did you now?" she says, playing along.

"The florist was boarding up early, and these needed a good home, and since I didn't have anyone else to give them to, I just thought I'd come by and say hello, you know, since I was in the neighborhood." His dimples appear momentarily beneath a short stubble of whiskers as he teases her. He looks around the room again, then lays the bouquet on the table next to her bed.

Cyd can't help but be moved by his thoughtfulness and his obvious discomfort. "I didn't realize you considered thirty miles down the road to be in the neighborhood. How lucky for me." She admires the flowers. "They're lovely. Thank you, Bobby. You shouldn't have."

"You gave us all quite a scare. Good job with that."

"I was craving some attention. You know I have needs."

"Next time you're feeling neglected, how about we settle for one of my famous neck massages or two-for-one margaritas? Let's pass on the near-death experiences."

"It was a shit show all right. I suppose you heard all the gory details."

She wasn't sure she should discuss Loren's behavior with Bobby, but they talked about almost everything—especially her feelings. What man wanted to talk about feelings? That's what was special about him, why she liked him so much. She didn't want to stop confiding in him now.

"I heard. I'm sorry, Cyd. I really am."

"I'm not sure what to do next. My head won't let me think too hard about anything right now."

"Then don't think. Helen said she's springing you tomorrow. You'll have plenty of time to figure it out. Let's just get you feeling better."

"I want to go to Phoenix."

"Say what?"

She hands him the letter and waits, holding the bouquet to her face, inhaling the freshness while he reads.

"Damn. This could be big. No wonder you want to go."

"I can't sit around here and think about what's happened, what's *been* happening right under my nose for God knows how long. Honestly, I feel pretty stupid right now. I didn't have a clue. Never caught a whiff."

"Why don't you go a little harder on yourself? Really let it rip."

One of the things Cyd loves most about Bobby, about their conversations, is his ability to keep her from taking herself too seriously. She considers what to say next.

"Do you want to drive me to Phoenix?" she asks, suspecting the answer she wants to hear is the same answer he wants to give.

"Yes," he says, without so much as a breath of hesitation.

He holds her gaze. His eyes are the color of the bay on a clear day. His rugged, angular face is worn from excessive exposure to sun and salt air.

"But," she prompts, knowing there's more.

"You know I can't leave now. I have to move my boat. They need me at the marina, not to mention The O. Can it wait?"

"Yes, it can. But I don't think *I* can. I need to go, Swanson. I need to move. I can't go home and lock myself in the house with Loren. And I don't want to go to Helen's. I just don't think I can sit still, you know? Of course, you do. That's why you spend half your life on a boat. I'm beginning to understand what that's about."

"Yeah, I do know. But you're hardly what I would call a

world traveler. I don't think you've left Lola since I've known you, other than to see Holly in Savannah."

Bobby knew her well. She was content to stay home. She and Loren used to take road trips when Holly and Bo were young, but she'd always been prone to motion sickness. Then, during Baker's illness, Cyd had been his primary support system. He was in and out of the hospital for three years. She couldn't have traveled if she wanted to. Then, immediately afterward, her mother needed her almost constantly, the decline in her health rapid and shockingly indiscriminate, most certainly exacerbated by stress and grief. First, random falls. Then, broken bones. Finally, trouble walking and the loss of fine motor skills, like holding a fork. Her mother was reduced to sitting in a special recliner or a wheelchair, watching game shows and praying the rosary.

Though two years had passed since her mother's death, Bobby was right. She'd gone nowhere. "This is different. I think it's a sign. The letter came today of all days," Cyd says thoughtfully, seriously.

"We know you can't ignore a good sign."

She smiles. "I feel bad leaving Nicky and Helen, though. They need my help."

"I don't know how they'll manage without you, but after seventy-five years, they can't throw in the towel now."

"Very funny."

She's smiling again. Bobby always manages to lighten the mood, just as Baker always had. Bobby's presence in her life, his friendship, has helped fill the void left by Baker's death, helped her cope. In many ways, he has rescued her.

Bobby continues thoughtfully, "A change of scenery might be just what the doctor ordered. The O isn't going anywhere, not in our lifetime anyway, and neither is Lola, hurricane or not. It will be right here waiting for you when you get back."

"It may be waiting, but I already know it will never be the same."

"Since when is the same so great?" he asks. There is an intensity behind the words. It catches in his voice.

Cyd studies him. His lips are full and impossibly rosy against a sliver of white enamel. He seems on the verge of saying more, but he doesn't.

"I think I need to do this," she says, her eyes locked on his.

"I think so, too."

Cyd feels an overwhelming urge to weep, over nothing and everything. She drops her eyes, steadying her breath. She almost flinches when he takes her hand in his.

"Listen, Sunshine, I just wanted to say that when I heard what happened they said you were okay but—"

The click of the door latch startles Cyd, and she reflexively pulls her hand from his.

Loren is there glaring at them, still in his wrinkled, stained shirt, his usually groomed hair sticking out around his ears.

What the fuck, Loren?

"Bobby," Loren says flatly as a greeting.

Bobby stands. "Loren, hey man. I just wanted to come by and check on her. I'm glad you're both okay."

"We're fine. You need to rest, Cyd. The doctor said," Loren starts.

"I was just leaving," Bobby says, taking a step back.

"Thanks for coming by, Swanson. Thanks for the flowers," Cyd says, trying to steal one more look, but Bobby is moving toward the door.

"You got it. Take care of yourself, Cyd. See you, Loren."

And before she can say anything more, the door swings closed behind him.

9

WEATHER REPORT:
WSVA Channel 6,
Savannah's First Alert Weather
Saturday, May 29, 7:05 a.m.

ANCHOR: "Meteorologist Holly Carr joins us from the weather center this morning to update us on an increasingly dangerous hurricane."

HOLLY: "That's right, Bill. Hurricane Abigail continues to gain strength as it tracks north and west toward Cuba. This storm is spinning over very warm water, which is providing perfect conditions for it to continue to strengthen. It is forecast to reach Category 2 status before impacting land again. Hurricane-force winds expand out eighty miles from the storm's center, and we are expecting a dangerous storm surge. Florida residents and businesses all along the West Coast are urged to heed their local warnings and complete their preparations as soon as possible."

10

Saturday, May 29, 2019
Panama City, Florida

The next morning, as a tray is set in front of her and
Cyd realizes she is starving, her cell phone rings. She
has already spoken with Holly and Bo and assured
them she is ready to go home. Everyone agrees it's best for her
to be discharged today to avoid any risk of having to ride out
the storm in the hospital. Every test and scan is clear, and
though she is sore and still a bit foggy-headed, she is anxious to
escape the confines of the room. She is told she needs to take it
easy for a few days, not too much exertion, not too much—how
did the doctor put it?—mental concentration.

This time, it is Annie calling.

"Darling," she says, nearly breathless with concern. "I am so
sorry I missed you yesterday. We didn't want to wake you. I'm
sure Helen told you, Tony and I flew back to Pittsburgh last
night. How are you feeling? I've been frantic with worry."

Annie and Tony bought a second home in Lola ten years
ago when Annie, an artist and a purveyor of all things beautiful,

decided to open an upscale gift shop around the corner from The Osprey. Though she's lived in the States for decades, she's English through and through. The women became fast friends when they met in a yoga class. Annie whispered one sentence to Cyd in the middle of a particularly challenging stretch—*We must stay bendy, darling*—and with that, turned Cyd into one of her most ardent fans.

Cyd tries to reassure her friend. "Worry is wasted energy, and I'm fine, really. I know how lucky I am," she says, then catches herself and adds, "How lucky *we* are."

"That's very big of you. I thought you might wish him dead after what he's done, the bastard."

"Part of me does," Cyd admits. "After twenty years of yoga classes, I should probably be better at nonattachment and opening my compassionate heart and all that enlightenment crap we're always striving for. Instead, I'm so angry I could rip Loren's head right off his brawny shoulders."

"Don't be too hard on yourself, darling. That's why we call it a practice," Annie says. "It would take two lifetimes of study and the compassion of Buddha to be okay with this. It's simply vile, what he's done."

"Thanks. And thanks for going by the house and bringing my things. Have you heard the latest? About the letter?" Cyd asks.

"Yes," Annie says, conspiratorially. "Helen told me. Quite exciting, isn't it?"

"I suppose. And I guess I need to tell Loren about it."

"Do you?"

"If I want to get to Phoenix, I think I do. The letter says I need to be there in person. I don't know what to think about any of it. The funny thing is, the doctor tells me that's one thing

I shouldn't do right now—try to think too much. Can you imagine? If he only knew."

"I'm so sorry you have to go through this," Annie says.

"I'm sorry I have to go through it, too."

"Listen, darling, there's something I need to tell you. As soon as I heard about the *situation*," she emphasizes this last word, "I remembered something from a few months ago. It came back to me when I heard about what Loren's been up to. It bothered me at the time, and now it makes sense."

"What is it?" Cyd has been out of bed all morning. Now, she begins to pace.

"I've been buying some pottery for the shop from a woman who winters on the island," Annie begins, referring to the barrier island not far from Lola. "She makes gorgeous glazed stoneware. You might remember it, that blue collection with the swirls."

In addition to showcasing her own art—custom, hand-stamped stationery made from the finest ink and papers—Annie's shop is known for carrying an eclectic collection of well-curated, handmade wares. Cyd immediately remembers the stoneware Annie is referring to. She had actually admired it.

"Yes, I know it. I almost bought a piece. Don't tell me."

"I'm telling you, it's *her*," Annie says in a near whisper. "Her name is Mila Menendez. I got to know her when she came in one day, about six months ago, just before the holidays. Her work is fabulous, as you know. I've been carrying it ever since."

"So that's just a coincidence? That you know this woman, this Mila?"

"We have a mutual friend, a woman called Susan. You don't know her. Susan rang me when she heard about the accident, to let me know that Mila wasn't badly hurt, but also to share a bit of gossip that she was with a man when it happened—*not* her husband. Too much of a coincidence. As she's talking, I'm thinking, bloody hell, it's Loren! Then, I remembered what I saw a few months ago. I realize why it stayed with me, why it struck me as odd at the time."

"What? What did you see?" Cyd sits, feeling weak. She's not sure if she'd rather know every detail or nothing at all.

"It's not so much what I saw, really. It's more the feeling I got. Mila and Loren were talking one day out in the alley next to the store. I didn't realize they knew each other, but it was more than that. Something in the way they were standing. It just seemed off. I chalked it up to my imagination but thinking back, there was an intimacy about it. That's why I noticed it. It was as if they wanted to be closer. As if they wanted to be touching each other."

"So you think it was going on then? When was that?"

"It was around the end of January. I remember because I was getting my Valentine's Day things from the storage room. I saw them through the back window."

"The end of January!" Cyd practically screams, rising to her feet. "It's the end of May! That fucker told me it had only been going on for a few weeks!"

Cyd is pacing again. Yesterday's nausea is replaced by a roil of fury directed at her husband.

"Oh, Cyd, darling! I hate to be the one to tell you, but I felt you would want to know. Now I'm thinking I've made a mistake. I should have waited. I've upset you."

"Damn it, Annie. What am I going to do?" Cyd drops into the chair, defeated.

"How I wish I was there with you! We could crawl on the big bed and watch old movies for a week." Annie has a beautiful hundred-year-old farmhouse and a spectacularly renovated bedroom, one of Cyd's favorite rooms anywhere.

"I'd let you drive me to Phoenix if you were here. I need to get my butt to Arizona and see what my Aunt Mae has left for me. You had a feeling about Loren, and I have a feeling about this. All the signs are telling me to go. I need to get out of here now, before this storm hits. They probably want us to evacuate anyway. Does that sound crazy?"

"It sounds a little crazy, but when your life goes tits up, maybe a little crazy is exactly what you need."

"That's it, Annie. I'll answer crazy with crazier!" Cyd exclaims, but the rush of enthusiasm leaves as quickly as it came. "Otherwise, Loren will have succeeded in taking something from me. Something precious. Something that I'll never get back."

11

Saturday, May 29, 2019
Lola, Florida

"I want to go to church," Cyd announces as soon as Loren has helped her into his truck.

"Church? Now?" He shoots her a sideways glance, and she can tell he wants to ask more. He's right to be confused. She doesn't normally go to regular weekly Mass anymore. Not unless they're visiting Loren's parents on a Sunday. Not since her mother died.

"Yes. Church, now. I can make the five o'clock Mass."

"Look, Cyd," he starts, then changes course. "Okay, I'll go with you."

"No, Loren, you won't. Go down to St. John's if you want to go to Mass, although the walls might start shaking when you walk in. But you are *not* walking into *my* church with me. Not today."

"Okay. Take it easy," he says. "If that's what you want, I'll come back to get you in an hour."

Loren had insisted on picking Cyd up from the hospital.

Helen reluctantly agreed, but only because her to-do list at The O had grown exponentially longer since the accident the previous morning, and she simply had to get back to the restaurant. It was Saturday, with the storm expected to come ashore sometime on Monday. Cyd had assured her she understood. "Go do what you need to do. I'll be fine."

Helen couldn't argue. The news about the hurricane had become more ominous over the past thirty-six hours. Cyd had steeled herself against the very strong desire to ask for a divorce on the spot and instead let Loren take her out of the hospital and into his truck.

Mass is about to start when Cyd walks in. The church is barely a third full. It is out of season in Florida, and the snowbirds have returned north for the summer. Cyd crosses herself as she genuflects at the edge of the pew, then rises with what feels like the agility of a ninety-year-old. Clearly, the impact of the airbag—of an entire car—has left its mark on her body as well as her psyche.

She nods to the couple at the far end of the pew and steps in from the side aisle. She lowers herself onto the kneeler and bows her head.

Hail Mary, full of grace, the Lord is with thee.

The next two sentences, the end of the prayer, flow through her consciousness as naturally as a sigh. It is her favorite prayer, a prayer to a mother.

She sits back in the pew. Another prayer, one from her childhood, comes to mind: *This is the day the Lord has made. Let us rejoice and be glad.*

She used to recite this Psalm to her children as she squeezed their small feet through the blanket to wake them for school. She followed it with *time to rise and shine*, imitating what her father used to say to wake her, only he always added a deep *ribbit, ribbit*, his imitation of a frog, as he tickled her toes.

The congregation stands for the opening hymn as the priest and the attendants walk solemnly toward the altar, hands in prayer.

Amen.

As a young girl, Cyd's attendance at Sunday Mass with her mother was nonnegotiable, but she rarely minded. She liked how the day was suspended for one hour, and she was transported in time, hovering between the ancient past and a mystical eternity. Even when she didn't want to go—and there were those mornings, too—she always found comfort in the ritual and felt better when it was over. It may be the persistent ache behind her eyes or the strong desire to scream in anger, but she feels no such comfort now. Her desire to be away from Loren has brought her here. She needs time to think, to be alone, and there's nowhere else to go. She closes her eyes.

. . . in my thoughts and in my words, in what I have done and in what I have failed to do . . .

As a child, her chest would rise with the first burst of organ chords as if a great breath had been blown into her. She would turn to see the small group gathered in formation at the back of the nave, ready to begin their slow march, the heavy-looking gold cross lifted high, and the vibrations from the immense pipes electrifying her entire body. The language never failed to move her. It was all so poetic and strange: *Glory be to God! Alleluia! The Lord, the Giver of Life. The Body of Christ.* So big. So unimaginable. So glorious.

Lord have mercy.

There was a time when she found solace here: going through the motions, standing, kneeling, crossing herself, all on cue, knowing exactly what would come next—the readings, the homily, the Eucharist, even the music. She liked knowing all the steps. She had wanted to be part of this sacred, ancient dance.

And then, suddenly, she had stopped wanting it. The whole idea of it felt like a deception. The Sunday after her father's funeral, Cyd refused to get dressed. She crossed her arms and announced that she would no longer be going to church. *I won't do it. You can't make me.* Her mom looked at her for a long time, eyes narrowed, but Cyd didn't flinch, and her mother didn't argue. They were engulfed in their grief, and neither had the strength to debate. It wasn't until years later—once she met Loren, who was also Catholic, and once she had an engagement ring on her finger for her mother to show off to friends—that Cyd went back to church, and even then, only occasionally and never by herself. After her children were born, they went as a family on Sundays, taking Iris with them. Otherwise, her yoga mat was her sanctuary. Her morning run was her prayer of thanks. Meditation was her ritual. Until today, Cyd hadn't been to Mass alone since the morning of her dad's accident.

Thanks be to God.

It feels hot in the sanctuary. Or maybe it's a hot flash. She can't even tell anymore. Maybe she's too on edge. It's as if she's been shaken to the point of separation, her insides curdled like a broken sauce. Did God save her life yesterday? Is that what happened? It doesn't feel as if that's what happened.

He will come again in glory to judge the living and the dead.

She must count her blessings. What does she have to complain about *really*? In this world full of suffering, she is beyond blessed. In the grand scheme, she doesn't have a care in the world.

It is right to give Him thanks and praise.

Yes, apparently, her husband has been having an affair. She knows it's happened—he's told her as much. He did it. He *did* do it. Yet, somehow, her brain will not process it. This fact is a piece of sand grinding a delicately balanced gear to a halt.

Hosanna in the highest.

Should she try to find a way to forgive him again? To forgive and forget—*whatever the hell that means.* She had forgiven him once, but she had never really forgotten. That much was impossible. But she had made a choice all those years ago, and in choosing to stay with him, she had realized the importance— the absolute necessity—of pushing the memory of what he had done out of her mind.

They were newly married at the time, and she hadn't yet told him what she suspected. He was always busy with work back then, trying to prove himself. She wanted to be supportive. She had made an appointment with the doctor that very day, to be certain. Once it was official, she planned to break the news over a quiet dinner. Maybe if he had known before he left that morning, things would have turned out differently.

By the time Loren returned from the conference three days later, Cyd had two new pieces of information: She knew she was pregnant, and she knew Loren had been unfaithful. Someone had seen them together and told Helen, who told Cyd. "What are the odds?" Helen had asked later, speaking more to herself than to Cyd. He—they—had been spotted two hundred miles from home. *Almost like a miracle.*

She had gone to stay with Helen, trying to decide what to do next. Cyd might have heard Loren out, but Helen, always her protector, was unmoved, and Cyd was too weak to argue. Cyd was distraught to the point of sickness. She could barely eat, and what little she managed to get down came right back up. Violently.

Loren had been doubly devastated when he learned that extreme stress could play a role in what happened next, though the doctor had said it was normal, that it was no one's fault, and assured them that they could certainly try again. Loren had been so sincerely remorseful, so traumatized, and Cyd shocked to the point of paralysis by the swift chain of events—it was all over in two weeks—that it was almost inevitable that they would go home together after her brief stay in the hospital. She was unable to make a life-changing decision at that point: to leave or to stay. She had nothing left—no energy, no determination, no vision. Leaving seemed impossible. And so, she stayed.

After a while, the story of Loren's brief infidelity became just that: a story, almost a work of fiction. It was the pain over the miscarriage that consumed her. Loren was there for her, then, in those days and weeks, constantly by her side, attentive and compassionate, loving. And her mind wouldn't let her hold all of it at once. She had to let go of something, so she let go of her anger. She accepted his comfort. Slowly, the whole painful chapter began to feel like another one of her nightmares. She began to believe in him again. She trusted him.

Soon, Holly and Bo came along, one right after the other. They were her reward, living proof that she had made the right decision. Loren was a good father. They had a beautiful family. They were happy. Forty-eight hours ago, if someone had asked, she would have said she had a good marriage. They had a happy marriage. That's what she would have said.

Our Father who art in heaven . . .

The letter—the gift from Mae, whatever it is—must be a sign. It arrived on the very day of the accident. But what does it *mean*, exactly? Are they meant to leave here, she and Loren together? She sees no other choice. She either stays and rides out the storm, or she goes now while the roads are still drivable. Who knows how long it will be before the roads are cleared—downed trees are common, flooding is almost a given—and then who will take her? It will be every hand on deck for the cleanup. It could take weeks for things to get back to normal.

She could fly, but the thought terrifies her. She's only flown twice, and, both times, she panicked to the point of sickness. Driving has become almost as unbearable, and when she thinks of what just happened—she should have seen the car coming—she simply doesn't trust herself behind the wheel. Helen says she needs to pay better attention, but even the best drivers, like her father, can be caught off-guard—devastatingly so. She needs no reminder of that fact.

After the storm, if the damage isn't too bad, she could appeal to Helen or Annie, but that would be unbelievably selfish. They will have too much to tend to here, in Lola, with their businesses. And Bobby, how would *that* look? Even if he could drive her, even if they are just friends, *that* is undoubtedly a terrible idea.

. . . have mercy on us.

The organist begins a melodic communion hymn. The congregation eases down onto the cushioned kneelers. Cyd rubs her temples. She feels dizzy, and the kneeling hurts her hips. She slips a water bottle from her purse, trying to be inconspicuous. A small boy, two rows in front, turns and stares until his mother notices and nudges him with her elbow.

Lord, I am not worthy . . .

And what *about* Bobby? Why is she thinking about Bobby

at a time like this? He's been in and around her thoughts since his visit last night. The way he had looked at her, so intently, like he needed her to know something, to see it in his eyes. What had he started to say before Loren interrupted them?

The Lord be with you.

And with your spirit.

The priest steps down off the altar. "May almighty God bless you. Go in peace to love and serve the Lord."

The processional cross is carried back down the aisle. Each parishioner crosses himself in turn, from the front to the back, as it passes.

A veil of dread falls over her. She had not really wanted to come to church. She had only wanted to buy time before going home with Loren. Her head hurts, and there's a level of exhaustion that's seeped into her very bones. She hadn't wanted to come, and now—now that it's time to go—she doesn't want to leave. The words reverberate in her head. *Go in peace to love and serve the Lord.*

She desperately wants to go in peace.

She sits again. The last of the closing hymn fades as she waits, staring straight ahead, aware of the murmur and movement of people leaving the holy space, heading back to their lives, picking up where they left off. The vibrations she felt minutes ago have faded, their energy gone.

Go in peace.

How can she possibly go in peace? In one fell swoop, Loren has managed to take not only her future, but her past. How blind had she been, and for how long? How much had she chosen not to see? What vast difference separated the reality of her life from her perception of it? She would never know.

The silence in the sanctuary is complete. She is alone. She

says one final prayer: *Please, God. Give me strength. Help me to know what to do.*

She rises, trembling, and genuflects once more. She walks down the aisle toward the heavy double doors that separate her from the outside world. As she pushes her weight against and through, she senses that she will not be back here for a very long time.

12

L oren is waiting in his truck when Cyd walks out of the church. As she pulls herself into the cab with some difficulty, she can't help but imagine what might have happened had it been this massive truck instead of Mila's car that plowed into Helen's little Subaru. *Mila—her name is Mila.*

"I want you to drop me at The O," Cyd announces as soon as she is seated.

"Why?" He stops himself. "I can wait for you."

"You can drop me off. I want to walk home. I've been lying in bed for twenty-four hours, and I am perfectly capable of walking one mile on a beautiful evening."

It is still surprisingly tranquil outside. There is a soft breeze and the humidity has dropped to a comfortable level. There is no sign of the massive hurricane that is barreling north with unstoppable ferocity, or that the likely path of the storm will encompass the town of Lola, Florida.

It's dinnertime when Cyd comes in the front door of The Osprey Cafe. Helen's mother, Sophia, is at the front stand, and she embraces Cyd with surprising vigor for a woman in her mid-eighties. She is plump and warm-hearted and quick with a hug. Sophia has always been like a mother to Cyd. After Cyd's father died, Sophia welcomed Cyd into her home and provided her with something as vital as air—a place to grieve and to heal.

Sophia reaches up and takes Cyd's face between her soft palms. She appears on the verge of tears, pausing for a moment as if trying to commit Cyd's face to memory. She says something in Greek, kisses each of Cyd's cheeks, and then hugs her again. Sophia always speaks Greek when she's emotional.

"I love you, too, Sophia," Cyd replies, deeply moved by the show of affection, although she has no idea what Sophia actually said.

Nick is at the huge stove when Cyd goes into the kitchen.

"Hey, Nicky," she says softly from across the counter, not wanting to disturb him during the dinner rush.

"C! Get your ass over here," he commands. He lifts her off the ground with his hug. "Damn, you scared me. I feel so responsible. I wanted to come to the hospital but Helen insisted I stay here. Damn, it's good to see you." He squeezes her tighter.

"Take it easy!" she says, laughing as he sets her back down. "You could do more damage than that car did."

"Come on, let's go into my office. Marco, watch the line for me. I'll be right back."

Nick leads the way into his small office off the kitchen and sits behind his desk. Cyd has seen him sitting just like this for nearly thirty years, reclined in the beat-up chair, his ankles crossed on the corner of the desk. This has been Nick's domain since his father died and left Nick, still in his twenties, in charge of a business that is as much a part of Lola's history as the oysters and the shrimp boats and the river.

She wants to tell him everything but knows this isn't the time. Instead, she makes sure he knows the details of the letter and her thoughts about leaving for Phoenix.

"You might come back a millionaire," he suggests with a smirk. "Then you'll be way too good for this dump. But how are you going to get out there? I know you're not getting on a plane, not even for a million dollars, not even if there *was* a flight to be had with this storm looming."

They both knew everyone who wanted or needed to get off the coast was swarming to the airports in Jacksonville or Pensacola. Getting a flight out was nearly impossible at this late date.

"Annie and Tony offered me their van. She called me this morning. It's parked in the warehouse and I can have it as long as I need it."

Tony had bought a custom van with the intention of taking Annie on road trips once he retired. In reality, the van stayed parked in the warehouse, Annie kept working in her shop almost daily, and Tony kept flying back and forth to Pittsburgh where he ran his manufacturing company. The van, sitting idle, was the perfect solution.

"So . . ." Nick begins tentatively. "Who's going to drive?"

"What choice do I have?" She is suddenly filled with rage and the plan she had settled on earlier now seems all but impossible. "I can't believe he's done this to us!"

"I can't either."

She drops her face into her hands. "I'm a friggin' mess, Nicky. Everything is happening so fast. Loren seems sincerely sorry. It's almost pathetic. Part of me wants to believe him. I can't just throw away a twenty-eight-year marriage, can I? That seems more impossible than anything!"

Nick is squeezing a small rubber ball always on his desk for this exact purpose: to absorb some of his intensity. He has always listened to her with an uncharacteristic amount of patience. As children, their four-year age difference gave him the right to ignore her—his little sister's annoying, ever-present friend. Instead, he had always been kind to her. He always treated her as an equal.

"I dreamt about Baker last night," Cyd says after a moment. "I wish he were here. He would drive me to Arizona. He would kick Loren's ass."

She can almost hear her brother's voice, *Let's go, Sis! But I control the music and the snacks!*

"You're right about that," Nick says. "Although Baker was always more of a lover than a fighter. And Loren could probably take him if you think about it."

Cyd smiles.

"I know you miss him," he adds. "We all do."

At times, like now, Nick has a slightly crooked tilt to his mouth, reminding Cyd of a younger Nick before he started wearing his perfectly groomed beard. It reminds her how long they've been friends.

"I have to tell you, Nicky, I didn't see this one coming."

"For what it's worth, I didn't either. Man, Loren." Nick's voice trails off.

Nick would be right to assume he would have heard something if Loren was up to no good. Cyd can imagine that he feels somewhat betrayed, too.

"I have no idea what I'm doing. I feel like I don't know anything about anything."

Nick looks at her with a kindness that nearly breaks her heart.

"I'm an idiot," she adds as if that settles everything.

"Yeah, you're an idiot," Nick agrees. "But that's nothing new. Maybe a road trip will be good for you. I'd love to drop everything and get out of here for a while."

He tosses a paper clip at her chest to get her to look up at him again.

He continues, "Look, C. We both know Loren loves you. This is fucked up, no doubt. But maybe he's really trying to make up for it. I'd like to believe that. Maybe you want to let him try."

Cyd can't speak. Nick's face is distorted by unspilt tears. He never knew about Loren's previous affair. No one did other than Helen, and Cyd isn't going to tell him now. She is trying her best to resist a full-blown breakdown. *Crying accomplishes nothing*, she tells herself. Her dad taught her to be strong. What she wouldn't give to talk to her father now, one more time, to ask him what she should do.

Cyd takes a deep breath, then sighs it out. The bustle of the kitchen is like comforting, familiar background music. She could sit in this one spot forever.

"I know you have to get back to work. I just wanted to tell you what's going on. I wanted to say goodbye."

She stands to go, and Nick walks around his desk.

"Come here," he says, smiling his half-crooked smile. "It could be a whole lot worse. You're safe, that's what's important. The rest of it, well, things have a way of working out."

She reaches up and hugs him.

"You're the best, Nicky. I'm sorry I'm leaving with this storm coming. I—we—have to go now, or we may not get out of here at all. The window of opportunity is closing."

"Thanks. We'll manage. Everyone knows the drill." Nick releases her. There is a slight warble of emotion in his voice.

Cyd looks at her friend. His downturned soft-brown eyes have been comforting her for as long as she can remember.

"Thank you, Nicky," she says, almost choking.

"You're welcome, C."

"What do you want for dinner?" Loren is in the kitchen when Cyd gets home. "I'll make you anything you want."

Fern is nearly hysterical with excitement. Cyd squats down to rub her golden coat and hug her thick neck. "I missed you, too, ol' girl. Yes, I did. Okay, okay." Cyd laughs as the big dog wiggles herself silly.

"We need to talk," Cyd says to Loren, holding the edge of the counter to pull herself up. "None of us is getting any younger, are we, Fern?"

Loren follows Cyd into the dining room. They each sit at their self-assigned seats at the table as they always have, as if nothing has changed. The window frames the bay like a painting, the view a tranquil, marshy panorama. Cyd resists the urge to lay her forehead on the table. Next to Loren sits Fern, completely content as he strokes her head.

"This came in the mail yesterday. Annie brought it to the hospital." She hands Loren the letter from the attorney.

He reads, then looks up. "This sounds incredible. What are you thinking?" he asks with trepidation, as if her answer might physically hurt him.

"I want you to drive me to Phoenix. Tony has offered us the van. We can leave right away, while there's still time."

Loren sits up straighter. "Since when do you want to leave during a hurricane?"

It's a fair question. They never evacuate. Very few of their neighbors do either. They all know it's frowned upon by city officials, but most long-time locals are too stubborn or over-confident or both. They feel they know how to prepare themselves and their property, they calculate the odds, and they stay put.

"I don't want to wait. I can't just sit here. Besides, it will only be harder after the storm. It may not hit here, but it's going to hit somewhere along the coast."

"Okay." He pauses. "I guess we can do that. We can pack tonight, and I'll get Ken to put up the shutters. We can go in the morning. Traffic will be murder, but the van has two gas tanks, so we can go about seven hundred miles without needing to stop."

Tony and Loren have had many conversations about the van. Loren knows just about everything there is to know about it.

He continues, "I'll leave my truck in Tony's warehouse and bring the van back here. We have a lot to do tonight if you're serious about this. Are you sure you feel up to it?"

Cyd observes her husband. She knows he is calculating, weighing things. Everything is a balance sheet with Loren. Each entry must have its offsetting entry. She can practically see the wheels turning. He's giving up something to get this chance. To get *her*.

"The doctor said you need to take it easy, to go back to your normal level of activity slowly. I'm supposed to be keeping an eye on you. Are you sure this is a good idea?"

"No, Loren, I'm not sure," she says, irritated and far from certain about anything. "I know what the doctor said. I'll go slow. I just need to throw some clothes in a bag. Sitting in a comfortable van for a few days will be a good way to recover. It's better than sitting in a boarded-up house waiting for a hurricane that may or may not come."

Cyd and Loren have been through their share of storms over the years. How many times had they sat in the dark as Cyd tried to hide her concern from Holly and Bo, playing board games by candlelight and listening to the wicked wind howl for hours? Their imaginations would fill in what they were unable to see with all the windows covered, the steel shutters turning the house into a large coffin. They would inevitably lose power and water along with it, relying on prefilled buckets set in the bathrooms to flush the toilets, and eating snack foods and pre-made sandwiches stored in a cooler. Cell service would go out, or landlines in the old days, and the only connection to the outside world would be a battery-powered radio. It was scary at times, but the adventure brought them all closer. Cyd doesn't remember ever being truly frightened as long as she and Loren and the kids were all together.

"It's settled then," Cyd says, pushing her chair back. "I'll start packing."

Loren runs both hands through his hair, squeezing the side of his head for a moment. He does not see Cyd watching as the briefest streak of panic crosses his face.

13

WEATHER REPORT:
WSVA Channel 6,
Savannah's First Alert Weather
Sunday, May 30, 6:03 a.m.

ANCHOR: "Meteorologist Holly Carr has been closely monitoring Hurricane Abigail, now a Category 3 storm. What is the latest, Holly?"

HOLLY: "Good morning, and yes, we have a major Category 3 hurricane moving into the Gulf of Mexico at this hour. We are getting early reports of extensive damage after the storm cut a devasting path across the island of Cuba overnight. There was some weakening due to the interaction with the island's mountains, but Abigail has quickly regained strength. Unfortunately, these are perfect conditions for the storm to continue to intensify. A ridge of high pressure may steer the storm more westerly, but right now, we have hurricane watches and warnings all along the west coast of Florida, from Tampa to the panhandle. Not only should people be aware of the deadly high winds, but tidal surge is a real danger for those close to the coast, with up to six feet of storm surge likely."

Part Two

Top of
the Breath

14

Sunday, May 30, 2019
Florida to Louisiana

When her alarm vibrates at 4:30, Loren is already up. Cyd rolls onto her back, relishing the stillness. She knows that once she rises, this plan of hers will be put in motion. It isn't too late to change her mind. They don't have to leave. They could simply board up the house and wait, as they always have. She could be here to help clean up once it passes. She could deal with Loren and the lawyer and every other decision some other day.

With one hand on her belly and one on her heart, she silently says her morning prayers. *This is the day the Lord has made.* She pictures herself gathering up her strength as her belly rises with each inhale. She has said this prayer almost every morning of her life. It is a habit held over from her childhood, though she realized when she was older that her dad never said the second line, the one about rejoicing. Her father wasn't a religious man. His prayers were his meditations on nature, born from his childhood in the Great Dismal Swamp, and his church was any quiet spot along the river under the shade of a live oak with his fishing pole in hand. He accompanied his wife to church on holidays or when requested, but he never took communion, and Cyd always felt a little sorry leaving him to sit in the pew alone while everyone else walked up to the altar.

In recent years, Cyd has added a very personal prayer to her brief morning ritual once she swings her legs around the side of the bed. It is prompted by the memory of her mother and the hammock-like contraption used by the caregivers to move Iris from bed to chair and back again. Cyd stops a moment each morning and stretches out her legs, points her toes, and rolls her ankles. She gives thanks for her strong body. She gives thanks for the ability to stand.

Her suitcase lies open on the living room sofa where she left it the night before. She had packed quickly, zombie-like, while Loren readied the van and made arrangements for the care of their house with the maintenance man at his office building. A stillness stretches beyond the back window, past the dock. In the dim light, she can make out the watery plateau extending from the edge of the lawn to a line of mangroves and grasses in the distance. A delicate mist lingers on the surface. Insects poke dots into the sheen. It is fragile. Exposed.

She stares into the open suitcase, unsure what to do next. Has she packed what she needs? What *does* she need? *Are you kidding me?* What she needs cannot be packed in any suitcase.

Cyd starts to zip the suitcase closed, then stops. Light reflects off a silver frame on the side table. She shifts aside one photograph—the one of Holly and Bo on the boat with Fern—and picks up the older frame. It is small and square, the black-

and-white image faded. Three young men with arms slung over each other's shoulders form a human chain and grin widely into the camera. They stand at the edge of a boulder-lined creek in plain T-shirts. A portion of a stone cabin cuts into one side of the frame, and a wall of rock engulfs the backdrop in the distance. The man in the middle stares out at Cyd. She stares back. "Come on, Dad. We're going on a road trip," she says aloud and slips the picture into the bag.

They pull out of town as the sun kisses the horizon, splendid orange and full of hope. The bay is deceptively serene. Cyd has listened to Holly's reports and read the news of Hurricane Abigail on her phone. Cuba was pummeled overnight. After briefly stalling, the storm is once again well-formed and rapidly intensifying in the warm waters of the Gulf. Cyd can practically feel it in her bones. The situation is growing more ominous for the panhandle region as the eye wobbles erratically up the gulf, increasing in strength while over water and making forecasting difficult. Most models show the storm making landfall late the following night, Monday, or in the early hours Tuesday morning, somewhere along the Gulf Coast.

Cyd says silent goodbyes to her beloved landscape and chants a string of Hail Marys from the perch-like passenger seat of the van. They plan to head west along Highway 98, running briefly by Apalachicola Bay and then along the Gulf of Mexico before cutting north to the interstate. Fern, like an old pro, settles herself under the small table behind the driver's seat where Loren has nested a blanket.

"Nice cave," Cyd says, looking back at the dog, her presence a comfort.

It would be so much easier if she could simply fly to Phoenix and back. At times, like now, she has to admit that her fear of flying—she prefers to think of it as a severe dislike—is limiting. After their freshman year in college, she let Helen talk her into spending spring break in San Francisco. Those were the days when she could drink enough courage to try just about anything and you could, unbelievably, smoke cigarettes on the plane. Helen had cousins there and she wanted to go sooooo bad, and *don't say you can't fly, that's not even a thing!*

So Cyd swallowed her apprehension, followed Helen onto the plane, and spent half the flight being sick in the claustrophobic bathroom. As she stumbled down the aisle to deplane, she swore she would never do it again. "Well if that's the case, I guess I'll have to visit you in San Francisco from now on," was all Helen had to say on the matter.

They spent their second day in the city, map in hand, exploring as much as they possibly could. When they realized the time—they were expected back for dinner—they hurried to the trolley car at Fisherman's Wharf. The waiting crowd was enormous, snaking a full block. One look at the queue, and they turned back the way they had come, up the hill. And then another. And another. Every time they thought they had arrived (*surely! finally!*) over the last bone-crushing crest, there loomed yet another monstrous slope. At first, they were laughing. What else could you do? But by the end of the ninety-minute walk, they practically crawled up the sidewalk. They collapsed on the tiny patch of grass in front of Helen's aunt's house, shaky from exhaustion.

That's how the last twenty-four hours felt. Every step was like dragging herself up a seventy-degree concrete slab with no end in sight.

Cyd is startled awake by a horn blaring just outside the passenger window. The van is creeping along a highway lined with vehicles across six lanes and as far ahead as she can see. The storm threat is evident as people flee the coastline, heading north and west. Cyd looks at Loren, sensing his concentration as he maneuvers the large unfamiliar vehicle through thick traffic. Trucks are lined end to end, and cars, filled to capacity, swerve from one lane to the next, trying to make fast progress. From the highway, Cyd can see the preparations. Businesses and homes are boarding windows. Sandbags line doorways. Shutters are pulled closed. There are lines at the gas stations.

She looks at the clock. It seems impossible that they have only been on the road for three hours. The radio is too loud for the early hour, playing Loren's choice of country music, something she recognizes but cannot identify. Their musical tastes have never been in sync. None of Cyd's jazz favorites are on Loren's playlist. Miles Davis, Dave Brubeck, Stan Getz—theirs was the music that transported Cyd back to her childhood living room: the turntable in the large credenza, her father in his favorite armchair, one knee over the other subtly keeping time with his foot, Baker sprawled on the floor studying an album cover. She puts in her earbuds and selects *Kind of Blue,* her favorite Miles Davis album. Her father's favorite. She closes her eyes again, shutting out the bright light and her harsh reality. She concentrates on the details of the opening piano chords.

She found the photograph of her father—the one now tucked in her suitcase—in her parents' closet not long after his death. There was something about the look on his face, a playful earnestness, his truest essence captured perfectly. From the moment she saw it, she cherished it. Since she first studied the image as a young girl, desperate for some physical remembrance, she kept it where she could see it daily: first on the nightstand in her childhood bedroom, then in her dorm room in college, then on the living room side table. He had posed with two of his Navy buddies while they were on leave and traveling. Her mother had told her this. On the back in her father's handwriting: *June 1955, Grand Canyon with Mickey and Dave, Wow!*

Once, Cyd asked her mother if she knew where the photo was taken exactly.

"No idea. Why?" her mom asked.

Cyd said she didn't know why. She just wondered.

"Did you ever want to go back there with him?" Cyd added, unable to fathom how her mom did not see in the picture what she saw—the look of utter amazement on her dad's face, complete awe, pure joy. How did her mom not want to experience that with him? Not want to be there with him *while* he experienced it? That was *all* Cyd wanted.

15

They arrive in Lafayette, Louisiana, in the early evening, twelve hours after they set out and four hours longer than it would have normally taken. They quickly realize a hotel room is not in the cards. Rooms have been booked days in advance by experienced hurricane dodgers.

"At least we have the van," Loren offers with a weary smile. He was right. Tony had spared no expense outfitting the van. They could live in it for a month if they needed to.

Cyd hadn't considered the sleeping arrangements. She is tired and tense, and her entire body aches with stiffness. Even Loren, with his seemingly limitless stamina, is wilted after the long drive. The van did indeed make the journey more comfortable, but Cyd's neck is like a violin string ready to snap, and her skull is stretched taut from overthinking. Despite her best effort to remain optimistic, she has spent much of the past twelve hours rehashing the decision that has put her in the position in which she now finds herself. One moment she wants nothing more than to save her marriage—the *last* thing she wants is to be a fifty-two-year-old divorcée. The next moment, she is sure she has lost her mind agreeing to have Loren drive her. It's as if she's rewarding his awful behavior. He's getting away with it *again*. The mere sight of him out of the corner of her eye is an unbearable irritation.

Regardless, she has committed to this trip and she needs to persevere until they get to Phoenix. She can deal with the rest later after she knows what *items of a personal nature* Aunt Mae has in store for her. In spite of everything that's happening, she can't shake the feeling that *this* is important. The timing of the arrival of the letter, almost at the exact time she was in the accident. She cannot ignore its significance. She simply *must* get to Phoenix.

Once off the highway, they find a parking spot on a side street downtown where they can stay for the night. They venture out to find a nearby restaurant. At least Fern, trotting happily beside them, is pleased with the decision. Cyd watches the sweet animal and wishes she could be as mindful of the present moment as her dog. Fern is a constant reminder of the joy that can be extracted from the mundane.

They see a restaurant with outdoor tables which seems very busy, either in spite of or because of the impending storm. It's always this way when a hurricane is coming. Everything goes on as normal, even as precautions are taken and preparations are made, then suddenly, everything stops. The world is suspended as if in mid-air. Everyone locks up, hunkers down, and waits.

A young woman greets them and leads them to a small round table toward the back of the patio. The server bends to pet Fern and offers to bring a bowl of water. Then she slides one of the chairs around the table so that both chairs are next to each other, facing the rest of the patio.

"There," she says, pleased with her work. "That will make more room for this pretty pup."

Fern wags her approval and sits down exactly where the hostess has made room for her.

Loren asks the server about the beer selection, and Cyd orders a glass of iced tea. A glass of wine sounds heavenly, but the doctor recommended she stay away from alcohol until all her symptoms—mainly the headaches and foggy brain—subside. It might hinder her thinking, he said. *We can't have that.*

"How do you feel?" she asks in an attempt at normalcy, seeing the fatigue on Loren's face.

"I'm good," he says, considering her briefly and then looking down at the menu.

"I texted the kids to let them know we got here," Cyd says.

"Good." Loren continues reading the menu.

Cyd sighs, feeling out of place, the surreal state of her marriage inescapable.

16

1987
Tallahassee, Florida

erhaps she had deceived Loren unfairly in the beginning. The circumstances of the night they met were
unusual. She wasn't drinking that night, unlike most
nights during her college years. She may have been hungover,
but only slightly, and she had definitely come down with a bug.

It was late in their junior year, and Cyd and Helen, as of
their most recent birthdays, were no longer teenagers. Helen
had insisted Cyd come out with her, despite her illness. A ginger-
haired boy who was working backstage on a musical production
had invited Helen to the after-party on the night of the last performance. The party was held in the courtyard of one of the
nicer restaurants in town, and Cyd knew Helen wanted the
good food as much as she wanted to see either the guy or the
play, so Cyd had gone along, reluctantly. She felt queasy and
didn't much care for musicals, but "It's what friends do," Helen
reminded her as she held up a halter top for Cyd to wear.

There, in the moonlit courtyard on an early spring evening,

sipping uncharacteristically on ginger ale, Helen's friend intro-
duced Cyd to a handsome graduate student. He was well-
dressed in a pressed, collared shirt and jeans that looked like
they, too, may have been pressed. There was an air of formality
to him, not a stiffness exactly but something close to it, as if he
felt out of place. His face was symmetrical, which bestowed a
classic type of beauty, and everything was perfectly in place, a
result of near-compulsive attention to detail she would later
learn. His thick black hair was precisely trimmed. The square-
ness of his chin and the straight line of his lips made him look
determined. Cyd always noticed a person's posture, and his was
impeccable. Maybe it was his sense of balance or the way he
carried himself—a smoothness of movement, a stealthiness.
Something about him was like a panther.

They talked, first in the group, then off to the side, just the
two of them—Loren, slightly nervous, Cyd, mildly flirtatious.
Perhaps it was the atmosphere—artsy and romantic—or the
cold medicine she had gulped down before she left her dorm.
Whatever the influence, Cyd was at once totally self-conscious
and completely at ease. He was mysterious and mature—so
unlike the college boys she was used to. She would later tell
Helen that she understood why they called it "falling" in love.
She actually felt like she was falling, as if she had entered an
alternate universe where the force of gravity wasn't as strong
or didn't work the same way, where you could be floating and
standing at the same time, tethered but adrift.

She might have enjoyed the experience more if she hadn't
needed to excuse herself to go to the bathroom, unable to hold
down what little food she had eaten. But her illness did give her
a good excuse to let Loren drive her home early. As it turned
out, he wasn't much for parties and was happy to leave, he as-

sured her, as he set down the remaining half of his one and only beer and escorted her away from the crowd.

They sat on a bench outside her apartment building and talked for hours. In spite of her cold, in spite of the vomiting, it had turned out to be a perfectly magical night. He told her about his upbringing outside Orlando with overbearing but loving Italian parents who called him by his full name—Lorenzo—and went to Mass daily. Growing up, he wanted to be a professional baseball player. Everyone told him he was good enough; they even wrote about him in the local paper. He gave a choked little laugh to accentuate what a silly and long-ago dream it was. Instead, he had settled on accounting and was working on his master's degree. He already had a position with the largest firm in Tallahassee while he was finishing his studies. One day, he planned to have his own practice where he could run things the way he wanted.

Cyd had enough self-awareness, even at twenty, to know things might have gone very differently that night if she had been drinking, if she had been acting like a typical immature college girl as she and Helen did most weekends. She and Loren even laughed about it in subsequent years, how he had caught her on her one sober weekend. "She never would have looked at me twice otherwise," he would joke when they told the story. But Cyd knew the truth of it. It was *he* who would not have looked twice. She had been given one first chance with Loren and, as Helen so eloquently put it back then, she had nailed it. She still thought of it as one of the best nights of her life.

Years later, she realized she had spent the first twelve years of her life certain she was the luckiest girl on the planet because of her father, and when she first met Loren, during their courtship and engagement and in the early days of their marriage, she felt the same sense of fortuity. It had all been so dreamy. They moved in together after a year, after she graduated, but only once they were officially engaged. They were Catholic, after all, and more importantly, both their mothers were Catholic. Iris literally beamed after church that first Sunday—the exact beam that was heretofore reserved exclusively for Baker—as Cyd lifted her left hand ever so daintily, wrist up, fingers down, posing for as long as it took for Iris's friends to tilt it this way and that. The stone was undeniably impressive, and oh, what a nice young man Cyd had found herself!

Not that Loren was an easy man—he could be demanding, meticulous, judgmental—but who was she to talk? She was unfocused, impetuous, gullible. And they were in love. Surely, that was the pillar upon which everything else rested. She had believed in him. He was the man she could depend on, the one who would make the right decisions, think ahead, plan things. He was the one she trusted to take care of them.

17

Sunday, May 30, 2019
Lafayette, Louisiana

Drinks arrive, and they turn back to the menus. A news alert flashes across Cyd's phone screen, and she picks it up to read.

"This storm is going to hit us. I hope Ken is able to get everything done at the house," she says, referring to Loren's maintenance man and friend. "I can't help but feel guilty for leaving like we have."

"The house will be fine. She's stood for a long time. Come on, babe," Loren says, reaching across and putting his hand over hers. His voice is smooth but there is a tenseness behind his eyes. "Let's just relax. We can make this into a fantastic trip. We need this. There's a resort in Phoenix called the Camelback Inn. Let's check in there and kick back for a few days."

"Can I get a massage?" she asks, rolling her head from shoulder to shoulder, hearing small pops as she does so. A spark of memory brings Bobby's cool hands to her neck. He often gives her neck rubs at work after a long shift, something that used to seem innocent enough. Now, the recollection alone causes her skin to tingle. She can hear the sound of his voice in her head, feel the way he held her hand, see the look in his eyes before he was interrupted.

"You can get a massage every day if you want." Loren's voice practically makes her jump. "Now let's forget about everything else and have a nice dinner. Look at Fern. We could take a few moves out of her playbook."

Loren seems to have read her earlier thoughts about the dog. Cyd looks down at the big golden heap between them, lying comfortably with her head lifted, watching the action around her, ready for anything but already perfectly content.

"Here's to massages every day," Cyd says with resignation, holding her glass of tea up to Loren's beer.

"Here's to a new start," Loren says. "Thank you for doing this, Cyd."

As they click their glasses together, Cyd hears the slightest noise, a vibration, and her vision is drawn to his lap. The way the waitress has arranged the chairs, he is sitting close to her. She can see his torso and thighs. There it is—undeniably—the light of his phone in his pocket, glowing through the fabric, and the vibration of a text message.

She looks from his lap to his face. Loren doesn't flinch. He has picked up the menu and he continues reading.

Cyd does the same, waiting. The space narrows around her. The sounds—of voices and silverware against dishes and footsteps and music—all fade into a muted background and there is nothing but her and Loren and the phone.

She waits.

She holds the menu. She glances at Loren's profile and then down at his lap. The light has dimmed.

She waits.

There it is again. The vibration, as loud as a church bell, and the light, as clear as the sun through stained glass.

And still, he does not move.

"Do you want to get that?" she says in her normal tone. Everything is oh-so-normal.

He looks up. So unconcerned. So unruffled.

"What?" he asks.

"Your phone. Someone is texting you, Loren. Aren't you curious who it is?"

He follows her eyes down.

"I'm sure it can wait. I'm starving. Let's order." He waves the waitress over.

"Are you ready?" the server asks innocently, her cheeks like ripe peaches. *What she doesn't know.*

"Yes," says Loren.

"No," says Cyd.

Loren looks at Cyd. Cyd looks at the pretty, young server and smiles.

"Take your time," the woman says and leaves them.

Cyd moves the napkin from her lap to the table.

"Cyd," Loren begins.

"I'm going for a walk. Eat without me."

He reaches for her arm as she moves, then pushes back his chair, but Fern is in his way and Cyd is weaving her way through the cluster of tables before he can get to her.

When she reaches the sidewalk, she starts to run. She *needs* to run. If she doesn't move, she will explode. She discovered this about herself after her father died. She has a temper. The thoughts start coming, and they keep coming, relentless, ugly, forcing her to do something or say something, something that cannot be undone. So, in order to quiet the thoughts, she has learned to run.

She zigzags down the sidewalk, out into the street and back again, moving around the other people and the sandbags and the orange cones. The blood is rushing to her legs and to her heart, and she has to move faster in order to absorb the flood of adrenaline, the pounding anxiety, the dam-breaking torrent of emotion. Her meditation practice has taught her she should be able to sit still. She should be able to focus on her breath and quiet her mind. Quiet the mind and hear God. *If only.* She runs as if she is being chased by a demon, as if her life depends on it, as if it is the last thing she will ever do. She runs for a long time, long after the sweat is streaming down her face and stinging her eyes. Long after her lungs feel like they might burst and her legs have turned to water. Only then does she turn into a corner park and drop onto the grass, heaving.

She lies for some time, long enough for the clarity of what's happening to sink in. *This is happening.*

Eventually, she stands, unsure of her legs, and walks slowly back to the van. She knocks on the big sliding door.

"Jesus, Cyd. What did you do?"

She knows what she must look like—a sweaty, stinking mess. "Let me by, Loren. Leave me alone. I need to lie down."

"Just let me explain. Please."

"Get out of my way," she snarls in a voice that threatens them both and pushes past him to the bed that occupies the back third of the van. She needs desperately to put her head on a pillow. "Give me some privacy."

Loren clips a leash on Fern and steps out of the van. Cyd washes her face in the small sink and wipes her body down with a cucumber-infused disposable cloth. She slips on a T-shirt, retrieves a small bottle from her cosmetic bag, and tips a sleeping pill into her palm. She stares at the pill, debating, recalling the doctor's instructions to take it easy, not exert herself, not think too much. She has already broken every rule. She needs to sleep. The thought of lying awake in the middle of the night with only Loren's breathing and her incessant thoughts . . . *to hell with it.* She swallows the pill and crawls into the strange bed. Unable to form another coherent thought, she lets the tears slip silently down her cheeks, unquestioned.

18

WEATHER REPORT:
WSVA Channel 6,
Savannah's First Alert Weather
Monday, May 31, 6:31 a.m.

ANCHOR: "Meteorologist Holly Carr is working overtime to keep us up to date on our top story at this hour. Hurricane Abigail is expected to make landfall somewhere along the Florida Gulf Coast as a Category 3 or possibly a Category 4 hurricane. I understand this is personal for you, Holly, that you grew up in Lola, Florida, which is in the cone of possible landfall."

HOLLY: "That's right, Natalie. (Clears throat.) I'm from Lola, so I must admit I'm especially concerned about my friends and family there, as well as for everyone in the path of this monster hurricane. The storm has rapidly intensified in the past twelve hours and is likely to be upgraded again to a Category 4 storm. You can see this wobbling path up the gulf. The longer it stays over water, the stronger it will likely become. Wind bands are already being felt along parts of the northwestern coast of Florida. You are urged to follow the instructions of local authorities and evacuate immediately if you are in an evacuation zone. Check with local officials for shelter information in your area. We expect heavy, possibly torrential, rainfall and wind gusts of 150 miles per hour or higher within the next twenty-four hours. As we know all too well, these are low-lying areas, and the storm surge alone is life-threatening."

19

Monday, May 31, 2019
Louisiana to Texas

Cyd wakes to the metal grind of the sliding door. The morning light cuts through the zipped-up darkness of the van's interior. She waits until Loren and Fern leave for a walk before she emerges from under the covers and rinses her face in the sink. Her head feels like it's filled with cement.

Dear, Lord, let me get to Phoenix. Give me the strength to get through the next two days. Please send me a sign. Let me know You are there.

The air conditioner hums in response. She sighs and crawls back into the bed.

They drive in silence for several hours. It is still slow going along the Gulf Coast. Cyd tunes in to Holly's mid-morning forecast. The storm is expected to make landfall in about sixteen hours somewhere between the big bend of Florida and the eastern coastline of Alabama. Regardless of where the eye comes ashore, the scope of the storm will be far-reaching. Holly speaks of low barometric pressure and reorganization over warm Gulf waters. Intensifying. Extensive. Violent.

Loren has made eye contact more than once and silently pleads for permission to speak. Her anger has been replaced with defeat. All Cyd wants now is to get to Phoenix and get out of this vehicle.

It is late morning when she moves to the back of the van, lies down on the bed, and rings Helen. No answer. Cyd can picture any number of scenarios in which Helen is up to her eyeballs in work, trying to safeguard The O. She leaves a brief message—"Just checking in. Thinking of you. Sorry I'm not there to help. We're in Texas. I love you all very much."

A moment later, her phone lights up.

"Darling! I'm so glad I got you. How are you holding up?" Annie says.

"Not great, honestly," Cyd whispers. "I'm trying to keep it together. If I try to talk, I might start screaming and never stop. It's all so tawdry."

"Listen, I learned something I think you should know. I called my friend Susan last night, the one who knows Mila. From what she said, I'm piecing together a story that doesn't quite mesh with what Loren has told you. I'm pretty sure it was Mila who broke it off with Loren, not the other way around. That's why he went to meet her like he did with the storm coming and all. She asked him to meet her, then *she* broke up with *him*."

Cyd turns on her side and pats Ferns's substantial head. The dog looks up at her with concern.

"Actually, that makes more sense than anything I've heard so far. I've tried to give him the benefit of the doubt, but he's obviously still in contact with her. There was a text last night.

He tried to act like he didn't see it, but I know it was her. And there was something he did before we left. I tried to chalk it up to my imagination, but when I asked him to drive me, I saw this look. It was just a moment, and he tried to hide it, but I saw it. It was like he was torn—he knew he should say yes to me, but he didn't really want to leave. Why would I think I should save this marriage? Or even could? I feel like such a fool. Oh, Annie! Oh, shit! What am I going to do?"

"Shall I fly to meet you? Just tell me where and I'll get there."

"No. That's very sweet of you, but no." Cyd rubs her fingertips into her forehead. The dull headache seems to have lodged itself there permanently. "The way I see it, I have only one card in my hand. I need to play it and get on with it."

"That all sounds very American, darling. Very capable. Take the bull by the horns and all. But don't feel like you have to do this all on your own. I am here if you need me. Any time. For anything." And with a final "kiss-kiss," the line goes quiet.

"That was Annie," Cyd says, taking her seat in the front again, looking at Loren's perfectly proportioned profile. These are the first words she has spoken to him all morning.

He glances at her quickly, then back at the highway, thick with traffic.

"I want you to listen to me before you speak, Loren. Listen, then choose your words carefully."

He looks at her again, longer this time, before returning his eyes to the road.

"In a few hours, our beloved town, our home, may likely get slammed with one of the worst hurricanes on record, and you and I have chosen to leave. I can't undo that decision, although a very big part of me wishes I could. In fact, I spent most of yesterday second-guessing myself, feeling selfish and so damn . . . unsure.

"But now, I've made another decision. I choose to believe that we are here and not there for a reason, just like I choose to believe that we crashed into each other Friday morning for a reason. I can't help but see it as a sign. A huge flashing red sign. There I was, just skipping happily along, living my oblivious little life—I mean, I was doing one thing and you were doing something else *entirely*—and the universe got my attention by literally crashing us into each other. And to top it off, it happened at 11:11. I know that means nothing to you, but it means something to me. The last thing I remember is looking at the clock and seeing 11:11 and feeling so damn happy. So, I'm going to ask you this just once, Loren. After twenty-eight years of marriage, if I ever meant anything to you, anything at all, I am asking you to respect me enough to tell me the truth."

Loren steals another glance. The space between them is a black hole of suppressed emotion—anguish, remorse, desperation, longing.

"You owe me the truth, Loren." She straightens herself. "Are you in love with her?"

He takes a deep breath and sighs it out.

"I met her in Annie's shop one day. I was checking on something, talking with Tony. She makes pottery, you know, platters and pitchers and things. We just started up a conversation. She was nice. Friendly." His jaw pulses.

"After that, I saw her a couple more times. I liked her. I did. I liked her." He runs one hand through his hair and looks briefly away, out the opposite window.

"One day, I went to see her on the island. She has a little workshop there." He clears his throat. "I don't know why I did it, but she asked me, so I went."

"That was in January?"

"Yes." His voice is barely audible.

"Over four months ago."

He does not look at her. "Yes."

Cyd studies Loren's face—his strong, familiar face—the face of the man to whom she has entrusted everything. Part of her is unable to grasp what Loren has done. More than half her life has been spent by this man's side and what does she know about him, really? Someone might as well ask her to believe the grass has turned blue.

"You're in love with her then." It is not a question.

"I'm sorry, Cyd."

For a second, Cyd thinks he might cry.

She takes a drink of water. Her hand trembles slightly as she lifts the bottle.

"Well. That's it then." She sits frozen. Not since her father's death has she felt such a bodily disconnect, as if she's been physically unplugged from herself. Neither of them says anything for several minutes. The air is thick. Her chest constricts.

"I want you to take me to the Dallas airport," she says finally, softly. "I'm going to leave you there. I'm going to continue on my own. I'm going to . . . leave you."

"Cyd," he starts, then lets the word hang.

Twenty-eight years of life and marriage have brought them here, together but separate. It is abundantly clear to both of them that there is nothing more to say.

20

Hurricane Abigail slammed into the small coastal town of Gulf Shores, Florida, in the early morning hours on Tuesday, June 1, as a massive Category 4 storm, mighty and vengeful. As it was happening, Cyd sat on an airplane for the first time in twenty years, trying to take deep breaths and keep herself from being sick. She pictured Lola—the narrow tree-lined streets, the old city dock, The Osprey standing guard in the center of town. In her mind's eye, she saw her sweet little house set delicately at the edge of the bay, and the worn, barnacle-encrusted shrimp boats that always nested along Water Street. She imagined what was happening there—to Helen and Nicky and Sophia at The O, to Bobby and his boat, to Annie's beautiful old farmhouse and her lovely store. She wondered what she might find—or not find—when she returned there. The thoughts only added to her nausea.

She tried to put Loren out of her mind. She focused on her breathing. She said prayers. As she leaned her head against the cool window staring out at the blackness, with the hum of the airplane engines vibrating from her ears to her belly, she couldn't help but see the stark analogy—a sign, dare she say—as she was hurled through the darkness toward an unknown future, her past being pummeled by a wrath of forces completely out of her control.

21

Tuesday, June 1, 2019
Phoenix, Arizona

When Cyd wakes Tuesday morning in a Phoenix hotel room, she tries Helen and then Nick. Both calls go directly to voicemail. As she watches the news coverage, she is barely able to recognize the footage taken on location, just down the road from the town where she has lived her entire life. It is indescribable.

She calls Holly. Together, they get Bo on the phone, and when she hears their voices, relief and gratitude flood her body. This is quickly followed by compassion, and perhaps a twinge of guilt, for her neighbors in Gulf Shores who are not nearly as fortunate as they are.

Cyd tells her children about their father—about their splitting up—as calmly and with as much reassurance as she can. Initially, she tries to gloss over the ugliest details. She tells them she decided to continue on to Arizona alone and that their dad would be returning home. Though they are both young adults, she instinctively wants to protect them, much as she did when

Baker was sick. She can still see their confused young faces trying to hide the horror upon seeing their uncle after some stretch of time, further eroded, wasting away. Both Cyd and Baker had tried to carry on as normally as possible for the children's benefit as well as their own. Baker never married, never had children. His niece and nephew *were* his children. They had all managed as best they could under the oppressive weight of what was happening, an illness as unstoppable and destructive as any hurricane.

Cyd then tells them, knowing she must get it out in the open before they hear from some other source, that their dad has met someone—yes, the woman he was with when the accident occurred—and that he has feelings for her, more than he admitted initially, and that they all need to accept that this is really happening.

Once she stops talking, Cyd realizes what is happening on the other end of the line. Holly is in tears, and Bo, too, is clearly upset.

They didn't always need her, or at least it didn't seem as if they did. Not in the way she needed her father when she was a girl, with a level of desperation. They had each other. Early on, Holly had taken on a maternal role, assuming responsibility for her little brother. As they grew, she stayed interested in his life, more involved than most sisters. In return, Bo adored Holly. He trusted her completely. Holly was so stylish and self-assured, even as a young girl, and so sincerely held her brother's best interest at heart, that Bo went along with almost anything she suggested. He still does.

"Oh, Holly! Don't cry, sweetheart," Cyd offers meekly.

"I can't believe this, Mom!" she exclaims.

"We're all safe. That's what's most important. Everything

will work itself out. I know it might not seem like that right now, but it will."

"Everything does *not* always work out, Mom!" Holly is sobbing now.

"Listen, Holl," Bo says. "I'll drive up. I can be there in time for dinner. Then, we can drive over to Lola as soon as the roads are clear. We can check on the house together. We can check on Dad."

Cyd's helplessness intensifies. Of course, they will want to check on their father. They will take care of each other as they always have while she gallivants across the country. The reality of what she is doing strikes her as borderline insane. Her children have always made parenting effortless, so effortless that Cyd often wondered what she had actually *done* as a mother. She felt somewhat dispensable. Their self-sufficiency hurt in a way she couldn't quite pinpoint. Or was she missing the point altogether? Loren had always been there for them. He had covered for her all those times when she was away caring for Baker and Iris. Or helping Helen and Nick. They love their father. Maybe Loren is the one they *really* need.

"That's a good idea," Cyd says, scrambling to reassure them. "I'm sure you're both worried about everything, including your father. That's very sweet of you, Lorenzo."

Cyd often calls her son by his given name, one he shares with both his father and grandfather. Bo is a nickname his sister gave him when her new brother came along a few months after her second birthday. "Lorenzo" was just too much for Holly's little mouth, so "Bo" it was.

Holly sniffles her agreement, then makes her mother promise to call as soon as she meets with the lawyer. She must promise to tell her what she's learned and let her know she is safe. "Are you really okay, Mom? I can fly out there. I hate that you're there alone."

Yes! Please come! I want you here with me!

Cyd raises a false cheeriness in her voice. "I wish you could both be here and Fern, too. I miss you all already, more than you know. But, no, sweetheart, you need to work. I'll be fine. I'll call you. I promise."

As Cyd hangs up the phone, numbness is the sensation she is most aware of—in her body and in her mind. Her senses have gone into overload, shut down like the loss of power during a storm. She drops back onto the bed and stares at the ceiling until it is time to leave for her appointment.

22

Cyd's nerves are frayed as she walks from the waiting room into the large office in the Phoenix high-rise. She is greeted by a husky man wearing a well-tailored suit and no tie.

"I hope you had a nice trip," Jonathan Walker says, shaking her hand and smiling warmly. "It's a pleasure to meet you."

He does not comment on the fact that she is here alone. She likes him immediately.

"Mr. Walker," Cyd says, attempting to keep her voice steady and act "normal" though she has lost track of what normal is. Any happy anticipation about the inheritance is gone, replaced by dread over the storm and despair over the state of her marriage. She is having trouble focusing.

"Please, call me Jonathan."

Jonathan asks about the hurricane. He is unsure where Gulf Shores is located, where Lola is located, reminding Cyd how far from home she actually is. He motions for Cyd to sit across from his immaculate desk and laces manicured fingers on top of a closed portfolio.

"I'm sorry about your cousin," he begins.

Cyd stares at him, momentarily confused, before the statement makes sense. She had forgotten the reason she was here in the first place—the most likely trigger that put these events into motion—was the death of Mae's son, Andrew, who she hadn't heard about or thought of in years.

"Oh, thank you," she stammers.

"Your aunt was not just a client," he explains. "She was a close friend. She and Peter were our neighbors in Atlanta. Later, my parents were investors in their company here, and we followed them to Phoenix. In fact, I met your father, Cyd. He would visit Mae in Atlanta on occasion and play golf with Mae and Peter and my dad."

Cyd knew her dad would drive up to Mae's once or twice a year, so it made sense that he would have met Mae's friends. Still, the mention of her father unsettles Cyd further and makes her sit up taller in the expensive leather chair.

"Yes, my dad liked visiting them. You must have been very young when you met him."

"I was, but I remember him. He was a good-looking guy, and I knew he served in the Navy, which interested me as a kid. He was a nice man."

"Yes," Cyd says. "He was that and so much more." Cyd can't help but feel proud of her father, even now. Everything about him was unmistakably decent and honest. It was no wonder he made a lasting impression on a young Jonathan Walker.

"Peter and Mae did well with their business here. They ran several independent living facilities which Mae sold after Peter passed. Mae asked to see me when she got sick, not long before she died. You may know that your cousin, Andrew, had problems. He suffered bouts of depression and struggled with drugs and alcohol. He was in and out of rehab for years and never able to support himself. Mae wanted him taken care of after she was gone, but she couldn't leave money to him outright, so a trust was set up to support him."

Jonathan opens the leather portfolio on his desk. Cyd can see neat handwriting on the legal pad. He reads for a moment, then looks up.

"After Andrew's death, the trust instructs me to pay out the balance to you and the other beneficiaries. Andrew did his best to spend his mother's money, but there are still some investments, enough to supplement a retirement. I can review those with you whenever you're ready. And then there's the house. There's enough cash to maintain it if you choose to keep it."

He pauses again, looking down, then turns a sheet of paper— a spreadsheet with valuations listed—so she can read it. Cyd has no words. The number at the bottom is one number she finds nearly incomprehensible.

"The house?" Cyd squeaks.

"Yes," Jonathan continues. "There's a house. Mae liked to call it 'the cabin.' Your aunt found it to be very peaceful. It's in Sedona, not far from here. Andrew used it on occasion, but he never loved it the way Mae did. He never wanted to live there. Maybe it represented the person his mother wanted him to be, you know, a man capable of caring for and appreciating such a place, a person he was never able to be."

Jonathan looks toward the window as if remembering something. "It has a beautiful view of the red rocks. Mae always said there was a magical energy in the canyon. She kept the house mainly for you, Cyd. She knew about your interest in yoga and meditation. Mae studied those subjects. She was interested in Eastern spirituality. She wasn't much for traditional organized religions." He gave a little laugh as if Cyd would understand why this was amusing.

Mae studied yoga? Cyd notices Jonathan is waiting, looking at her, serious again.

"Sedona was an important part of Mae's life, and apparently, she thought you would appreciate it, even love it, like she did. I remember her saying that you were your father's daughter. Those were her words."

Cyd's hands start to shake. She pushes them down to her lap.

"That's why Mae wanted you to come here if you were able," Jonathan continues. "She wanted you to see the house. She didn't want you to sell it without seeing it first, although you have every right to do that. It's yours now. But she told me, from what she knew about you, well, she wanted you to see it at least once, if possible."

Jonathan Walker removes a manilla envelope from the leather binder. He turns it over. A smaller envelope and a set of keys tumble onto the desk. He slides the keys over.

"These are to the cabin."

He turns the smaller envelope so the writing faces Cyd, and he moves that across the desk as well. On it, in a faded, cursive handwriting, are two lines:

To Cyd

Love, Mae

"This is the key to the box," Jonathan says.

Cyd takes the envelope and clears her throat. "The box?"

"Oh, didn't I mention it? She left a box." Jonathan looks to his left. There, on a table in front of a sofa sits a wooden box the size of a large shoe box with a small brass lock. It appears to be quite old.

"I haven't seen the contents," he continues. "I know there are letters. Your dad wrote to Mae over the years. He kept her informed about you. And about Baker, too, of course."

"You see, Cyd," he continues, more seriously now. "There's something more Mae wanted me to tell you. Since she couldn't tell you herself, she felt it was important for me to tell you in person. After your brother died . . ." His voice trails off, and he lowers his gaze, seeming to need to collect his thoughts.

My brother?

He looks up again. "You see, Cyd, your brother was not actually your brother."

"Excuse me?" Cyd croaks, unsure of what she has just heard.

"Mae was Baker's mother. Your mom and dad adopted him because Mae was very young, barely nineteen and unmarried. Your parents, by contrast, were settled and financially comfortable. Of course, it was different back then, a young single woman getting pregnant. It was pretty scandalous. Her family was poor, as you know. Your grandfather was dead by that time. Mae was on her own, alone, barely able to support herself, much less a child. It must have been very scary."

Cyd struggles to concentrate. She moves her shoulder blades down her back and grips the arms of the chair. Jonathan leans forward on his desk as if concerned for her safety.

"I take it that you didn't know about this. Mae was certain that you didn't at the time of Baker's death, but I didn't know if you'd learned anything since then."

"No," Cyd says in a faraway voice. "My brother . . . Baker was adopted? Baker was Mae's son?"

"Yes, he was."

"Who was the father?" she hears herself ask, unsure why she should care.

"I don't know. Mae didn't give any details about him. Apparently, he was never in the picture. He may have been older, perhaps married. Remember, it was the fifties in the South," he adds as if that explained everything.

Cyd is unable to speak.

Jonathan continues, "Mae knew Baker was sick, but not until the end. At that point, Mae was very sick, too. She wanted to go to Baker's funeral, but she was too weak. It was very hard on her." He pauses, then asks, "You didn't know your cousin very well, did you, Cyd?"

"No. I never spent any time with Andrew other than when we were little."

"He struggled his whole life with drugs," Jonathan explains. "Mae tried many times to get him the help he needed. She sent him to expensive rehabs. In the end, they were estranged for a long time. He would come to her for money and she would give it to him, and she set things up so he had an allowance after she was gone. But Mae had long since accepted that Andrew would never have a normal life."

At the hospital, Helen had reminded Cyd of their mutual impression of the young Andrew: *he seemed off, weird.* Looking back, Cyd realizes he was most likely painfully shy. Later, her mom mentioned his addiction in passing. It hadn't meant anything to Cyd; Andrew was practically a stranger. Back then, she hadn't made any comparison of Andrew to Baker. Why would she? Now, there is a sad and undeniable similarity: Mae had two sons, not one, and they both struggled with drugs and alcohol for most of their lives.

Baker had been an alcoholic before Cyd understood the meaning of the word. She guessed he began drinking before he was out of middle school. Before their father died, Baker's drinking had become so disruptive to their family life that he had moved out of the house. It was a few months shy of his high school graduation. His drinking escapades had become unbearable. Cyd had watched from a cracked bedroom door on several occasions, awakened by the commotion as a confrontation between her furious father and her protective, defiant mother unfurled with Baker between them. He was seemingly oblivious to the chaos he was causing, stoned and drunk, wanting only to get past his battling parents to his bedroom. Cyd had never seen their father as distraught as he was during these episodes.

One night, after such an encounter had played out—shouting and crying and knocking into walls—Cyd waited until everything had gone quiet. She tiptoed down the hallway to Baker's bedroom and went in. He was face down on his bed, shoes still on, snoring like an old man. The room reeked, pungent and sour, overlaid with stale smoke.

Shortly thereafter, Cyd came home from school one day to find her mother sitting stone-still at the kitchen table. She started to speak, to ask what happened, then stopped herself. She went to Baker's room to find it empty. The posters on the walls—the one of Jim Morrison and the velvet one with the blacklight wormhole—were gone. The top of his dresser was cleared, and his closet, except for a few odd shirts and pants he never wore, was emptied.

She heard a noise and turned to see her mother behind her. "Come on out of there," she said, holding onto the doorknob, ready to close it behind them. Cyd studied her mother without moving. She looked coiled, as if sheer will alone kept her from exploding, from breaking into a million fragments. Cyd had questions, but her twelve-year-old mind couldn't formulate them. She felt she should hug her mother, though she rarely did, or that her mother should hug her, but neither of them moved. Cyd simply walked out of the room in silence. Their feelings about that day would remain a mystery. They had never discussed it.

After that first week, Iris spoke as if Baker's leaving home was the most natural thing in the world. Cyd overheard her on the phone telling her friend how well Baker was doing. "He's very independent. He had me over just the other day. That apartment of his is a lot nicer than the first place Jesse and I had." She didn't mention there were three guys, maybe more, sharing a tiny two-bedroom, and any time Cyd had gone there, it smelled like pot.

Baker's explanation to Cyd had been evasive. "It's not a big deal. Dad and I agreed it's better for everyone if I go. Besides, I'm not far. I'll be back to torment you, so don't get too comfortable."

But he never came back. Not really. Not until he got sick.

Jonathan Walker cleared his throat, perhaps to get Cyd's attention, then continued, "After Baker died, Mae asked to see me. Maybe she had been holding out hope that one day she could tell Baker and you the truth. Your mother was . . ." He pauses again, perhaps considering the right word. "Your mother didn't want Baker or you to know about this. She didn't want anyone to know. Mae said your mother was terrified of how Baker would react. I suspect Mae was, too. Your mother cut off contact with Mae and the rest of your father's family, your other aunts and uncles because, of course, they all knew."

"My brother was my cousin?" Cyd realizes tears are streaming down her face. She isn't exactly sure why she is crying.

Jonathan reaches into a drawer and hands her a small packet of tissues.

"I'm sorry to have shocked you like this," Jonathan says.

"I have been through everything in my parents' house. I cleaned it out after my mom died. There was nothing—no documents, no letters—nothing about an adoption." She struggles for a link. "But maybe it makes sense that there wouldn't be. I can see my mom doing this, wanting to keep a secret like this. She was so concerned about appearances."

Her head begins to swim.

"Are you all right?" Jonathan asks, handing her a bottle of water. "Can I get you anything?"

"Thank you," she says. "I'm fine. This is just all so unexpected. It never crossed my mind. But now that I think about it, I've never seen a picture of my mom pregnant with Baker. There are some of her pregnant with me, but not with Baker. I've never thought of that before." Cyd knows she is babbling. She takes a clipped inhale and tries to settle herself.

"Mae was relieved that your parents wanted to take the baby," Jonathan continues after a moment, assessing her. "She was young and scared, and she trusted your father completely. She told me how much she loved your dad."

He pauses again, reading his notes. "Mae lived with her older sister and brother-in-law in Baltimore while she was pregnant. Your parents took the baby as soon as he was born. Your mother believed Mae was mentally unstable for a long time afterward, and that's why she tried to keep away from her. Mae admitted she had been in very bad shape, mentally and emotionally. Then, she met Peter. It was their relationship that saved her. Peter knew everything about Mae's past, and he loved her unconditionally. After they had Andrew, your dad convinced your mom to let Mae be involved, a little bit anyway, as I understand it."

Jonathan seems at a loss for words. He looks directly into Cyd's eyes. "Mae felt she made the right decision back then. That's what she told me. She knew she was near the end of her life, and she seemed at peace with the decision."

Cyd is crying again, softly, for a loss she can't define. Intellectually, she knows this is all ancient history. None of it affects her now. It's simply a story. And not a particularly uncommon one, really. So why does it feel like so much more?

"I'm sorry to upset you. I know you have a lot on your plate with the hurricane and all," Jonathan says sincerely.

"I'm fine, really. Thank you. I am dealing with a lot right now, truth be told. More than the storm. This all feels like too much to take in. I don't know why, exactly."

"I want you to know one thing," he continues, still holding her gaze. "I remember very clearly the day Mae gave me these things, these instructions. She was a special lady. I know she loved you. She hoped you would understand."

23

Tomorrow is guaranteed no one.

Cyd repeats the sentence to herself like a mantra, trying to let the words relax her as the driver weaves expertly through Phoenix traffic headed toward Sedona. It has been a mantra for her since Baker's death. Can it be *ten years*? Cyd had been so busy caring for her mother during those subsequent years that she hadn't had time to take a breath much less to grieve properly. And now, an entire decade—gone.

Her head aches. Depleted—that's what she is. And overloaded. She almost wishes she was back in the hospital, left to rest, still postponing her reentry into the real world. Why had she been in such a hurry to leave? She can barely imagine her reasoning. She remembers the doctor's orders: Take it easy for a week. Limit heavy mental concentration for a few days. *Ugh.*

Thoughts of her recent hospital stay bring memories of a different hospital and the hours spent at her brother's side. Cyd had been there through it all, along with their mother, waiting for the inevitable.

For Iris, the stress of losing her favorite child, her son, must have been almost more than she could bear. Baker had, indeed, been her favorite. There was never any doubt in Cyd's mind. It had been an unspoken truth in her family for as long as Cyd had memory—Baker was their mother's favorite, and Cyd was their father's. It's no wonder that was the case, she thinks now, in light of what she has learned about Baker's background. Gaining and then losing her son was undoubtedly the greatest joy and the greatest sorrow of her mother's life. Cyd had watched helplessly as the process of Baker's dying played out, taking a devastating toll on Iris's health. For three years, emergencies arose and then resolved, but there was never any improvement. Just an excruciating decline. There were nights when Cyd insisted that Iris go home and eat some decent food. She needed to rest, Cyd told her, or she'd get sick, too. *What good would that do anyone, Mom?*

In the end, Cyd was left to care for their ailing mother alone, and she felt her brother's absence every day like a hole in her chest. Cyd especially missed Baker's extraordinary sense of humor. She knew Iris did, too. The two women needed something to help alleviate their pain, to somehow make light of the unbearable situation in which they found themselves— invalid mother and ill-equipped caregiver daughter, both grieving an extraordinary loss. Cyd would try to imagine what Baker might say to make their mother laugh about her own debilitating condition, to make them all laugh as they had in happier years. Remarkably, Baker could find humor in anything, his inner flame ignited by the laughter of others. He once told Cyd that in order to divert his attention from what was happening to his body, he would lie in bed at night and think up jokes. He could get them howling by making fun of his colostomy bag (imagining it as a floating device), or his uncontrollable weight loss (letting his shorts fall down as he walked), or his visits to the chemotherapy clinic. He could actually make them laugh about chemotherapy. *How?* Cyd knew he had endeared himself to everyone involved with his care—his doctors, the many nurses, the other patients. It was like a superpower.

But Cyd did not have her brother's wit, and when she reached for something to say to fill the enormous gap left in Baker's wake, she was left feeling cheated, the words she searched for remaining just beyond her grasp. She was often angry, too. Angry that Baker hadn't taken better care of himself. Angry that everything fell on her and her alone when he got sick. There was no wife to help care for him. Not even a long-term girlfriend. He hadn't been very good husband material. His humor only carried him so far.

When Baker got his diagnosis, Cyd was the first person he called. He had asked her to break the news to their mother. He thought it would be better coming from Cyd, giving Iris time to process it all before talking to him. Cyd wasn't sure about his reasoning, but she had agreed to do as he asked. Their mother wasn't one to fall apart, but this was uncharted territory. Cyd had found herself overcome by an unfamiliar feeling of protectiveness toward her mom, a woman whose fortitude had always trumped her small stature. It was as if Iris had suddenly become a less substantial version of herself, and Cyd wasn't sure she could handle what she was about to go through.

She still felt angry all these years later, as if she'd been duped. She remembered clearly what Baker had said during that first conversation, relaying his doctor's optimism, making light of the situation in spite of the cancer diagnosis.

"Don't worry, Sis." Baker practically chuckled over the phone as Cyd tried to process the shocking news. "And, tell Mom not to worry. This isn't going to kill me."

Three excruciating years later, he was gone.

Cyd reaches into her handbag and retrieves the key to the cabin from the side pocket. Then she digs deeper, feeling along the bottom of the bag until she finds it. She withdraws the small furry token that she has carried around for the past ten years. She clips the cabin key onto the small chain, letting the white rabbit's foot dangle down. It had been Baker's. He, too, carried it everywhere. First, in his pocket, before he was able to drive, then attached to his car keys. He kept it with him for as long as Cyd can remember, and then, at the end, he gave it to her.

In the back seat of the car, the sun's relentless glare accentuates the pounding across her forehead, thumping to the rhythm of the tires on the pavement. She tries Helen's number and the call goes directly to voicemail. She fingers the silky keepsake and closes her eyes. It really *is* too much. Her brain has shut down like the end of an album when the record keeps spinning but the only sound that comes out is the scratch of needle on vinyl.

Still, the thoughts beat their way in. Was agreeing to take Baker from Mae when she was at her most vulnerable really the best solution? Had Mae ever regretted the decision, perhaps wanted to undo it? Is that why Mae wasn't around when they were children?

Cyd pictures her mother, petite and always perfectly presentable, so concerned about what people might think. Was the truth so disgraceful that she needed to take the secret to her grave? Why not tell Baker after he was grown? He might have gotten to know Mae. She could have explained herself, perhaps helped him to understand. Did he deserve to know?

And what about Mae? Who *was* this woman? And why did she want Cyd, a niece she hadn't seen in decades, to know all this information now? She can't quite make sense of it. There is something barren about the story, stark and sharp, not unlike the arid landscape outside her window, holding its secrets close, hidden from outsiders.

Her father's face appears in her mind's eye. She can smell the odor of him—Old Spice and salt air and sweet tea. She can still feel the strength of his embrace and the scratchiness of his kiss on her forehead. It's all so hard to comprehend, to square what she has just learned with the people she thought she knew. She had never known her father to lie. And yet, he *had* lied. He had saved his sister from a life she didn't want and presented his wife with everything she dreamed of. He had done what was asked of him. But what had *he* wanted?

Her father had left home before dawn that Sunday morning, the 5th of July, after one last gathering with his friends and neighbors in the town park. He took his fishing gear with him. The police arrived at the house just as Iris was leaving for Mass. Her husband's car had been found a short distance off a remote stretch of marsh-lined road, they told her. With uncanny bad luck, he managed to hit a lone tree head-on, his neck broken on impact. He may have swerved to avoid hitting an animal, a deer perhaps, in the early morning fog.

After the initial shock of her husband's premature death, Iris picked up her life without any evidence of self-pity as Cyd watched in disbelief. She cooked dinner and invited friends over for coffee and resumed her volunteer work at the church thrift store. She talked to Baker on the phone on the nights he didn't come for supper—he had moved out by then. Cyd would overhear her mother relaying the events of the day in an inconceivably normal tone, even laughing at times in response to something Baker said. Cyd listened in dismay, her stomach in a constant burning knot. Cyd's response to her father's death had been a mixture of disbelief and terror that struck with the intensity of an electric shock, creating a stew of grief and re- morse she could not digest. Iris seemed unable or unwilling to help Cyd cope with a loss as severe as an amputation, and the distance she had always felt between herself and her mother widened to a chasm.

Baker had tried in his own way to console her. He would come into her room and sprawl on the floor as he had done when they were younger, offer to play Monopoly or take her into town for pizza. But Cyd was unable to respond. If there was a will or an inner strength with which to hold herself up, it was, at that young age, unavailable to her. Any interest she once held in athletics, piano, even schoolwork—in any activity that had inspired her father's admiration and praise—disintegrated along with her father's presence. She dwelled inconsolably on the simple, everyday things they had done together: giggling uncon- trollably while playing a silly game of Sorry!, or practicing golf swings in the backyard by whacking at whiffle balls, or listening to jazz music after supper. How had she not spent more time with him? What else had she been doing? The regret would linger for years.

Helen had been there, of course, faithfully, unflinchingly, and even then, as a young girl, practical and wise. Cyd began spending even more time at the Kondilises' house. No one asked anything of her. They just went about their lives—cooking, eating, arguing, laughing—and let Cyd disappear into the middle of it. Sophia Kondilis treated Cyd as if she were another one of her children, no more or less special, which made Cyd *feel* like she was one of her children, and for which Cyd will always cherish her.

Nicky, too, had been perfect. He'd paid her just the smallest bit of extra attention, nothing anyone else would notice, but which Cyd clung to, grateful and desperate. He had given her a sympathy card, writing how sorry he was for her loss, that he knew what it meant to have a good dad, and how sad he would be if he lost his father—an eerie premonition of what awaited his family, also much too soon. In his own intuitive, attentive way, Nick acknowledged the depth of her suffering and somehow made it more bearable.

Cyd opens her eyes and examines the expansive Arizona desert. She caresses the small furry foot between her fingers and stares down the long stretch of highway. Unsure of where she is or where she is going, the only certainty seems to be that she is a long way from nowhere.

24

The ride to the cabin takes a little over two hours. As they pull into Sedona, the rhythm of the motion slows, and Cyd realizes she has nodded off. Her thoughts turn immediately to Lola, and once again her phone call to Helen goes to voicemail. She says another silent, fervent prayer for the safety of her friends and neighbors.

The driver turns off the main road and winds up toward the hills. As he does, her aunt's attraction to this place becomes obvious. The colors deepen. The famed red rocks bolt up like a stone cityscape, red-orange as promised, but so much more— light pink and milky gray and soft, chalky brown. It is fantastic, surreal. She opens the window, wanting to feel closer to what she is seeing. The air is clean and subtlety fragrant. She wants to inhale all of it. She wants it to seep into her pores.

From a narrow sandy road, they pull up to an adobe-style house. The house is tucked behind a line of twisted juniper trees and framed by the red rock formations in the near distance. Cyd gets out of the car and stretches her arms overhead, harnessing the aroma of plants and stone, filling her lungs to capacity. She drinks in her surroundings, captivated by the beauty and the power. It is all so glorious, and she is so very insignificant. She lowers her arms. There is nothing but the desert, the magnificent rocks, and a glorious stillness.

The driver sets her bags at her feet as Cyd turns her attention from the view to the house and its substantial double front doors. The outside walls are thick and cream-colored, and as soon as she steps under the eave, the intense heat diminishes like magic. The lock clicks open, and she pushes against the dark wood—the weight of it a comfort—and steps inside.

Directly opposite the front door, across a single room that comprises the main living area and an open kitchen, there is a two-story triangular bank of windows with a direct view of the great protrusions. Though the house is small, the open floorplan and the expansive panorama create the illusion of *space*. Closest to the house, there is a sparseness which, in the near distance, gives way to larger trees and then to increasing elevation. There are towers and mesas in every direction, grand and mysterious. Standing there, her vision focused outside the huge glass panes, it is as if the great red rocks are in the room with her, like party guests, as if you could rise from the sofa and walk right up to them. They are part of the house.

An unmistakable energy swirls up and around her. There is a tingling up her spine and down her arms. The rocks surround her, comfort her, whisper their long-held secrets. They are real. They are permanent. Everything else is fleeting.

Cyd finds a pervasive calm throughout the entire home as she explores the cabin. The decor is simple and elegant, with Southwestern art hung sparingly and floors of thick Mexican tile. The palette mimics the desert—pale walls offset by honey-colored doors and ceiling beams. There is a large Navajo rug dyed with the colors of the landscape and an antler chandelier over a dark walnut dining table. Cyd can easily see the woman from her childhood, her mysteriously glamorous Aunt Mae, gliding through this house.

The silence is broken by the buzz of her phone. It lights up with a picture of Holly caught turning her head toward the camera, movement evident by the swoosh of her hair out to the side. Her face is bright and set with large thick-lashed eyes. Cyd snapped the photo a few years ago as they walked past an old brick wall, just as Holly turned to look at her, mid-stride. It had been a carefree mother-daughter shopping day.

"Mom! Where are you? I thought you were going to call me after your meeting. Is everything okay?"

Cyd recognizes real concern in her daughter's voice. She knows she would be worried, too, if the tables were turned.

"Oh, sweetheart, I'm sorry. So much has happened. I decided to leave Phoenix. I'm in Sedona. I just got here."

"Sedona?" Holly asks, understandably confused.

"I know. I have things to tell you. But first, what is the news from home? I haven't been able to watch anything since early this morning."

"I've seen the reports from Gulf Shores. There's nothing left there, Mom. It's devastating. People have died. And we don't know much about Lola yet."

Holly's voice reveals her shock at what she has seen. The neighboring town where Cyd had driven at Nick's request— where the accident occurred—has taken a direct hit.

"I watched a little first thing this morning, but no more," Cyd explains. "I was with the lawyer and then in an Uber. I fell asleep during the drive here."

"*Where* are you, exactly?" Holly repeats the question, clearly upset.

Her daughter has always been sensitive. Cyd longs to take her in her arms and comfort her. Instead, she soothes her daughter's fears as best she can, as she's been doing for the past twenty-seven years. Cyd gives an abbreviated summary of the whirlwind of events—the inheritance, the house, and the locked box she has yet to open. She finds herself leaving out the revelation about Baker almost instinctually. She realizes she is experiencing a mini-version of what her parents must have dealt with—what good would come from telling her? Did her children *really* need to know these outdated details?

"You and Sean need to come out here," Cyd says, referring to Holly's long-term boyfriend, changing the subject to a more optimistic topic. She looks around the beautiful room, still trying to grasp the fact that she is actually sitting in Mae's house. No, in *her* house. "And Bo, too. This place is incredible. I can't wait for you all to see it." As the words leave her mouth, she wonders if it's true. *Will* they be able to come here? It's nearly two thousand miles away. Can she even manage to hold on to it long enough for that to happen? How will she ever afford this place?

"Wow, Mom. This is exciting. I can hardly believe it. Maybe things will work out after all. Life is full of surprises, isn't it?"

"That it is," Cyd agrees. *That it is.*

Once she assures Holly that she really is fine, they say their goodbyes. Cyd picks up a large book from the coffee table in front of her. A photograph of one of the red rock formations is on the cover. She leafs through the pages, reading the descriptive names of the unique formations that dominate the area—Bell Rock, Cathedral Rock, Coffee Pot Rock. She reads about the swirling vortexes of energy that are believed to exist in the canyon, some upward moving and some downward. They are said to enhance the practice of meditation and even promote healing and spiritual growth. The news of this mystical energy comes as no surprise. Cyd felt it the moment she stepped out of the car. Had Mae studied this phenomenon?

She crosses her legs under her and confronts the wooden box. The initials *MJW* are engraved on the top, dating it prior to Miss Mary Jane Williams becoming Mrs. Mae Williams-Grant. She removes the small key from the envelope, turns the lock, and lifts the lid.

There is a stack of letters, many identical in size, bundled together the width of a brick. She sets the letters aside. There are old postcards and photographs with faded black-and-white images, small and square and deckle-edged, similar to the one of her father and his friends. There is writing on the back of some of the photographs—dates and names—also faded. Cyd glances quickly at some of the photographs, certain most are from Jesse and Mae's childhood home. There is a white rabbit's foot key chain, nearly identical to the one Baker carried for years, and a thin linen handkerchief with light blue embroidery neatly pressed and slightly yellowed. She rubs the soft fabric between her fingers, wondering who else has touched it. Perhaps it had belonged to her grandmother, a woman she never knew. She sets the rabbit's foot and the handkerchief on the table next to the box with the photographs. There is a very real, very physical sensation of being pulled back into the past.

She picks up the stack of letters once again. On top, clearly meant to be seen first, is an envelope of a different style with her name on it, *Cyd Carr,* in the same script as the envelope containing the key to the box.

Cyd unfolds the stiff paper. The letter is dated January 27,

2009, ten years ago. She takes a moment to place the date. It was a few months before Mae's death. She had just turned sixty-eight years old. Baker had died six months earlier when he was forty-eight. Her mother, already sickened by grief and illness, would pass away eight years later.

Cyd pulls her attention back to the present, inhales deeply, and begins to read.

25

My dearest Cyd,

*You now know part of my story. I might have told you
myself, but the good Lord has other plans for me. I am
anxious to move on. Once this last task is finished, I'm
ready to go. It is time for me to meet my Maker and pay
the price for my sins.*

*This is not the first time in my life I have wanted to die. If
I had gotten my way, I would have been gone a long time
ago. Instead, God decided I should stay a bit longer and
live out this life fully. I am surely grateful, but I never
understood why. I certainly didn't deserve it. Maybe that
question will soon be answered. I like to believe all our
questions will be answered in the end. Or maybe, even
better, they will no longer matter.*

Cyd stops, surprised by this sentiment, one she shares with
Mae. Is it another strange coincidence, a similarity with a woman
she barely knew, or does everyone want all the important questions answered in the end? She has always hated unanswered

questions. According to her dad, "*But why?*" were her two most overused words.

She continues reading.

You and I suffered a deep loss the day your father was taken from us, a cut to the bone. I have missed Jesse every day right up until this one. He saved my life. He was the reason I tried to get better because he wanted that for me so much. His strength and love lifted me up and made it possible for me to go on with my life when I could not see the point in taking another breath.

You were cheated when your father was taken. You only knew him through the eyes of a child. I hope now you can know him in full like I did. He was the most honest, self-less man that ever there was. He was strong and decent in every way. You have him in you. I saw it. My wish for you and my belated gift to my brother, my hero, is that these letters will help you to know him.

I don't expect you to understand the decisions we made. We all did the best we could, I suppose. I was mad, truly mad, for some time. It's a wonder I came out of it. I had given up on myself. But your father never gave up on me.

Your mother did the best she could, too. I think Iris and I could have been great friends had things gone differently. We liked each other at first. Your dad called us "his glamour gals" in those early days. But then, Iris went a bit mad herself. She did the only thing she knew, which was to protect her family. I never blamed your mother for anything. I was grateful to her.

I don't know at what point in your life you will be read-ing this. It might even be your children who inherit this box and are reading this letter. I can only trust that it will work out as the good Lord intends. "Man plans, the Lord laughs," Mama used to say.

One last thing, child—funny, I still can't help but think of you as a child. I spoke to your father many times about you. I know how he felt about you. He loved you like no one else. I saw how he looked at you and you at him. I can tell you, without a doubt, you were the light of his life. He saved my life and you, in turn, saved his. Well done, Sweetsie, well done. I know you have made him proud.

Your loving aunt,
Mae

Cyd drops the pages to her lap. No one had referred to her as *Sweetsie* since her father. It was his playful interpretation of Sweet Cyd, shortened to Sweet C, which morphed into Sweetsie. Obviously, Mae remembered the endearment. The words bring Jesse into the room. She can hear his voice, feel his hug and the roughness of his whiskers, see his encouraging smile, the one he saved just for her. "My sweet Cyd," he would say. "How's my Sweetsie?"

The irony of the nickname was lost on her as a child, but now Cyd understands, given her reputation of being anything *but* sweet, how perfect it was that her father had chosen it.

Her mother liked to say that Baker was the best baby any-one had ever come across. He simply didn't cry, she bragged, as if she and God together had created this miracle child. He didn't cry to get lifted from his crib in the morning or when he was placed in it at night. He didn't scream to get what he wanted or throw a tantrum if something was withheld. Baker was the sweet one.

For Iris, for whom order and tranquility were everything, Baker truly was the perfect child. Iris had grown up in a house full of commotion, Cyd's father explained. He was always trying to lessen the gulf that seemed to separate Cyd from her mother. Iris rarely spoke about any of it—the fact that her own mother had died when Iris was two, leaving her to be raised by an aunt and uncle on her father's side. She had been plopped amid her six cousins—an unruly bunch, apparently—while her father worked all hours as a waiter in his uncle's restaurant. She had lost her father, too, soon after meeting her husband-to-be. Iris craved nothing more than her father's company and, since that was unavailable, solitude, which she found at church and in the library. Iris, named defiantly by her mother after her favorite flower rather than after one of the grandmothers as expected, was a quiet only child who grew into a serious, hardworking woman, conscientious, well-read, and Catholic. Cyd wondered if Iris loved Baker so intensely because he made her laugh in a world where little else did.

In contrast to Baker's agreeable, happy childhood, when Cyd came along seven years later, it was like an alarm set off. The pregnancy was difficult and the delivery ended in an emergency Cesarean. The whole affair had taken such a physical toll on Iris that the doctor discouraged her from trying to have any more children. It was probably just as well, Iris once said, since Cyd exhausted her mother from the start. She barely slept. She wanted to nurse at all hours and screamed ferociously to make her desires understood. Her mother's description of her as an infant stayed with Cyd. She saw in herself a tendency to be difficult, impatient, even defiant. Was that the way she was, or was that the way her mother saw her?

In Cyd's mind, it was no wonder Baker was the sole recipient of their mother's true devotion. She heard all about it for as long as she can remember: Baker was born delightful, and he stayed delightful. Even when he was drunk, he could be endearing and lovable (up to a point), never mean or cruel. Baker's excessive drinking began in high school and, to Cyd's knowledge, never stopped. He was one of those people who shouldn't drink at all. There was a fragility to him. He went from sober to slurring with little in-between. As he got older, he must have accepted this shortcoming, and to deal with it, he either drank nothing at all or settled in where he knew he could pass out in relative safety, like his apartment or backyard. He rarely went to a bar— he could save money while avoiding the problem of how to get home. Over the years, his tendency to isolate himself for extended periods of time concerned Cyd. She guessed he spent a lot of time drinking alone.

Eventually, Cyd came to see Baker's humor as more of a deliberate shield than a natural gift, a well-honed defense system meant to keep people from looking any deeper. It saddened her to see that Baker's friendships, while plentiful, were somewhat superficial and mostly short-lived. People came and went—guy friends, girlfriends, customers, jobs. He left Lola and moved around for years until he got sick. The older he got, the more reclusive he became. Cyd saw less and less of him. She knew a lot of people cared about him and loved him. But, in the end, his world had shrunk to a painfully small circle.

Cyd lifts her eyes to the wall of windows, reflective against the dark outside, as the memories brush past her like spirits. She doesn't want to continue reading. It would be so much easier with Helen sitting next to her for moral support. She doesn't even have the comfort of Fern at her feet. On the verge of tears, she tries Helen's phone again. Nothing. She presses the palms of her hands against her eyes, takes a deep breath, and pulls a letter from the box.

26

The envelopes are arranged with the most recent on top, so she reads in that order, moving backward in time. For the most part, they are uneventful, like letters she had written herself back when people actually wrote letters. (The real fun was watching with anticipation for the return note to arrive in the mailbox.) These letters, the ones written by her father, documented the nearly twenty-five years before his death—he had been only forty-three years old when he died. As she reads, Cyd knows immediately why Mae wanted her to have them, not because they are riveting or dramatic or eloquent—they aren't. But because they relay, ever so sweetly, the rhythm and flow of life as told by a brother to his little sister. All the beautiful little things that make up every day and, eventually, an entire life.

The weather is a much-covered topic since her father was a farmer at heart: *This has been the hottest, wettest August the state has ever seen. At high tide, the docks are nearly covered. I guess that's why the mosquitos are as big as rats this year. Reminds me of when we would camp down by the creek.*

He wrote about whatever was happening at home: *Iris has*

been working on some throws for the church bazaar. She sits in her chair all evening, but they sure do seem to appreciate her hard work.

Cyd smiles at the stories of her and her brother: *Baker's been making us all laugh by dancing on his toes. Saw it on the television once and he's been imitating it ever since. That kid sure is funny when he gets on something.* And, in another: *Cyd made another perfect grade on a math test. And she's getting so tall. She's right in line with Iris now.*

The letters bring forth memories of her childhood Cyd didn't know she possessed. Each one is an episode, like a weekly television show, of the mundane and the wondrous that was their life as a young family. Mae was absolutely right. These letters are a gift unlike any other—the first twelve years of her existence documented in her father's words. They also present a precious glimpse into her parents' marriage from a vantage point she couldn't have seen as a child and of their early years together as a couple.

He conveys the excitement of their first months together: *I can't wait for you to meet Iris. I know you two will be fast friends. She's real quiet, but smart when you get to know her. She's read so many books they could fill up a library. Reminds me of you and those glamour magazines you were always reading.*

There were dark days, too, after the miscarriages her mother had suffered in the first years together. Cyd only learned of these events when she lost her first pregnancy. Her mother had meant to comfort her, telling Cyd she understood how she felt. In one letter, her father wrote: *I'm real worried about her, Mary Jane. Some days she sits at the kitchen table all day long. She's still in her nightgown when I come home from work, sitting right where I left her that morning. I don't know what to do for her.*

According to her dad, Cyd's parents began their marriage in

agreement over children. "We would have had ten," he said once, and Cyd was quite sure he was serious. Instead, there were three miscarriages before Baker was born. Cyd suspected her mother was severely depressed during that time. Once, toward the end, when Cyd took her mom to the doctor during the height of her illness, she admitted as much. Not looking at Cyd, Iris answered the doctor's questions: Yes, she had some experience with depression and yes, she was struggling now, as she had when she was younger. Yes, she would like him to prescribe something that might help with the feelings she was having, with the relentless despair that pervaded her days. Cyd remembered the three lost babies then, and her own miscarriage, and filled the prescription without asking her mother anything further. Cyd wishes now she had been more compassionate toward her mother, more understanding of the many difficulties she had endured during her life.

As she reads, Cyd sees the letters as a study of a wife and a friend. She admires the portrait these observations paint: one of a strong, charitable woman, devoted to her family and her community, self-sufficient, determined, and generous. Why hadn't she been more aware of it while her mother was alive? Why had she felt as if a competition existed between herself and her mom? It seems obvious, now, that Cyd had refused to see—or had been unable to see—her mother as a woman, as a complex, multifaceted *person.*

Cyd stops once, a sudden choke of emotion in her throat, after finishing the only letter in the box written by her mother. Tucked in the envelope is a small headshot of Baker, one taken at school. He smiles sweetly into the lens, the faint dimple in his left cheek visible, his hair short and freshly cut. Iris had written on the back—second grade, April 1967—two months before Cyd was born. In the brief letter, her mom wrote that Baker had made his First Communion.

We all did the best we could, Mae wrote in her letter. Is that all there was to it? Maybe that's all there should be. Isn't that what she always told her children, to try to do their best?

Cyd drops the note to her lap, unspilt tears making it impossible to continue—tears for her father and for Mae, for her mother and Baker, and for her younger self, too. The past—*her* past—seems very distant, almost like a life she's only read about, not actually lived.

Another line from Mae's letter floats into her thoughts: *This is not the first time in my life that I have wanted to die.*

Had Mae changed her mind about giving up the baby? Mae said she didn't "blame" Iris, but surely that came later. Cyd knew her mother could be very judgmental. And, she was a staunch Catholic. *You did not have sex before marriage. You did not have an affair with a married man.* These rules were nonnegotiable in her mother's world. Mae's behavior would have been scandalous. Her mother would have wanted to keep it a secret at any cost.

Is that why her mom hadn't confided in her, even after Baker was gone, even though it might have brought them closer? They were two adult women, both of them mothers. They should have been able to talk about it.

In honest retrospect, though, it wasn't surprising that her mom had never confided in her. What was there to say, really? It was over and done. Cyd said those same words to herself many times over the years—why dredge up the past? What's done is done.

And what about Baker, the beloved son and brother at the center of all this? Did he ever suspect? Had he known and not told her? Did this have anything to do with his drinking?

As the questions multiply, Cyd realizes she will never know the answers. Everyone is gone. There is no one to ask.

She turns to the last letters in the box. A few from Jesse and Mae's older sister, Lucy, and from their mother, Cyd's grandmother, whom she has only ever seen in photographs. She reads them all. In the end, there are no answers. There is nothing about the adoption, or the deep sorrow Mae had admitted to in her letter to Cyd, or anything suggesting a rift between her mother and Mae. It is as if the story has been sanitized.

She sits with the letters strewn about her. It seems she should feel a sense of closure. Instead, it feels like another betrayal. Intellectually, she knows it's not about her. It's just a messed-up situation. A baby out of wedlock. A secret adoption. Lots of families have worse skeletons in the closet. But it's all set something in motion—a reexamination of her entire past through a new lens, a mental autopsy of the validity of everything she thought she knew about her parents and her brother.

And Loren. Involuntarily, she is reminded of Loren's deception, and—snap!—the sickening feeling is back. The pain is visceral. She is hurled back to the hospital moments after learning about Loren's affair, grasping for something to hold on to, something real, something true. How did she not see it? How could she have been so totally blindsided?

She is lost in thought, sitting in the light of a lone lamp, when her phone lights up with a text bubble.

Swanson: *Hey. Just checking on you. How are you feeling?*

She doesn't dare think too long. She dials his number.

"Hey there," he says, sounding surprised and pleased.

His voice is soothing, almost lush. She releases her shoulders and sighs out a week's worth of tension.

"Hi," she says.

"Are you okay? I've been, you know, wondering how you guys are doing. If you got out of town without any trouble, wondering how you—"

Cyd cuts in to rescue him. "I'm fine, really I am." She considers her options. Which direction to take the conversation. *To hell with it.*

"I'm alone, Swanson. I left Loren in Texas. I flew to Phoenix, if you can believe *that.* I actually got on a plane." She had almost forgotten that last part, her *real* accomplishment. "I'm feeling quite sassy about it, truth be told."

"Miracles never cease," he says, repeating back to her one of her favorite axioms. She can hear the smile in his voice. "How was it?"

"I didn't puke." She finds herself smiling back.

"Progress all around."

"And that's not all. I am the proud new owner of a house in Sedona. My aunt left it to me. I'm sitting in it right now."

"No shit. Sedona? I've heard it's pretty incredible."

"It is. I mean, I haven't seen much, but the house is beautiful. It's right in the middle of the red rocks. It was her special getaway spot. How perfect is that? And there's something almost magical about the place. They say there's all this ancient energy swirling around. I feel something. I do. I know it sounds like gobbledy-gook, but I really do feel something."

"Hey, if you feel something good, that's a win in my book. You don't have to try to explain it away." He hesitates. "So Loren is gone?"

"Don't get me started. In spite of all the good energy here, it wouldn't take much to get me riled up all over again. Yes, he's gone. Or rather, I'm gone. I just decided I had to get away. I had to get on that plane."

"A new adventure."

"I haven't thought of it like that, but yes. I have no idea what I'm doing next, so I guess that qualifies as an adventure. Ready, fire, aim," she says and laughs.

They go on to fill each other in on the past few days. He tells her he was able to get a flight out after taking his boat to relative safety upriver. He flew from Atlanta to Chicago and planned to watch the storm pass from a safe distance. Bobby lived on his boat. He had nothing holding him in Lola. Nothing and no one.

"Send me the address of the house," he says. "I'll look at it online."

She promises to do that, then says, "Thanks for calling, Swanson. I really do appreciate it."

"You got it, Sunshine."

She doesn't hang up. She can hear him breathing.

"Swanson?" she says in a near whisper.

"Yeah."

"I miss you, too."

It is late when Cyd crawls into bed—Mae's bed—and she brings the box with her. She pulls out the stack of postcards. One is from her Aunt Lucy, with a picture of the Empire State Building lit against the 1960s New York skyline. Another is of the Golden Gate Bridge from their mother, Lucille. *How about this!* she had scribbled on the back.

A colorful card catches her eye and she pulls it from the pile —a postcard with a photograph taken at the edge of Grand Canyon. The composition is from the rim and encapsulates a vast portion of the great chasm under a sliver of blue sky. The colors, though faded with time, are incredibly vibrant as if taken from an antique palette. The date written on the back is 1955, the year before Jesse had met Iris on a beach in Florida. Her father's handwriting is on the back:

Sis,

Sure do wish you were here. Standing on the edge looking down, you can't believe it. It's the most glorious place I've ever seen. I know you would love it as much as I do. Someday, I'll bring you.

Love, J

Cyd studies the image on the card then flips quickly through the old photographs recognizing it instantly—one taken of Jesse and his two friends, almost identical to the one Cyd has kept on display for decades, the one she brought with her on this trip. The two pictures were obviously taken at the same time on the same roll of film. Jesse Williams stands tall and invincible, chest out, wearing the same wide grin Cyd often sees on her son's face, the similarities between grandfather and grandson unmistakable. She had stared into those eyes for years. The emotion they hold beams across time and space like the howl of a wolf.

As Cyd returns the papers back to the box, arranging the letters so that everything will fit, she notices something sticky. She pulls the oldest letters from the bottom of the pile. A second envelope, thinner and smaller, is stuck to one of the others. She carefully pries the smaller envelope apart and reads the address:

Miss Mary Jane Williams
Virginia Correctional Center for Women
Goochland, VA

Cyd carefully opens the thin envelope and removes a fragile sheet of paper folded in thirds. The letter is dated February 15, 1960, less than three weeks before Baker was born, tiny as a bud and over two weeks early—at least that was the version of the story recited by Iris throughout the years. The letter is in her father's handwriting:

Dear Mae,

I've made arrangements to come again the last week in February. I'm counting the days. You have to be strong, Mary Jane. I know you're strong. You need to reach deep down for everything you've got. I know you can do it! You have to take care of yourself. Lucy tells me you're barely eating. If you can't do it for yourself or for the baby, then please do it for me. I promise you, things will get better. You will get through this and soon, you will have your whole life ahead of you. You are a beautiful young woman. I will be here for you—Lucy and Iris and Mama, too. All of us are here for you. You cannot give up, Mae! You are stronger than that! You've been through too much to give up now. I don't want you to get sick. Please eat. Please. I love you. I will see you very soon.

Jesse

Cyd recognizes her father's writing, but it is sloppy and slanting as if the words might slide off the page. She rereads the letter.

What the fuck?

Her head hurts and though her body is exhausted, her mind does not yet want to let her succumb to sleep. There is nothing more to be done tonight. She sets the letter aside and checks the time. It is midnight, which means it is 3:00 a.m. in Florida. Too late to try Helen again. She switches off the light. She prays for her friends in Lola. She prays for wisdom and compassion. And she prays for sleep. Not necessarily in that order.

27

The knocking is what eventually wakes her. It is dark. She feels to the side, but Loren is not in the bed. She gets up slowly, tentatively, and feels along the wall, searching for a light switch. The floor feels strangely cold on her bare feet, like hospital linoleum. Her eyes are wide open, but she sees nothing, only darkness. A great relief comes when she feels the flat panel and finds the toggle, but the light is dim, barely visible, and she flips the switch up and down several times. A sickness rises in her stomach. Moisture tingles the back of her neck. The knocking continues. But from where? It seems to be coming from everywhere. She looks frantically around the unfamiliar room, but the light is so dim. *Why is the light so dim?* Then she sees Loren. Thank God! He is right there! She steps toward him, reaching, wanting him to hold her, but as she does, he moves away, keeping the distance between them. He is still, not stepping backward, and yet the distance between them remains unchanged as she moves toward him, frantically reaching. *What is that knocking, Loren? Do you hear it? Loren!*

28

Wednesday, June 2, 2019
Sedona, Arizona

As she is pulled into consciousness, she realizes someone is knocking on the front door. She sits up, breathless. The great stones glow in the distance, drenched in color like kings draped in red robes.

The door. It must be a neighbor who saw the lights on last night. She pulls her robe from the suitcase and runs a brush quickly through her hair.

She is wrong. It is not a stranger she finds waiting when she cracks open the big door. Instead, she is greeted by dimples and sapphire eyes and a mischievous grin—special delivery right to her doorstep.

"Swanson! I don't even know where to start! What? How?" She swings the door open and throws her arms around his neck. "I knew this place was magical, but you can't get from Chicago to here that fast without a flying broom. What gives? Come in, you!"

The relief of having her friend here, and having him know her well enough to know that coming is exactly what she needs, turns her giddy with gratitude.

"I may have fibbed a little last night. I talked to Annie on Monday. She told me you were getting on a plane in Dallas. I figured you might need some moral support. I flew to Phoenix yesterday before I called you. I wanted to surprise you."

"I'm certainly happy that you did." She pulls him into the room with one hand and sweeps the other arm toward the wall of windows. "Not bad, right? This is why Aunt Mae wanted me to come out here. She thought I might put it on the market without seeing it first. She called it 'the cabin.' I may be a Florida girl, but I think I could get used to this."

His hand is still in hers as she leads him to the sofa. She drops onto the cushions and curls her bare feet under her in one smooth motion.

"We'll go find some coffee in a moment," she says, patting the seat next to her, turning serious. "First, tell me, how are you? Do you know how your boat is? What do you know about Lola?"

"My boat is safe. Cell service is out around the area, but I've talked to a few people. Word is trickling out of Lola. The media swarm has started, too, but all the major news coverage is out of Gulf Shores since they took the direct hit. It's a disaster. About as bad as it gets. Lola got hammered, no doubt, and it's going to take some work getting things situated, but we got lucky. Unlike Gulf Shores, the town is still there."

Cyd can picture in detail what Bobby is hinting at. She's likely seen more news footage of such destruction than most people. She's seen her fair share in person, too, having lived in Florida her entire life. As anyone in Gulf Shores would attest to now, a hurricane is often described as sounding like a freight train barreling directly through your house. And it goes on for hours. She can imagine what it must have been like for those who chose to ride out the storm and for those trying to return to the rubble left in its wake. She shivers at the thought of how narrowly they averted the worst of Abigail's wrath.

Bobby goes on to tell her what he knows. The O was flooded and will be closed indefinitely. It was high tide when the storm hit, so the rising water along with the rain flooded much of downtown along the river. And there were several twisters in town spun off from the hurricane. "Those things are nasty. Indiscriminate," he says. "Annie and Tony may have gotten lucky. I don't know about your place."

"I don't have television or internet here. I feel lucky to have cell service. Let's try Helen again. I haven't been able to reach her."

Cyd picks up her phone. She pauses briefly before tapping the icon next to Helen's name. It is a picture of a picture—an old photograph taken when Cyd and Helen were in grade school. It was Halloween. Cyd was dressed like a piece of candy corn, and Helen was a Tootsie Roll. They were grinning widely, excitedly. It feels like yesterday and another lifetime all at once.

Cyd touches the phone and waits. Nothing happens, and after a moment, a double beep sounds, and she is cut off.

"It could be days before the service is restored," Bobby offers. "She'll call you when she can." He rises from the sofa and walks to the windows. "Hard to imagine having a bad day when this is what you wake up to. What do you say we just screw around all day? See what trouble we can get into?"

He turns to face her. His smile is as irresistible as always.

"Let's start with coffee and some food. I need to build up my reserves if I'm going to try to keep up with you," she says. Any unpleasant remnants of the dream or Mae's mystery or her own uncertain future fade into the background.

They spend their time luxuriating in the rare gift of an entire day without schedule or obligation. They drive into Sedona and order coffee and Bloody Marys and way too much food—pancakes (Cyd's choice), huevos rancheros (Bobby's choice), a plate of bacon (just because), and a giant cinnamon roll (why the hell not).

They eat leisurely over effortless conversation where nothing of serious importance is allowed to ruin their lighthearted mood. They chatter and laugh and reach over to each other's plates to scoop or stab and decide another round of drinks is in order after the embarrassingly empty plates are cleared.

They browse a large antique mall where they try on old hats, and Bobby walks out wearing a used Stetson in remarkably good shape. They wander through an art gallery, pointing out paintings that they then stare at side by side, chins resting in fingers.

"Notice the feathery brushstrokes around the bulbous nose," Bobby whispers conspiratorially.

"*You* may think this is just a red square," Cyd initiates at another, "but I see what the artist *really* intended: the meaning of life!"

"The horizon can be high, it can be low," Bobby prompts.

And Cyd finishes, "But it can never be in the center!"

Later, they sit in the shade of the pergola on the back patio, stretched out in the Adirondack chairs.

"So," he begins. "Someone has a birthday coming up."

"Yes, someone does," she answers, her head tilted back, her eyes closed.

"So what are we doing this year?" he continues.

"I was planning on forgetting about the whole thing."

"I think not. We've celebrated our birthdays for the past five years. This year needs to be the blowout year."

She sits up suddenly and grabs his wrist.

"Oh my god, Swanson! I nearly forgot. It's your fortieth this year!"

"Damn right, it is." He is lying back. He doesn't move.

"Shit." She settles herself again.

"What?"

"I love that our birthdays are a day apart; you know I do. It's just that with everything going on, I'm not up for a celebration. But *you* need to! You absolutely need to. You can tell me all about it afterward."

"Hmmmm. So that's what you've come up with?"

"Don't pressure me!" she whines. "You know I can't resist you pressuring me."

"That's what I'm counting on."

There is a substantial pause.

"Speaking of counting, have we ever talked about your life path number?" she asks, a sliver of sun cutting through the wood beams warming her face.

"Uh, maybe. Tell me again," he says groggily.

"Your life path number is eleven. That's a good one. I'm a seven."

"Explain, please."

Cyd is sure he is humoring her, certain she has made him endure some version of this rambling at one point or another over the years, but she continues. "Your destiny number. It's kind of like your zodiac sign. It tells you what your tendencies are, you know, your personality traits, metaphysical shit."

"And how do you get eleven from June 6, 1979, may I ask?"

"You take the digits of your birthdate and keep reducing them until you get a single digit. Unless you come up with 11, 22, or 33, then you stop there. Those are the master numbers. You don't reduce those."

"I'm not following," Bobby says, still relaxed but definitely intrigued.

She questions if she *has* ever told him—*maybe not*—and her enthusiasm increases. "So, June 6, 1979. If you add up all the digits—the month is six plus the day is six, that's twelve, plus one is thirteen," she mumbles. "Plus nine is twenty-two, plus seven is twenty-nine, plus nine, thirty-eight. Three plus eight equals eleven. That's your number. Eleven."

"And why is eleven a good one?"

"Eleven is linked to psychic abilities and spiritual enlightenment. Of course, you're an eleven. People are naturally drawn to you. I should have known," Cyd says with certainty.

"And what about seven?" Bobby asks. "You said you're a seven."

"I am. June 5, 1967. Eleven plus twenty-three is thirty-four. Three plus four is seven. Sevens are a bit of a pain in the ass, really. We're searchers. We seek out answers. We want to understand aaaall the mysteries."

"That sounds like too much work. I'd rather be psychic."

"I need to find a little order among the chaos. I think I'd lose my mind if I believed we're all just little steel balls spinning meaninglessly in some cosmic game of roulette, everything just left to chance. I have to have something to hang on to. Something that makes some sense."

"And numbers make sense to you?" His eyes are closed, and he sounds sleepy.

"At least numbers don't lie, Swanson," she says, succumbing to her fatigue. "At least there's that."

29

There is a faint but distinct trailhead out back, beginning where the loosely arranged desert garden on Mae's property melds into the overgrown, open terrain, and which presumably ends at the base of the expansive, jutting rock formations. When Cyd awakes, groggy and content, Bobby is walking in the yard near the start of the trail in his cowboy hat and shorts.

She watches him before he notices that she is awake. It is strange to see him here, away from the water, wearing something other than a baseball cap to shade his eyes. He is lean—almost too thin, kept that way from his relentlessly high level of energy—and strong, not from the gym but from the physical work on his boat. He is a man who is always moving, even when he is still. There is a relaxed alertness about him. He's interested in everything and doesn't want to miss any of it. Cyd remembers feeling that way, too—a lifetime ago, when she left Lola for the first time and went away to college. She thought she'd been wasting time and life was passing her by. She and Helen had gone a bit crazy at first, like two caged animals set free. As a result, her early college days were a blur of parties, drinking, and lots of cute guys.

Then, she met Loren and everything changed. Two years later, Helen's dad dropped dead—literally dropped to his knees in their driveway early one morning and died. Mr. K—everyone who knew him called him Mr. K—had suffered a massive heart attack. He had made it to the side of his truck and collapsed, alone. If someone had been with him, maybe he could have been saved. They all believe that to this day. But it was 4:30 in the morning, and he was on his way to his restaurant like he was every morning. It was the reason why Helen returned from Greece so suddenly, aborting a dream she had carried since childhood, leaving behind a woman who may have been her one true love. Once Helen's dad was gone, both women knew Helen would stay home. She would stay at The O and help her brother and her mother. It was never even discussed.

When Cyd slept over on a Friday—which was often—she and Helen were allowed to ride in Mr. K's old truck to "help" open The O. They'd sit three across in the wide cab, windows down, the heavy morning air gently pulling them awake. They would go in through the front while the whole town slept. Mr. K would pull out his big ring of keys and turn the heavy bolt. There was always one brief moment when the three of them would stand in the quiet darkness of the entryway, the dining room barely visible on either side, and Cyd's breath would catch in her throat with anticipation, maybe even fear. She can feel the stillness of that moment all these years later, the magic of it, just before the darkness gives way to the light and the day is set in motion to bring whatever it will bring. It is like being suspended in mid-air after leaping off the quarry ledge before hitting the water.

"Hey there, Sunshine."

"Hi. Have I been asleep long?" She stretches her legs and arms in opposite directions.

"As long as you needed to be. What do you say we go for a walk, check out that trail?" Bobby asks coming toward her, reaching a hand to pull her up.

It is late afternoon and warm in a way that Florida never is —drier, more spacious. The long slant of the sun is turning the rocks from deep red to vibrant orange. Cyd is up and searching for her sneakers while Bobby fills a water bottle.

They walk deliberately toward the formations, Bobby slightly ahead on the narrow trail. It cuts alternately through shrubs and cacti under a cloudless sky, then under canopies of ash, juniper, and pine, where it is surprisingly well-shaded. Cyd takes in the fragrant air, wanting to capture the strange, fantastical beauty of the place.

They haven't walked far when a flicker of movement draws Cyd's attention upward. A hummingbird darts down and then up again, disappearing into a tree. She stops momentarily, searching the tree limbs, wanting Bobby to see it, too, but it is gone. A few steps later, the tiny creature returns, following just above Cyd's shoulder, bringing with it a jolt of pure joy.

"Isn't he wonderful, Swanson? I think he likes me!"

The bird then swoops ahead, leading them like a mini welcoming committee. Twice, it comes so close that Cyd thinks it might fly right into her. She follows it with her eyes in amazement.

The path continues to steepen, twisting up the side of the red stone hills, the dust coloring her shoes reddish-brown. They make their way around to the west side of one tower where the foliage is sparse and squat. Looking out over the immense stretch of valley, Cyd realizes they have climbed quite high. There is a flat ledge ahead, about ten feet above where they are standing. Bobby follows her gaze.

"Do you think we can make it?" he asks, then guides her ahead with his hand on her low back before she can answer.

Using her hands to keep her balance, grabbing a branch and then a rock to steady herself, she climbs. He waits patiently as she carefully finds her next step. When they reach the ledge and sit down, she is thrilled with her accomplishment.

She is, quite literally, sitting on the side of a cliff. The energy is palpable. As far as she can see, there is a desert canvas broken through by great eruptions of rust stone towers—majestic, pushed up by the hand of God—there is no other explanation. It defies imagination.

Bobby, too, is staring out into the distance. He reaches over and takes her hand. She turns to him and smiles, feeling strangely shy. Though he looks straight ahead, she is sure he is seeing her.

She settles herself, and her breath naturally slows. Soon, there is no distinction between where her body ends and the air begins, and it is only when Bobby rubs her hand with his thumb that she is aware of his touch. Gradually, she feels a familiar vibration rise out of the stillness and shimmer through her body.

She first felt this sensation as a young girl but thought nothing of it. It was just one more thing to notice about her changing body as she teetered at the edge of puberty: a tingling that ran the length of her spine and up the back of her neck, a nearly imperceptible buzzing in her ears. Sometimes, it was an intermittent pulse. At other times, it settled into a steady stream, a pleasant tingling. Helen called it her voodoo buzz. Later in life, she came to know it as an energy—a thrilling, soothing energy.

In the depths of her grief over losing her dad, in the middle of the night when she felt most depleted, if she was very still, it might come to her like a whisper in the dark. From then on, she associated this tingling with her father. Later, she attached it to all of those she had loved and lost. It reminded her that they were still with her.

The sun is big and low in the sky. The layers of rock glow and soften. A wave of despair begins to build in her chest. She feels as if she is looking out at her future—a foreign landscape she has no idea how to navigate. It would take no more than a nudge to send her tumbling over the emotional ledge. She does *not* want to do this now. She does not want to ruin this beautiful day by melting into a puddle of self-pity. She turns to Bobby and kisses him on the cheek. Before he can respond, she has pushed herself to standing.

On their way back to the house, seemingly out of the ether, the hummingbird reappears like a spark, dipping and darting, practically kissing Cyd as she had kissed Bobby. Cyd smiles to herself, uplifted by the tiny creature, grateful for the entire surprising day. She is reminded of something she taught her children when they were young: If the only prayer you ever say is *Thank you*, it's enough.

"Thank you, Bobby," she says. "Thank you for being here."

"Nowhere else I'd rather be," he says, not looking back as he leads them down the trail, the hummingbird fluttering just above his shoulder.

30

Later, after a dinner of cheese and crackers, while searching through one of the closets, Cyd literally squeals with excitement. She pulls out the flat box and presents it with a bow—the word Sorry! in the familiar bold black script facing him. It had been her favorite. She loved playing with her dad as a girl. "Game on, Swanson!"

After a few rounds—with lots of teasing and squealing the word "sorry!" more times than she can count—she can no longer stifle her yawns. She leads him down the short hallway to one of the two smaller bedrooms off the great room.

"You can put your stuff in here," she says, closing the blinds for privacy against the darkness outside.

When she turns, he is right there. She practically bumps into his chest.

"Will you stop for just one minute?" he asks.

He isn't touching her, and yet she can almost feel his body against hers. They have touched each other many times over the years in the way that good friends do—a hug, a kiss just off to the side of the lips, the occasional neck rub—never more than that. And yet, if she is honest with herself, it was always more than that. Their immediate mutual attraction was something she hadn't felt toward any man since Loren. It was impossible *not* to be attracted to him—that was her justification. And the fact that Bobby seemed fairly oblivious to his effect on women made him that much more irresistible. She *did* find him extremely attractive, inside and out. That much she could admit. But she was married, and even if she wasn't—*come on*—he was twelve years younger. He could have just about any woman he wanted, and he had *a lot* of them over the years. She knew they both cherished their friendship, and she left it at that. Or she tried to. She never spoke of her feelings for Bobby to anyone, not even to Helen, though Helen made it clear with an offhand comment years ago that the two of them were fooling no one.

Cyd's default reaction to them standing together now—so ridiculously close she can feel his breath—is to formulate some smart-ass comment, some take on one of their shared jokes, but his intensity stops her. There is the look he wore the night he came to see her in the hospital, just before Loren interrupted them. She can neither speak nor move.

He takes her waist and holds her eyes with his. His voice pours out smooth as caramel sauce. "You know I'm crazy about you."

"I know you're crazy." Cyd is afraid to say anything more. She no longer trusts her mouth.

"Maybe. But that doesn't make me all bad, does it?"

"It makes you pretty bad." She searches his eyes, trying to interpret his thoughts. In the silence that follows, she feels he is waiting for her to say more. "I suppose I'm no better, Swanson. We're a fine pair, the two of us."

"Why is that?" He pulls her ever so slightly closer.

"I know I don't need to state the obvious," she begins tentatively, very much aware of his hands on the curve of her hips. "I am still married."

"There's only one thing that's obvious to me," he says with a hint of a smile pulling at the corners of his mouth.

"A lot has happened in a week. The accident, the storm, this house. The doctor told me not to think too much."

"I'm not asking you to think."

"This is all so . . ." She doesn't know what "this" is, so she trails off.

"There's this saying in swimming," he begins. Bobby grew up in the water. He swam all through high school and in college, too, until he decided to leave and live on his boat. He finishes his thought. "You can't swim fast if you can't swim slow." He says this gently as if he is moving through water this very minute.

Cyd repeats the words in her head. "I might have to think about that for a minute."

"We can swim slow. As slowly as you need."

She is held in place by the firm pressure of his hands on her hips and the proximity of his face to her own.

"I'm going to kiss you now," he says, but he does not move.

"Okay." Her voice is barely above a whisper.

He pulls her into him and moves his hands to either side of her face, lacing his long fingers through her hair and around her ears. The kiss is as sensual and tender as any she has ever felt. Somehow, she is not at all surprised. *So this is how he kisses.*

After some time—a time she knows she will always remember—he pulls away from her slightly. His dimples make a brief appearance.

"Damn, Swanson." It comes out in a breathless hush. She is smiling, too, or perhaps it is more of a conspiratorial grin.

"Slow or fast. It's entirely up to you."

This voice is not the regular Bobby voice. It is changed. They are changed. *Are* they changed? The question frightens her.

She takes a breath. "I'm going to say one thing and then I'm going to force myself to walk upstairs to my bedroom—alone," she says. He still has his hands on her, stroking her upper arms with his thumbs. She is literally shaking—half with desire and half with disbelief. "And I don't want you to take this the wrong way."

His eyes are sparkling. Clearly, he is enjoying himself.

"I love you, Swanson. You know I do."

She lets that statement sink in for a moment. Of course, she loves him. She adores him.

She continues, "You are one of my favorite people on this planet. Our friendship is one of the highlights of my life. I don't want to ruin that."

"Nothing is going to be ruined. *That* you can be sure of."

"I'm holding you to that," she says, struggling to keep her voice steady. Suddenly, it is all so urgent, so serious. She feels tears forming behind her eyes.

"Come here," he says, pulling her to his chest and wrapping his arms around her. This hug is familiar to her. This is territory she feels capable of navigating. "I fish for a living. I am a patient man. We can go slow. As slowly as you need. All I'm asking is that you let us go."

He releases her and takes her face in his hands once more. This time, he surprises her. He kisses her gently in the middle of her forehead, not unlike her father had done many times.

"Goodnight, Sunshine. Sweet dreams."

31

Bobby is already up and in the kitchen when she goes downstairs. He is lean and scruffy and when he kisses her—which he does without hesitation as if they have done this very thing many times—she can smell the desert on him.

"Good morning. Did you sleep well?" He turns her and kneads her shoulders from behind exactly as she likes. "I ran out for breakfast burritos and coffee. Are you hungry?"

"Too many questions," she moans, stretching her neck to one side and then the other. "Oh, right there . . . yes . . . oh that's good."

After a moment, he stops and turns her around to face him. He is studying her. She returns his stare momentarily, then is the first to break it.

"Let's go out back," she says, releasing him. She picks up the bag of food and one of the coffees he has set on the counter. He follows her past the stone fireplace and out the glass door. The valley looks like freedom, golden and radiant in the early morning light.

They sit in silence, both taking in the grandeur. She knows he is waiting for her, patient as always.

"I need a favor," she says, aware of the pulling sensation that had started its tugging two nights ago. "I found something in the box Mae left me. There's a letter that I know she did not intend for me to see. She was in prison while she was pregnant. I don't know why or for how long. It just goes to show you really don't know anything about other people. We're all living in our own little bubbles, drifting along encased in our own separate little worlds."

"That's one way to look at it, I suppose."

"I'd like to go into town and rent a car. I want to drive to the Grand Canyon. I may stay for a couple of days."

"Oh, okay." He waits a beat and then adds, "I'm happy to drive you wherever you need to go. You know that, right?"

"I do know. Thank you. I just need to do this on my own."

They continue to sit in silence. She swallows a bite of warm flour tortilla and soft scrambled eggs and wonders if all the food tastes better in the desert.

She feels compelled to add more. "The doctor told me I'm not supposed to exercise or think too much. How ridiculous is that? I feel fine, and I have to do this, Swanson. I need to find some clarity around what I need to do next with my life. It's like something is calling to me from that canyon. I have a photograph of my dad when he was there, long before I was born, that I've been looking at since I was a little girl. I'd like to see where it was taken. He felt something there. I need to feel it, too. Maybe then, I will know what I'm meant to do. There must be a reason that all this is happening. I just don't know what it is."

The silence is broken only by the faint hum of a motor clicking into operation in the distance. Cyd is suddenly nervous about what he might say next.

"You don't need to explain it to me," he says. His posture is as relaxed as ever, but the energy flowing between them has shifted somehow. "I want you to do what you need to do. It sounds to me like the current is going to take you, so you might as well let go of the oars. It makes things a lot easier."

"You came all this way." Her voice trails off.

"And I'd come a lot farther. You know I'm crazy about you."

"I know you're crazy," she replies, unsure how to respond, afraid to say more.

Could it be this simple? Cyd loves that Bobby has always been uncomplicated around her. Impossibly easy. They have spent time together several days a week for over five years. They have worked together and sat in bars together. They have talked for hours. They share private jokes and special intimacies. She likes being privy to things about his past relationships, things the women involved would *not* want her to know. And she confides in him, too, about things she can't or won't tell Loren, or doesn't want to bring up with Helen or Annie. Thinking back on those conversations, her old worries seem so trivial: She missed her kids; she hadn't been a great caregiver to her mother—*shouldn't that come to her more naturally?* She was losing her looks. She had no ambition, she had no talent. The list went on. But he never seemed to tire of her ramblings. There was an understanding between them. With him, she was free to misbehave, to temporarily shirk her responsibilities— not be the wife or the mother or the caregiver-daughter—and her secret was safe with him. Bobby would listen without trying to solve anything.

"Give me a break," he would say. "Since when are you supposed to be perfect?"

They finish their breakfast mostly in silence. As she rises to go upstairs, she feels Bobby's eyes following her. There is an awkwardness she rarely feels around him. She knows she would be disappointed if the tables were turned.

When she comes down the staircase, bag in hand, he is standing at the large bank of windows, his back to her. He doesn't hear her at first. She stops and takes in the surrealistic scene. She is standing in this house—it is, unbelievably, *her* house now. This man, who is not her husband, is here because he cares about her. She could stop all this crazy nonsense she's planning—to drive alone across the desert and traipse across the wilderness where any number of things could go wrong—and simply enjoy what is right before her.

She is just about to take the last step down when her phone rings. Bobby knows enough to know her ring tones—songs she has allocated for each of her special contacts. Neil Diamond's "Holly Holy" for Holly, "Mr. Bojangles" for Bo, and for Loren, the whistling start of "Don't Worry Be Happy," which struck Cyd as the funniest thing the day Bo had helped her load the ringtones onto her phone. It was so *not* Loren. Now, as both she and Bobby hear the familiar tune blaring from the back pocket of her shorts, it seems almost like a cruel joke.

Bobby turns from the window. The song continues to play. Cyd searches Bobby's eyes, but the glare from the windows obscures her vision. She wills the phone to stop. The device whistles on.

"I'll wait outside while you get that," Bobby says. She hears the forced casualness in his voice, and before she can respond, he is out the back door.

Cyd's arms have turned to stone. She sets the bag on the floor and fumbles for the phone.

"Loren?" she begins before realizing what a stupid question it is.

"Cyd! I'm glad I got you. I had to drive to find a signal. The phone service is almost useless. How are you? Are you all right?"

This rambling takes her by surprise. She suddenly needs to sit and walks to the dining room table. Her thoughts scatter like unruly children.

"Yes, I'm fine," she stammers. "What's happening there? How is the house?"

"It's not good. We've lost the chimney. Rain has come in. The boat is halfway underwater. The entire town is flooded. It's not good, Cyd."

Cyd feels his panic cutting across the airwaves. It is unlike Loren to panic, she thinks, before remembering how little she truly knows this man.

She collects herself, then answers, "It's only stuff, Loren. At least everyone is safe. Are the kids there yet?"

Loren tells her that he has spoken to Bo, and both Bo and Holly plan to drive to Lola as soon as possible. They want to help, he explains, and they want to see him. Cyd listens as Loren runs down an initial checklist of what work needs to be done on the house with his usual proficiency. When he stops, she says nothing.

"Cyd," he begins again.

She knows he is changing the subject. She finds herself, inexplicably, wanting to hear something from him, but what? That he will reverse the clock? Tell her it's all been a terrible misunderstanding? Let her return somehow—magically—back to the life she had so carefully constructed, to that place of blissful ignorance? Is that what she wants?

"I want you to come home. Please."

The realization that she has, indeed, wanted to hear these words—for her bruised ego, for her broken heart, for her sanity—hits her like a torrent. Her chest thumps and she feels lightheaded. How is it possible that he can still get to her like this? She starts to interrupt him, then reflexively lets him continue.

"I've tried to explain so we can move forward. I've always loved you. You know I have, from that first night when you threw up ginger ale and cold medicine."

Cyd knows this reference to their first date is meant to soften her.

"The last thing I ever wanted to do was hurt you or the kids. There's no amount of hatred or disappointment you could have for me that I don't have for myself. I can't undo it, Cyd. All I can do is be sorry and swear to you that it won't ever happen again. I don't know what else I can do."

"Just stop, Loren," she squeaks, choked by tears. "I cannot listen to this same story again. I believed you once. I've already given you a second chance. Or more. How many others have there been? How many are there that I never learned about? You no longer have the right to ask me to do anything!"

She is sobbing. She gulps in a breath, trying to regain her composure.

"I'm hanging up now," she says after a moment. "I will come home when I'm ready and not a moment sooner. In the meantime, you need to talk to your children. You have hurt them as much or more than you've hurt me. Don't call me again, Loren. If I want to talk, I'll call you."

She hangs up the phone and drops her head between her knees. *Stop it, stop it, stop it!*

She hears the door and looks up. Bobby is backlit by the morning light.

"Can I do anything?" he asks, but he does not come toward her.

Cyd swipes both palms across her eyes. "No. I'm sorry. I'm okay."

They are silent as they drive into town. When they pull into the parking lot, Cyd turns to face him.

"I'm sorry, Bobby. I don't know why I let him get to me." She tells him he can stay at the house while she's away even though she knows him well enough to know he won't. She babbles on as if talking alone will hold him in place, prevent him from vanishing as quickly as he had appeared. "If you're gone when I get back, it's okay. I have no idea what I'm doing. I feel like I don't know anything anymore. Something is telling me to go. That's all I know to do right now."

Bobby has not turned to face her. He does not get out to open her door or move to kiss her. Cyd freezes under the steady stream from the air conditioning vent, suddenly afraid to breathe.

"What is it?" She reaches for his hand and takes it from the steering wheel. His fingers are slender, rough, and soft. He lets her do this but otherwise doesn't move. "What have I said?"

Finally, when she thinks she will burst from dread, he turns. He takes her other hand in his.

"Listen, Sunshine." His voice comes out strained. He clears his throat ever so slightly and begins again. "You need to go and do whatever you need to do. I want you to. I've tried to tell you how I feel about you, but I don't want to be another one of your problems. You've got enough on your plate."

Cyd starts to speak but is stopped when he puts a finger to her lips.

"I'm going back to the hotel. I will wait there for three days. You know how to reach me. If I don't hear from you, I'll understand. Maybe it's time I get back on my boat and head north. I've already stayed a lot longer than I intended to in that small town. Besides, I can't stand to watch what he's doing to you."

He gets out of the car and sets her bag next to her rental. They stand, his hands on her waist. Her mouth has gone dry. The tortilla lies heavy in her stomach. She's afraid she might start weeping all over again. Part of her wants him to kiss her like he did last night and beg her not to go. Another part knows the reason she cherishes him is because he would never do that. Yet another part understands this may be the last time they will stand like this, holding onto each other, electrified, connected at a deep, unknowable level, on the brink of something she can't yet define and may never get to explore.

"Don't do anything I wouldn't do," he says, looking down at her with violet-blue eyes, making her question everything she thought she knew to be true.

He kisses her gently, then waits while she gets in the car and fastens her seatbelt. When she looks back one last time before turning onto the road, he is still standing there, gazing in her direction. It takes everything she has—every modicum of self-control, every shred of self-respect, every ounce of determination—for her to step on the accelerator and pull into traffic.

Part Three

Exhale

32

Thursday, June 3, 2019
Flagstaff, Arizona

F lagstaff, Arizona, sits at an elevation of seven thousand feet, with the San Francisco Peaks as a majestic backdrop. Driving into town, Cyd finds a rustic center square bordered by railroad tracks and Route 66, with several blocks of lovely old buildings anchored by a 1920s railway depot turned visitor center. The sandstone brick facades, beautifully preserved, hold the warmth and strength of the surrounding landscape and stand as a testament to the determination and spirit of those who designed and built them over a century earlier.

Cyd emerges from the rental car with mixed emotions. Bobby may not want to add to her newfound troubles, but he has. He is another decision to consider on what feels like a long and growing list. Nevertheless, she can't help but feel triumphant, having conquered the thirty-mile, hour-long scenic drive through Oak Creek Canyon with relative ease.

She is content to stroll without an agenda, admiring displays through large store-front windows. As she passes a hip-looking brewery and the stately Hotel Monte Vista, all of it a lifetime away from her familiar Florida beach towns, she experiences a surprising sense of belonging. The Peaks beckon in the distance, and it occurs to her that she could live somewhere other than Lola. She could choose something different. The realization is a pleasant surprise, unexpected, like a breeze on a still day.

But could she live somewhere else, *really?* She had never had any desire to leave Lola, not like Helen had. When Helen left after college, Cyd suspected she might never come back. It was a sense of family obligation and love that drew Helen back after her father died. Helen was needed—*is* needed—in Lola. But Cyd? Her children have made their lives elsewhere. Her work at The O is not what anyone would describe as a career. The actual state of her house is unknown, and she's not sure she wants to live there even if she can. Everything about her house is also about her marriage, a marriage that will be the shame-filled talk of the town by the time she returns. In Lola, she had been a daughter, a sister, a mother, and a wife. Those roles no longer apply. Maybe Lola is no longer where she belongs.

A sigh escapes involuntarily, and a crushing emptiness rushes in. The thought of going back is paralyzing. She simply cannot imagine the life that awaits her there. There's money from Mae, yes, but not enough to keep a second home and travel back and forth. And she'll still need an income. This is not a case where Cyd will tell her boss to kiss off, as Helen teased when she first heard of the inheritance. There is simply not enough cash. She can sell the cabin—she may have to—but that feels disloyal. And she's had one of her nagging feelings that the cabin itself is a sign, maybe a sign directly from Mae—maybe from her dad, too—sent from beyond to let her know she is not alone, that they are with her. But a feeling, a premonition—

whatever it is that is tugging at her—is not going to pay her bills.

Cyd shakes herself back to the present and recommits to the task at hand. She finds an outdoorsy-style clothing shop where she selects a pair of hiking boots and a lightweight jacket. The salesgirl convinces her she needs special socks to keep the gravel and dust out of her shoes. She also chooses a pair of long yoga pants, Maui Jim sunglasses, and a baseball cap with a mountain range logo that reads, *Flagstaff Est. 1882.*

Pleased with her purchases and determined to keep her mind on the here and now—*you are finally going to the Grand Canyon!*—she is ready to continue her drive. As she heads back toward the car, another shop draws her attention. Its windows display rugs and artworks like those in Mae's house. Cyd enters, taking in the contents of the small space. The shop appears empty except for an older woman behind the counter. She looks up and makes eye contact. She gives a nod of greeting, but nothing more, allowing Cyd to browse uninterrupted.

After a few minutes, as Cyd is about to leave, she notices a round glass cabinet containing several shelves of jewelry. She studies the contents and then looks over to the woman.

"Excuse me," she says. "Would you mind opening this case? There's something I'd like to see."

Cyd points to the item and the woman removes it, taking it from the small box and handing it to her. Cyd admires the small silver pendant. It is a hummingbird, about the size of a quarter, flat on the back side, rounded and carved on the other. The body is mother-of-pearl, opaque, like swirled cream.

"A local artist makes these," the woman says. "She puts a little card in with each one, explaining more about the piece."

She gives Cyd a small folded card. It reads: *The bird is a powerful spirit guide, one of strength and freedom. It will keep you in close connection with the higher Spirit.*

"It's beautiful," Cyd says, turning it in her hand. There is a weight to it, despite its small size. There are carefully etched feathers in the tiny silver wings.

"I agree. And I love that her pieces have significance behind them. A bird helps the one who wears it bear hardships in life."

Cyd continues reading: *It represents beginnings and endings, the natural passage of the cycles of life. You are reminded not to flap too furiously to get to your destination but to respect the importance of finding the treasure presented each day.*

"I'll take it," Cyd says without hesitation. "And I'd like a chain for it, too."

The woman helps her select a chain, and after she's paid, Cyd says she'd like to wear it out of the store.

"Here, let me help you," the woman says, coming around the counter and fastening the chain around Cyd's neck. The bird lands low on her breastbone, just above her heart.

Cyd steps back and touches it. The silver is cool against her skin. "Thank you," she says.

"I hope you will wear it in good health," the woman says.

"I intend to," Cyd says, once again raw with emotion. She steps into the warmth of the cloudless Arizona morning, more determined than ever to follow in her father's footsteps. She touches the pendant with her fingertips. *Let's go, my little friend.*

33

Thursday, June 3, 2019
Grand Canyon National Park,
South Rim, Arizona

The drive from Flagstaff to the entrance of Grand Canyon National Park is under two hours through a diverse landscape, from pine forests to expansive grasslands, with the stunning mountain range in the distance. Cyd is surprised by how truly desolate it is. It isn't until she nears the park's south entrance that the highway opens to the town of Tusayan, the gateway community whose history is linked to the founding of the park in the early 1900s.

Once at the park's perimeter, she pays her entrance fee and drives along the narrow road until she sees signs to the main parking lot, deciding to start there before finding her room. Fortunately, she was able to book a cabin inside the park due to a last-minute cancellation. It was unusual, she was told when she called for a reservation from the car. The cabins sold out months in advance. Soon, the children would be out of school, and the park would be inundated with crowds. She is indeed very lucky, the woman on the phone had assured her before they hung up.

Cyd parks in the vast lot and follows the flow of visitors down a walkway past a modern building that serves as the visitor center. Around the corner, a low stone wall runs the length of a wide sidewalk. She is swept along, people to her left and right, heading toward the barrier wall along the canyon rim. She spots an opening where the path continues out to an overlook. Groups are gathered there, posing for pictures with their backs to the view, or looking out as they walk around the large circular terrace taking in the vista. She has arrived at Mather Point.

As she nears the edge of the terrace, she can see the mesas in the distance, but her view is limited by the midday crowd. When a space opens next to the stone barrier, she walks up to the edge of the overlook and peers out.

Her breath catches in her throat. A hum fills her ears as if she has plugged them closed with her fingers. Her senses are instantly singularly focused. Nothing exists other than what lies before her—a vastness unlike anything she could have imagined. This is an expanse so immense, so wide, so deep, it is beyond comprehension. There is no beginning and no end, just layer upon layer of rock and sediment for as far as she can see, dug through to expose the very heart of the earth. The colors are endless, at once muted and brilliant: purples and blues, oranges and golds, deep green and stark white. There are cliffs and gullies, mesas and buttes, and sandstone walls penetrating a vertical mile from top to bottom. She had no idea such magnificence existed. Even the astonishing beauty of the Sedona red rocks seems small in comparison to the eternity that stretches out before her. She is suspended, mesmerized.

In the far distance, at the very bottom of the vast crevice, a tiny string of blue weaves its way through the rocky gorge, disappearing around a distant bend. This is the Colorado River, the great river that attracts whitewater rafters from around the world. The powerful, dangerous Colorado River is now, from her vantage point, no more than a single thread laid across a blanket the size of a city block. How could it possibly be? A seemingly tiny stream has cut through the crust of the earth, leaving in its wake a divide as vast as the night sky. What amount of time exists that would allow that small ribbon of water to create this galaxy of wonder?

Her mind will not let her take it in. Emotion fills her chest. Here is a miracle laid bare before her eyes. Surely, this is the glory of God, not in any church but right here in front of her. There is nothing intangible about it. She can smell it. She can hear it. If she chooses, she could leap and fall into the endlessness of it. How long would it take to hit the bottom? It is bottomless. She wants to scream with joy and pain and wonder and defeat and confusion and gratitude. All of it. She is finally here. She has arrived at the place that has called to her since her childhood, since the day she first studied the eyes of her father in the small photograph, somewhere near this very spot. She has the sensation of holding her father's hand—hers is small, and his is large and strong and warm. In one grand whoosh, all the emotion of the week erupts within her, threatening to buckle her. She is fixated on the expanse before her. She squeezes the hand. *Hold me, Daddy. Hold me tight. I need you.*

Someone pushes against her, drawing her from her reverie. Cyd turns reluctantly and walks away as others swarm to close the space she has just vacated.

Cyd stumbles back the way she came, weaving her way through the crowd of visitors, dazed. A walkway runs along the rim and she follows it, looking for a quiet place to compose herself. The experience of being here—the intensity of it—has caught her off-guard. She finds a log in the shade of a cotton-wood tree and sits, the sensation in her chest physically painful, a brokenness, a hollow at her very core. Her body needs to fill it somehow, but it seems impossible, like trying to mend a fractured bone with sheer determination. The reality of her situation is suffocating. Regardless of what she finds or doesn't find in this place, her reality awaits her. She will return to a life she cannot visualize, that she hasn't yet tried to imagine. She sits, dry-mouthed and shaky, unsure of her ability to make a sound decision about anything, not even what to do when she gets up from this log.

Her breath constricts as if she may start to hyperventilate. She closes her eyes and tries to slow her breathing, which has become ineffective, a sort of panting where she cannot get enough air. She focuses on her senses: the sounds of the people moving and talking, the warm breeze against her arms, the fragrance of dry earth.

What did you feel when you were here, Dad? Were you happy? You looked so happy. Were you searching for something? Did you find what you were looking for? Show me, Daddy. Help me to find it, too.

When Cyd was three years old, she'd been plagued by a strange and unexplained series of fits. At first, they were dismissed as temper tantrums, but soon her parents thought something might be seriously wrong, an undiagnosed disorder of some kind. Her behavior was unlike anything they had heard of or been exposed to. They were at a loss for what to do.

Something would set her off or, even worse, nothing at all.

Cyd would fall to the floor and kick and scream, sometimes for ten minutes or so, other times for an hour or more, once for two miserable hours, her mother told her. She screamed and cried, eyes squeezed shut, stiff with fury, seemingly oblivious to everything around her. She responded to nothing—not to threats or soothing, not even a small slap across her face which Iris had administered out of desperation. Once she started, there was no way to make her stop, they told her. She would rub her tiny bare feet back and forth against each other so violently she would draw a bit of blood across the top as if she had scratched them. Jesse would pick her up, still kicking, and set her in a warm tub. She screamed so loud and for so long that, for several years afterward, her voice was deep and scratchy, so odd for a little girl, as if she had just gotten over a bad case of laryngitis.

Once it began, the fit had to run its course, it seemed, however long it might be. Then, red-faced and soaked with sweat, she would drift back, the hold released. Only then could her father take her in his arms and comfort her.

Cyd repeated this strange and terrible behavior once every month or so for nearly a year, and then, just as her frazzled parents were ready to seek professional help, she stopped. The outbursts simply stopped as abruptly as they had started.

Cyd remembered nothing of these episodes, but the description of them frightened her when she was old enough to understand. Eventually, her parents were able to make light of that time, almost joke about it. Her father declared her "passionate," and her mother simply shook her head and rolled her eyes. But Baker had confided, when they were older, and with uncharacteristic darkness, "I'm telling you, Cyd, it was like something out of a horror movie. You were possessed by the devil, I swear. You were this sweet-looking thing, this tiny blond angel, and then you turned into some kind of monster. No one could snap you out of it. We all tried. It was like . . . I don't know . . . it was like something just had to come out. And then, suddenly, you were back to normal, like nothing had happened. It was fucking weird, I'm telling you. It was scary as shit."

Hot tears form behind her closed lids and she slides off the log and onto the ground. Pressure fills her throat. The memory— or rather the story of the memory—comes to her now as it does on occasion, in times of crisis or extreme distress. It seems to lie dormant just under the surface, whatever *it* was, whatever *it* is, waiting to take her down.

Breathe. She knows she must get control of her breath. She pulls herself up from the base of her spine, trying to create space, to counteract the constriction that has taken hold of her. She has learned this in yoga class. She knows what to do. She begins at her core, putting her attention there, at her low belly, pulling the air in slowly, filling her abdomen, then her rib cage, then all the way up to her collarbone. She draws in as much air as she can, then sniffs in even more, forcing her lungs to expand to full capacity. She stops, holding her breath, resisting the urge to let go. Holding. Holding. The pressure builds.

Don't collapse . . . first from the upper ribs . . . then the middle . . . slowly . . . lastly, the belly.

With control, she squeezes the last of the air from her lungs. It is stale. It is useless.

Push it all out. Let it go.

She settles herself, literally breathless, and puts all her attention on that space, on the stillness she has created. This moment, just before the next breath, before the start of something new, when she is emptied, when everything is completely still, this is where her strength lies, her salvation. This is the stillness at the bottom of the breath.

She continues to concentrate on her breathing, and after some time, the panic fades. The racing in her mind diminishes. The constriction in her chest is gone. She comes back to herself. The hollowness is still there, but it has lost its chokehold.

Cyd spends the afternoon exploring the small village atop the South Rim. There is the Bright Angel Lodge, with its deep brown hand-adzed logs. At the opposite end is the sprawling El Tovar, built from Oregon pine and local limestone. It seems to be an extension of the canyon itself.

Next to the El Tovar is an unusual adobe-style building, reddish in color, with tiny windows and multiple roofs. It serves as a tourist gift shop, but it is obviously authentic, modeled after the ancient dwellings of the Hopi Tribe. Even the name—Hopi House—is enticing to Cyd. Inside, there are peeled log beams and corner fireplaces and small niches cut into the walls. Native American rugs and blankets hang from walls throughout the multiple rooms. Obviously, Aunt Mae had admired this ancient, labor-intensive art form, the intricate designs, the vibrant dyes. Cyd reads the small cards attached to each work of art, fascinated by the mostly elderly Navajo women who weave them.

In the entryway, she notices an old photograph of Mary Colter, the building's perfectionist architect, and stops to read the information. She studies the picture of the chief architect, who also designed Bright Angel Lodge further down the rim, and wishes she could have known her, feeling a sense of sister-hood as she learns that Mary, too, had suffered the untimely loss of her father when she was a young teenager. And, in another touching coincidence, she discovers that Mary Colter's full name is Mary Jane, the same as Mae.

Later, in anticipation of sunset, Cyd settles herself at the rim's edge near the start of the Bright Angel Trail. The air has grown cool and the wind is insistent. She situates herself on the low stone wall, cross-legged, gazing across the gorge, fixated. As the daylight fades, a stillness descends, and the vibration returns— a mighty hum, all-encompassing, reverberating out and back, connecting her to the rocks and the great expanse of starlit sky. With it comes an immense relief, a sureness that she has made the right decision in coming here. She sits for a long time until it is completely dark and the crowd has dissipated.

As she walks down the dimly lit path to her cabin, she realizes that she's been out of touch all day. She hopes no one is worried about her, Holly in particular, but decides she will not call anyone tonight. She has entered a realm she does not want to disturb, a disconnect, as if she is floating, hovering ever so slightly. She is acutely aware of her breath and her posture and of the energy running up and down her spine. She feels the presence of her father and mother, Mae and Baker. They are here with her. They have met her here, all of them.

34

Friday, June 4, 2019
Bright Angel Trail,
Grand Canyon National Park

I t is still dark when Cyd slips into her new yoga pants in the dim light of the cabin. She folds the socks over her hiking boots as the girl at the shop had demonstrated. She fills a canvas bag with the few things she thinks to carry: sunglasses, sunscreen, water bottle, two hard-boiled eggs, and a bag of trail mix—*if ever there was an appropriate time*, she had thought when she grabbed the package off the rack in the lobby store. She slips the framed photograph into the bag. She isn't sure what to expect as she descends. Though she skimmed the brochure the man handed her at check-in, she has not given much thought to planning her day. She simply wants to walk into the great abyss.

Bright Angel Trail begins just past the historic Lookout Studio. Cyd had studied the building the previous day—a stone house balanced precariously on the canyon's precipice, clinging miraculously to a wall of sandstone. How it actually clung to its perch for a minute, much less a century, boggles Cyd's mind. The wondrously simple structure blends so seamlessly with the side of the cliff it seems Mother Nature herself placed it there. It is another one of Mary Colter's creations.

There are very few people out at this early hour. The canyon walls emerge in the distance as if rising out of still water, slowly coming into sight from top to bottom. It is cool, and the wind kicks and swirls in intermittent gusts. Cyd digs her hands into the pockets of her jacket. The path is not terribly steep at first, but it is unpredictable. The surface stones vary from dust to gravel to bowling ball–sized boulders. She has to catch herself with each step, bracing against the pull of gravity, her knees already sending up little pangs of protest.

As the light increases, the outline of other hikers is visible on the hairpin turns above and below. Most move in pairs or groups of three or four, but there are a few singles as well. The path narrows in spots, and the drop-off is deadly steep. There are no guardrails. She watches her movements carefully, stepping over and around cracks and large stones, staying away from the outer edge of the path, trying not to skid on the loose gravel or trip on a protruding rock.

It isn't long, within the first hour or so as she makes her way carefully down the trail's dozens of switchblade turns, that she stops, amazed by what lies before her. A massive pale stone wall appears so near it's as if she's practically bumped into it, though how far away it actually is, she cannot guess. The wall rises straight and smooth, so enormous it encompasses her entire field of vision. The white sandstone sheet is stark and bright compared to the chunky red layers on which it stands, as if a colossal chisel has been used to hack away the immense vertical surface. The upcoming blue of the morning sky accentuates the beauty of the cream rock, pulling the colors of the stone to the forefront—pale rose here, silver and gunmetal there. The wall literally drips with pigment. Spires rise at the top, and on the side rocky turrets jut up like ghostly figures frozen in time. It is a breathtaking display of nature's artistry at work over millions of years.

"Excuse us." A voice breaks the silence.

Cyd realizes she has stopped in the middle of the trail, dumbfounded by the magnificent sight ahead of her.

"Oh, no, excuse me. It's just so wonderful, isn't it?"

Cyd steps aside for the older couple, each with a walking stick.

"It's one of my favorite views in the canyon," the woman says. "It looks much different here than it does once you get further down. I could stare at it for hours."

"It's my first time here," Cyd says. "Everywhere I look, I can't believe my eyes."

"It is incredible," the woman says. "We come as often as we can." She looks at the man—her husband, Cyd guesses—and smiles warmly.

"Yes, we do," the man says. "As long as we are able, we'll keep coming back. It's addictive, you know."

"I see what you mean," Cyd agrees.

"Enjoy your day, dear," the woman says, and the couple continue down the trail.

Cyd stands still for a few more minutes, sipping on water. The air is getting warmer. She puts her scarf in her bag. She has worn the light jacket, a long-sleeved shirt, and a tank top, and plans to peel off layers as needed.

At the first rest stop, she finds a wooden shed set a short

distance off the trail—the pit toilets—and a small log pavilion. Nothing else. She notices the couple who had passed her coming down sitting on a stone step. The woman smiles when she sees Cyd and waves her over.

"So how did you enjoy your first mile and a half?" the man asks.

"It's unbelievable," Cyd says. "Just when you think it can't be any more beautiful, you look up and it takes your breath away. Or maybe I'm just out of shape. This trail is not easy. You really have to watch your step."

"Oh, yes," the woman says. "The walking sticks help. We've learned the hard way."

"Yes, indeed," her husband agrees. "So what made you decide to come down?"

"I've always wanted to come," Cyd says. "My father visited when he was in the service. He loved it."

"I think every American should see this place at least once, even if you just stay up top like 95 percent of the visitors. It's a national treasure, to say the least," the woman says, looking out at the vista. They sit about a third of the way down the side of this section of canyon with a clear view of the switchback trail snaking up in one direction and down the other.

"It's a good thing you got out early," the man says. "You don't want to be behind the mules, I can assure you."

"He's right about that," the woman agrees. "That's another lesson we learned the hard way."

The couple laugh easily, their affection obvious. Cyd is certain theirs is a long-term marriage. "How many years have you been coming?" she asks.

The couple look at each other and nearly break into a giggle.

"Believe it or not," the woman begins, smiling at Cyd, then

at her husband, then back at Cyd, "we came here on our honeymoon in 1967. A lot has changed since then."

The woman hesitates, then the man joins in. "But not the view," they finish in unison, capping off the hokey private joke with a little laugh.

"Wow," says Cyd, caught up in their enthusiasm and resisting the urge to tell them that 1967 was the year she was born. "That's quite a commitment all the way around. You two must really like each other, as well as the canyon."

They reach toward each other and the man squeezes his wife's hand. A sense of loss grabs at Cyd's throat. What has this couple been through? How much heartache? How many disappointments? Doubts? Temptations? Has either of them strayed? How much have they changed over the years? Surely they are two very different people from the ones who reached for each other's hand fifty-odd years ago. It can't just be luck that has kept them together.

"Are you all right, dear?" The woman's voice startles Cyd back to the conversation. "Can we get you anything?"

"Oh, no," Cyd says. "I'm fine. I was just thinking, the reason I wanted to come here was because my father visited when he was in the Navy, around 1955. He loved it. I wanted to see what it was that captivated him. I never had the chance to ask him. He died when I was young." She hadn't meant to go on. The words emerge unedited.

They sit and talk for some time. Cyd learns that the couple has two children, five grandchildren, and one great-grandchild on the way. Cyd tells them about Holly and Bo. She tells them her husband had to stay in Florida, so she decided to try the hike on her own.

"Actually," she adds, wanting to know more about this lovely couple, "we're going through a hard time. I decided it would be good for me to be alone. Do you ever do that? Take a break from each other, if you don't mind me asking? I don't mean to pry."

The woman, Ruth, laughs easily. Cyd now knows their names—Daniel and Ruth.

"Of course we take breaks!" Ruth says. Daniel is chuckling, too. "I go to rug-hooking camps all over the country at least a few weeks every year. And Danny spends hours in his shed. He makes beautiful furniture. I don't know that we would have survived without our independent hobbies. It's very important to have things you keep all to yourself. Wouldn't you agree, honey?"

"My wife is always right," Daniel says, giving Cyd a wink.

Cyd spends the next mile and a half walking with the couple, descending the canyon wall, chatting some, then falling into silent contemplation. What secrets has Ruth kept to herself? What sorts of things would she consider *not* okay to keep from her husband? Did she ever feel caged? Like she needed to get away from her husband in order to feel more like herself?

At the next rest area, they tell her they have come as far as they planned for the day. Ruth is having pain in her ankle and they don't want to push it. They insist Cyd take some extra food—an apple, a baggie of bite-sized carrots. When Ruth hands Cyd a package of cheese crackers, Daniel pretends to want to stop her. "Hey, those are mine!" Then he confesses endearingly, leaning into Cyd, "Those are my weakness. I snuck them in when she wasn't looking."

"It's been so nice meeting you and talking with you," Cyd says. "You've inspired me to come back, and I will think of you every time I do."

At the last moment, just as Cyd turns to go, Daniel says he

wants her to have his walking stick. He's managed to amass an entire collection over the years, he assures her, and she will need it on the way down more than he will on the way back up. Cyd resists, but both Daniel and Ruth insist. Cyd is choked with emotion, grateful for this touching gift, both to use and to keep as a memento.

"Thank you for everything," Cyd says, hugging each of them in turn with a sincerity that surprises her. She's normally not a hugger of strangers.

"You are more than welcome," Ruth says as she hugs Cyd firmly in return. Cyd is sure this is how Ruth hugs her own children and she feels lucky to be on the receiving end of her sincere fondness. "You take good care of yourself."

"This place will bring you answers if you just listen," Daniel says, holding her shoulders and looking at her warmly.

Then, with a wave, they go back the way they came.

35

After a second small rest area comes another stretch of steep, cliff-side switchbacks before Cyd finds herself at the bottom of this section of the canyon. In front of her, the trail is a faint divide across a long basin. In the distance, layered walls of limestone, sandstone, and shale rise up on three sides. The sky is bright and clear. She is out of her jacket and knows she will soon be down to her tank top as the sun hits her full-on, no longer cut off intermittently by the rocky protrusions. She puts on the sunglasses and twists her hair up off her neck and into the hat.

A mash-up of thoughts come and go, unprompted, like background noise. Bits of the letters pop into focus, then Loren's words in the van—*we just started up a conversation, I liked her*—followed by thoughts of Helen and everyone in Lola, the clean-up they are all undergoing and the hardships that lie ahead of them. She thinks about Bobby, and a shiver travels down her spine as she relives the sensation of his kiss. He will wait. But not for long. She sees her father's face, and she hears Baker's infectious laugh. She remembers how her mother's hands looked in the casket, wrapped in rosary beads. The thoughts are like the ever-changing clouds floating overhead, without form or purpose. She keeps a steady pace, setting the stick with each step. Sweat prickles the back of her neck, and she repeatedly shifts the bag from one shoulder to the other as her body begins to rebel against the exertion.

The sound of voices interrupts Cyd's daydream, several at once, overlapping and lively. Cyd glances over her shoulder to see four young people coming up behind her. Their smooth, muscular legs seem battery-powered.

Cyd says hello as they start to pass her. They all have backpacks similar to the ones she saw in the outdoorsy shop in Flagstaff, like nylon suitcases strapped across their shoulders. As one of the girls comes alongside Cyd, her backpack bumps Cyd's shoulder and both women stumble slightly before regaining their footing.

"I am *so* sorry!" the young woman exclaims. "I'm such a klutz!"

"Yes, you are!" the other woman says. She turns to Cyd. "She's downright dangerous with that thing. She forgets she's got it on or something."

Both the women laugh, shoving each other, not unlike Cyd and Helen do at times. They look to be in their mid-twenties, around Holly and Bo's ages, Cyd guesses. There are two good-looking young men with them. All four look like they just bounced out of an REI catalog.

"It's no problem," Cyd says, laughing along with them, trying to keep pace with the group. "I'm pretty klutzy myself. I wouldn't even attempt to carry one of those things. I would have taken out half the people on the trail by now."

Within a short distance, introductions have been made all around, and Cyd is happy with the distraction and lively conversation. They remind her of her own children and their friends, people she never tires of. They are from the Bay Area, each working in some sort of tech job—Cyd doesn't quite follow their explanation and doesn't want to ask for clarification. They are all adorable, she decides, and she is pleased they are interested in talking with her, saving her from herself.

The three women fall back, moving at a more relaxed pace, as the boys begin to outdistance them. Megan, a cute redhead, and Kate, the shapely blond who had bumped her, chat easily with Cyd. They all work together and have taken off for the week on a road trip. Kevin is Kate's boyfriend, they explain, but Megan and Matt are just friends. They plan to spend the night in the canyon and hike back tomorrow. Matt is the only one of the four who has been down in the canyon before.

"Isn't it a-may-zing?" asks Kate, speaking to no one in particular and emphasizing each syllable. Her blond hair is pulled into a ponytail and sticks out the back of her cap, swinging as she walks.

"I loved it the minute I saw it," admits Cyd. "I looked over the rim and couldn't believe my eyes. I still can't. It really is spectacular."

"I know," agrees Megan. "I wish we were staying down here all week. We talked about going whitewater rafting but it's too expensive. Maybe next year. Are you staying the night, Cyd?"

"No," says Cyd, gesturing to her one small bag. "I'm not prepared. I didn't even think about that, but it does sound a-may-zing!" The girls laugh at Cyd's impression of Kate. "Seriously, I think it's a great idea." Out of habit, she almost adds, *My husband would love it, too,* but catches herself.

"Your husband didn't want to come?" asks Kate.

"Don't be so nosey," says Megan, shooting her friend a disapproving look.

Cyd smiles, amused by their mini-telepathic connection. Kate had practically read her mind. "No, it's fine. Actually, I just wanted to come alone. It seemed like a good idea at the time anyway. I didn't know I was coming here until a few days ago. I've had a lot going on."

Megan shoots a look in Kate's direction. The girls realize Cyd has picked up on their shared, wordless communication.

Megan hesitates a moment then says to Cyd, "I thought we should have come alone but we had already made plans with the guys. I think she needs some space away from Kevin. Some permanent space." Megan sounds like a concerned big sister.

"It's not that simple," Kate says. "Maybe I should have broken up with him a long time ago. I guess I don't want to be alone or something stupid like that. I don't even know . . ." Her voice drifts off, absorbing into the great walls.

"Relationships are hard," Cyd offers. "All relationships, not just love interests. I think knowing which people are worth the effort is the real trick. Sometimes it's better to let go."

"That's it exactly!" Megan says, enlightened. "He's not worth the effort, Kate."

"It's easy for you to say. I care about him." She is quiet for a beat, then adds, as if she feels the need to explain further, "I love him."

"He's a jerk," Megan says under her breath so that only Cyd hears.

They continue walking and talking, almost constantly, unlike the intermittent conversation with Ruth and Daniel earlier. The girls' youthful energy is strong and direct, like good espresso, and gives Cyd an emotional and physical boost, a distraction from her increasing fatigue. It has been about forty-five minutes of brisk walking across the basin and nearly three hours since she started out. Ahead, she sees the copse of trees and inviting greenery she had seen from the rim. She knows it is another rest area and a popular turnaround spot, nearly five miles from the trailhead at Lookout Studio.

"You girls go ahead, keep up with your friends," Cyd says. The boys are pulling farther away from them on the path. "I'll see you up there, if you're going to take a rest, that is."

"Oh, yes," says Kate. "We're taking a break. I have to pee!"

Megan again gives Kate a friendly little push and the girls scoot ahead, calling for the boys to wait, their backpacks bobbing in the sunshine.

36

Once the girls leave Cyd to herself, it is immediately evident how much faster she had been walking to keep pace with the younger hikers. Her hips, knees, and neck all demand that she sit down. A mirage-like patch of green, Havasupai Gardens is a literal sanctuary in the middle layer of the canyon on a geologic shelf known as the Tonto Platform. The stark landscape of this area of the canyon stretches in every direction, while nestled at its heart is a welcoming patch of grasses, cottonwoods, and willows. Vegetation thrives thanks to Garden Creek, a water source that is fed by a natural spring. Many of the hikers who have either started out earlier, passed Cyd along the way, or come down from the north are now enjoying this oasis, lounging in the shade and snacking at the picnic tables.

Wandering through the garden respite, Cyd resists a strong desire to pass out under a tree. The thought of a nap is intoxicating. What if she didn't have the energy to retrace her steps back up the trail? She remembers the doctor's instructions—no strenuous exercise for a couple of weeks. This was most likely considered strenuous exercise. The insanity of what she is doing takes hold like a fever. *What were you thinking?*

Squelching her anxiety, she hunts for a comfortable place to sit. An older man is alone on a log bench eating something, perhaps a sandwich, and Cyd's stomach growls to life. Her first inclination was to find a spot on the grass alone. Instead, she finds herself strangely drawn to the man on the bench.

"Hello," Cyd says. "Do you mind if I sit here?"

"Hi there." The man, who looks to be in his late sixties, turns and smiles genuinely. "Why would I mind? Please, sit. There's plenty of view to go around."

She hears the remnants of an accent. Kentucky, maybe.

"There certainly is," Cyd says, looking across the expanse in the same direction, the distant walls of stacked brilliance rising to meet an azure sky. She has been looking at the layered gorge for hours now and it seems to transform by the minute, constantly transitioning. The changing light creates a slightly different and equally incredible canvas every time she looks up. It seems to be reflecting her own ever-changing emotions.

"You coming down from the South Rim?" the man asks.

"Yes, and I'm pooped. I really have no idea what I'm doing. It was a spontaneous decision. It is incredible, though. I never imagined such beauty."

The man's sandwich is on his lap on an open piece of wax paper, a sight that almost makes Cyd laugh aloud. It reminds her of the sandwiches Iris made for her and Baker so many years ago, and those she had made for her own children. It occurs to her that she has never seen anyone else wrap their sandwiches in wax paper, at least not since she was in grade school, which of course is ridiculous, since what else is wax paper for if not to wrap sandwiches? The man catches her looking and raises his eyebrows, his eyes betraying his amusement.

"I know it's not much but I'm happy to share. I have another one. Can't guarantee how nutritious it is, though," he says, tempting her curiosity as he reaches into the backpack sitting at his feet.

"Oh?" Cyd smiles back, her mouth watering.

"Peanut butter and Nutella," he says with a straight face and a twinkle in his eye, holding out another sandwich folded neatly in the opaque wrapper.

"PB and N? No way!" Cyd is unable to resist either the pleasant man or his nicely wrapped sandwich. She scoots closer to take the package. "Normally, I wouldn't take food from a stranger, but Nutella? Are you kidding me? Hand it over."

"Breakfast of champions," the man says, taking a bite of his sandwich and returning his gaze out across the canyon floor.

"Nothing better," Cyd says, opening the paper on her lap as he had done. She takes a bite, and before she has swallowed completely, purposely using the effect of the gooeyness in her mouth, she adds, "I'm Cyd, by the way."

"Hi, Cyd-by-the-way. I'm Clint."

"Nice to meet you, Clint. You sure make a helluva Nutella sandwich."

"It's my specialty. I was thinking of starting a food truck. All my friends are encouraging me."

"Are they? You must have friends in low places."

"We can't all be visionaries, Cyd-by-the-way. Some of us have to be followers. And purchasers of Nutella sandwiches sold from food trucks. That's how the balance of the ecosystem stays in check."

"I see your point. I'm glad to know I have an important role in the larger order."

"That you do." Clint takes the last bite of his sandwich. He reaches into his backpack, comes up with a refillable bottle, and takes a long swig. He looks back at Cyd and her small bag on the bench next to her, his eyes teasing her again. There is something familiar about him, as if they've met before, though she knows they haven't.

"You look like you're traveling pretty light there, young lady. Do you have water? I'd hate to have to call for an airlift due to a dehydration-induced coma."

"Ah, fear not, oh ye of little faith." Cyd reaches into her shoulder bag and finds her own small bottle. "Yamas," she says as she holds it up toward him. "I mean, cheers."

"May your Swell bottle always runneth over," Clint says, holding his bottle up toward Cyd before screwing the cap back on.

They settle into silence, staring at the view like star-struck fans. Cyd really did find the sandwich delicious. She can't remember the last time she had eaten one, certainly not since the kids were little. Bo loved Nutella but she only bought it occasionally. She wondered now why she would do that. Why did she deprive her son of something so simple and delicious? A sadness rises up as she thinks of the long-ago missed opportunity, the finality of it like a gavel hitting wood.

"Hey, you okay over there, Cyd-by-the-way?"

Cyd realizes with embarrassment that she had just let go a deep, long sigh.

"Oh, yes, I'm fine," Cyd says. "I was just having a moment of regret. I should have made my children more Nutella sandwiches when I had the chance. What was I thinking?" She takes another bite as if to emphasize her point.

"Something about being down here in this little gully brings up all kinds of old garbage, at least that's what I've found. The past follows you down the trail like your shadow and then attacks when you have no possible escape. That's part of the charm of coming down here, don't you know? You get to confront all your Nutella demons."

"Do you come often?" Cyd asks.

Clint hesitates for the briefest of beats. "I've been coming once a year since my wife died. This is my fifth trip. I hike down and spend the night under the stars. I look up and think about life in all its messed-up glory, then hike back the next day. It's my annual pilgrimage."

Clint looks away from Cyd as if speaking to the distance cliffs.

"You always spend the night down here?"

"Sure do. It's a long walk. I figure I might as well stay a while and enjoy the scenery. There's a campground down near the river. You've made it to the halfway point, but it's still another four miles to camp and they're not particularly easy miles. There will be a group of us out there tonight. Some keep going right on across. It takes a good two or three days, but you can go down the South Rim and up the North Rim." He pauses and looks at Cyd. "Am I telling you something you already know? I tend to ramble."

"No, please, ramble on," Cyd says. "I don't know much about the canyon or the trails. Honestly, I have no plan—not the best idea I've ever had, I'm now realizing. I wasn't thinking. That's something I tend to do."

"Sometimes the best-laid plan is no plan at all," Clint says. "It should be a beautiful, clear night. I have a tent but I'm thinking I might sleep out in the open. Nothing like a blanket of stars, especially these stars. They fly them in special, you know. Not to be missed."

"I've heard rumors to that effect."

"This place here, this little oasis, was used by the Havasupai Tribe for who knows how long. They actually gardened here, harvested crops, thus the name, Havasupai Gardens. There are also remnants of some stone structures, probably built by the Puebloans who were here even earlier, thousands of years ago. Later, around the turn of the century—the previous one that is—the Americans came in and fixed up the trail a bit. They built the cabins at Phantom Ranch in the early twenties. They planted these cottonwoods, too." He gestures to the grove of trees around them—the small grassy sanctum in the middle of rocks and dirt offering a perfect interlude after the first five miles on the trail.

"There are underwater springs here that wind down to the Colorado River. Pretty cool, as they say," Clint adds.

"It sounds wonderful. I would love to stay longer but I have nothing—some water, an apple, and some appropriately named trail mix. Oh, and half a PB and N." Cyd holds up the second half of the sandwich. "But I'm clean out of camping gear."

"You can probably walk a little farther today if you want," Clint says after a moment. "But you have to be careful to head back before it gets too late. That's very important. It's a good four-hour walk back up from here, and that's if you keep moving. You don't want to be walking up that trail at dusk. That'll be your last Nutella sandwich if you're not careful."

"The campsite is another four miles?" Cyd asks, not sure why she wants to know.

"Yup. It's just over the river. Bright Angel Campground. Not far from there is Phantom Ranch. There's a small canteen there. You can even buy beer."

"I had no idea," Cyd says. "There's a whole world down here. I really need to get out more."

Clint braces himself on his knees and straightens slowly.

"There's a fine balance between optimal energy and gluttony," he says, brushing crumbs from his lap, then folding the empty wax paper and putting it back in his bag. "Never have been able to eat just half."

Cyd studies him as he rearranges his backpack. He is distinguished even in his dusty hiking boots and cargo pants, solid, like the granite wall behind him. His thick hair, dark mixed with silver-white, is neatly trimmed, and his hairline is cut definitively across his forehead. He looks fit but moves as if he might have sustained injuries in the past, perhaps to his back or his neck. Maybe he played football. It isn't difficult to picture him as a teenager, posed with a ball tucked at his elbow. His face is square and appealing, his skin taut like fine leather in need of conditioning and, though Cyd had seen an almost childlike delight in his eyes, there is a weariness there, too. He seems burdened by more than his backpack.

"Hey, Cyd!"

Cyd turns to see two young women bouncing along the path.

"Hi, girls. I made it," Cyd says, standing. "And I've been educated and well fed by my new friend, Clint. Clint, meet Kate and Megan. I nearly dropped trying to keep up with them for the past mile."

"Hello, hi," the girls sing out in unison. "If you're not ready to leave yet, we've got a great little picnic spot in the shade. Come over and join us."

Clint and Cyd follow the women behind some bushes to find Matt and Kevin spreading a cloth on a patch of grass.

Cyd stops in her tracks. Kevin has removed his hat and sunglasses. She gets her first good look at his face. It is as if she is transported back thirty years. Before her stands her brother in his mid-twenties—the same slight build, the same pale eyes and blond hair, the same *face*. She feels tears begin to pool. The resemblance is uncanny. *What are the odds?*

"Prime real estate you've got here," Clint remarks to the guys.

Cyd resists the urge to walk up to Kevin and wrap him in her arms, to weep, to hold on for dear life. She truly cannot believe her eyes.

"Hey, there, young lady. You look like you've seen a ghost. You ok?" Clint asks.

Clint is looking at her with some concern when her eyes refocus.

"Oh, no, I'm fine. It's just—I have to tell you, Kevin. You look exactly, I mean *exactly*, like my brother when he was your age. It's the damnedest thing. I've never seen anything quite like it. He's dead now. He died." She stops herself as they are all now staring at her. She realizes her emotions have hijacked her face. One thing you do *not* have, Helen likes to tell her, is a poker face.

She wants—she *needs*—to sit down.

Kevin laughs uncomfortably, obviously unsure how he should respond. "He must have been a good-looking guy," he says as he returns to helping Matt.

Cyd takes a breath, trying to calm herself.

"That happens to me all the time," Kate interjects cheerfully, either unaware of the awkwardness Cyd has created, or purposefully deflecting it. "I must have one of those faces. I swear, I look like someone's sister or old roommate everywhere I go."

The mood restored, they all sit around the cloth. Food materializes from ziplock bags and tinfoil as conversations overlap and arms grab and pass food from every direction.

Clint is talking about one of many scammers who sought to enrich himself by profiting from the canyon. Around 1890, a man named Ralph Cameron helped improve the trail they'd all just hiked. He then began charging a toll to tourists even though the trail had been forged by the Native American Havasupai Tribe long before Cameron came along.

"The canyon has a long history of con men coming in here trying to make a buck," Clint says. "Cameron even tried to acquire mining claims to this very spot."

Cyd is interested in what Clint is saying but distracted, finding it hard not to stare at Kevin. She wants to touch him, to hold him by the shoulders and study him. Instead, she observes him from the corner of her eye, allowing herself a full-on glance when she can do it unnoticed. She can barely contain her racing heart. The resemblance is unnerving as if she's entered a dream state where the past is overlaid onto the present.

It doesn't take long for Cyd to realize that Kevin has none of Baker's sweetness or likability. He is quiet and strangely sullen, given the circumstances of his being in this beautiful place with his friends and his cute, bubbly girlfriend. But Baker wouldn't have done something like this, something as normal as hiking with friends, Cyd realizes. This thought makes Cyd sad. She still misses her brother, especially around her birthday. And all the news about Mae has brought him to the forefront these past days.

Baker's cancer and the physical deterioration that came with it had been devastating and surreal. He had accepted his plight long before Cyd had. The possibility that her brother might die in his forties was a fact she couldn't grasp. It was too far-fetched, as abstract as one of Bo's paintings where the scene is real but the interpretation makes it almost unrecognizable. Cyd hadn't accepted her brother's dying until he looked up from his bed and said weakly, "We all have to go at some point, Sis."

By that time, he was emaciated and in constant pain. He had finally stopped telling jokes. He refused any further treatments and died a few days later in his childhood bedroom, pumped full of morphine.

Laughter jolts her back to the present. The kids—as Cyd now thinks of them—are friendly and open and seem genuinely interested in listening to Clint's stories. Even Kevin is engaged. "Cool," he says at one point.

Cyd tries to keep her attention on the conversation. She learns the kids, too, are headed to Bright Angel Campground where they plan to spend the night.

"You should come, Cyd!" Kate blurts out, as Matt is telling Clint about their plans. "We have plenty of supplies. It'll be fun. We can stay up late and tell ghost stories!"

Cyd notices that Kevin shoots Kate a quick, sharp glance. Kate drops her eyes as if she's been scolded aloud. Megan shoots a look at Cyd that clearly reads, *See what I mean.*

"Oh, I don't know," Cyd says, though she is immediately tempted. Then she adds half-heartedly, "I don't want to be any trouble."

Cyd knows it is borderline crazy to consider spending the night, but she likes these people and she really does want to stay in the canyon as long as she can. She has questions, questions she plans to send out into this place in hopes of gaining some response, questions she's only just begun to formulate. She can't help but see this young man who looks so bizarrely like Baker as yet another sign. Maybe she should stay.

"It's no trouble at all," Megan insists, and Kate nods along. "It's settled then!"

"Well, okay," says Cyd. " I don't know why not. Thank you. It sounds like fun."

"YOLO!" Kate exclaims, unable to contain her natural state of innocent excitement. When Cyd looks at her, confused, she explains, "You only live once!"

"Okay, then. YOLO!" Cyd laughs, a bit uncomfortably as Bobby's words come back to her. *Three days.* This is already day two. What if she is too late getting back? Maybe it's better if he's not there when she returns. Maybe Bobby is right. She has enough on her plate.

"See what this canyon does," Clint says as they gather their things. "The energy, it gets in your veins. You're already hooked."

"I do have an addictive personality. Either that or it's the Nutella talking," Cyd says, still questioning the wisdom of her decision but undeniably revived.

37

The hike down to the campground is as spectacular as the first part of the trail. It's not long before Clint encourages the kids to go ahead, then settles into a slower pace next to Cyd.

"We'll be coming up the rear," Clint says.

"Like the old people that we are," Cyd adds with a wave, as the four youngsters pull ahead on the trail.

As warned, the trail is definitely *not* easy. There are more switchbacks and no shade through a section aptly nicknamed Devil's Corkscrew. Cyd is grateful for Daniel's walking stick, and she tries to focus on the stunning scenery rather than her aching hips or burning feet. She's unsure of the exact temperature—at least the mid-90s—and she is no stranger to heat, but this relentless sun is brutal. June is the driest time of year, she has learned, which makes for fantastic night skies, but there is not a cloud to be found. The top of her head bakes under the fabric of the hat. She might as well be laid out on a cookie sheet.

After an hour or so, her enthusiasm has given way to a steady barrage of self-doubt, or what Helen likes to call her *Itty Bitty Shitty Committee*. She still has time to turn around. No one would fault her for giving up. She shifts her one small bag yet again. It is a boulder slung over her shoulder. The neck pain is relentless. The ibuprofen she took with lunch has done nothing for the spasm radiating across her low back. She begins to fear her legs, already rubbery, might give out if she doesn't sit soon. She watches Clint's broad back in front of her and tries to keep pace.

She has walked for miles with no hint of the scene where the photograph of her father was taken. She's certain it was not taken at the rim—she explored the entire length of the South Rim yesterday—nor was it taken along this rugged trail. There is absolutely no sign of the water that is in the background in the picture. It is a fantasy to think she will find one specific spot in a canyon that's larger than the state of Rhode Island. She hears Bobby's voice in her head. He was right when he said she is no traveler, and here she is, walking nine miles into the Grand Canyon on a whim and spending the night with five people she's just met, completely unprepared, searching for *what* exactly? A message from a ghost? She left Bobby behind, she *hurt* him for this wild goose chase? Has she lost her mind? The absurdity of it feels like a cruel joke.

All she knows for certain is that the life she has known, the one she thought she would be living for years—maybe for *all* her years—no longer exists. The assumption that any of it was permanent now strikes her as incredibly naive. She feels as if the canyon is swallowing her whole, digesting her, reconfiguring her. What will be disgorged when the process is complete, she cannot imagine.

A not-so-young couple comes up behind them, gliding by as Cyd steps aside. The woman moves effortlessly in spite of the large backpack strapped across her back. *How in the hell?*

Cyd suddenly feels done in, as if she might faint.

"What time is it?" she asks, bending over to catch her breath.

Clint tilts his wrist. "It's 1:08."

Cyd throws her head back and swings her arms wide.

"It's 1:08! Thank God, it's 1:08!" She plops an arm on Clint's shoulder. "You have no idea how much I needed it to be 1:08, Clint. Maybe there's hope for me after all."

"If only all women got so excited when I told the time, my life might be entirely different by now."

"It's not the time, Clint. It's that the time is 1:08. The number . . . 108, as in . . ."

In her heady state of excitement over this much-needed, perfectly timed sign from the universe, she's not sure where to start. It is the number of all numbers—sacred, powerful, auspicious. It is the union—actually seen in its written form—of one with infinity: the number 1 which represents the individual, joined or looped together by a 0, as in the circular nature of life and all things in the natural world, to the number 8—which is the infinity sign turned upright—which is God or the universal energy or the all-knowing or the divine or whatever magnificence one wants to imagine.

Clint interrupts her mental ramblings. "As in the golden ratio."

"Yes!" Cyd exclaims. She sits down on a boulder and digs out her water bottle. "You know it then?"

"As in shells and sunflowers? Yes, I know it."

"And the eye of a hurricane!" Cyd exclaims, temporarily forgetting the throbbing extremities that are her aching feet. "Who doesn't love a perfect spiral?"

Cyd has been fascinated by the golden ratio since her father— lover of aesthetics and proportion, the man who never met a math problem he didn't like—first explained it to her when she was a little girl. It is a math equation, yes, but it is so much more. The divine proportion—she always loved that description. There is beauty in its perfection; placed throughout nature by God and used in art and architecture by the greatest of artists.

"Did you know the distance between the moon and the Earth is 108 times the diameter of the moon?" Clint sits beside her, also getting out his water bottle.

"A mala has 108 prayer beads," Cyd offers, referring to the rosary-like strands of beads used in many religions, including Hinduism and Buddhism.

"The diameter of the Sun is 108 times the diameter of Earth," Clint adds.

Cyd does not hesitate. "And 108 nadis converge to form the heart chakra."

"I have no idea what that is but I know there are 108 stitches on a baseball."

Cyd is laughing. "I have no idea how you know that. Nadis are energy centers. The diameter of Stonehenge is 108 feet."

"I majored in mathematics. The sum of the first twenty-two digits after the decimal point in pi equals 108."

"That's a good one. The Buddhists believe there are 108 types of feelings."

"And 108 is a Harshad number," Clint offers succinctly.

"A what number?"

"Harshad. A number divisible by the sum of its digits."

"Stop," Cyd laughs. "You win."

"You mean I don't even need to get into the decimal parity of the Fibonacci sequence?" Clint asks, straight-faced.

"Now you're just being ridiculous. But you can't leave me hanging. The decimal what?"

"Decimal parity. You break numbers down into single digits.

For example, fifteen is one plus five, so fifteen becomes six.'"

"Are you friggin' kidding me?" Cyd squeals. "I do that! That's how you take your birthday and get your life path number!"

"If you mean what I think you mean, then yes. That's decimal parity and if you take the repeating digits of the Fibonacci sequence—"

"Uncle!" Cyd exclaims. "Enough! You're going to make my head explode."

"You started it."

"Fair enough."

And with that, somewhat refreshed, Cyd pushes herself to standing. She looks at Clint and points to the trail ahead. "Onward," she says, trying to motivate herself through sheer mental determination, hearing her dad's encouragement in her head, and clinging to Clint's assurance that they are almost at their destination.

Soon, the terrain opens from the confines of a tree-lined gorge to the expanse of the mossy-brown Colorado River along which the trail continues. This is the same sliver of water that Cyd observed from the rim at Mather Point. It is nearly incomprehensible that she has walked from there to here, and she fights to keep from breaking down on the spot. They are close, she knows, but they are not there yet and she is unsure how much further she can go. Finally, when she fears she is quite literally at the end of her rope, she glances up from the dusty path and sees the sway of glistening cables spanning the river like an outstretched hand: the last remaining obstacle between her and the campground, the gloriously elegant Silver Bridge.

As they approach, Clint points out the pipeline supported by the narrow suspension bridge. He explains how the water travels from the springs along the North Rim, across the river,

and then back up to the South Rim. Without this extensive pipeline, there would be no hotels or visitor center or Hopi House.
The bridge gleams, encouraging her, beckoning her to come
forth. As she approaches the anchorage and looks down through
the metal grates, barely two feet wide, she feels Clint's steady
hand on her lower back. "You got this," he says. "I'm right behind
you."

"You got this," she repeats aloud.

Cyd takes hold of the rail to steady herself and, with the
river flowing fierce and vibrant below, takes the first tentative
step to cross over to the other side.

38

When they arrive at the camping area, Cyd and Clint find Kevin and Matt pitching tents around a leveled circle lined with boulders. There is a picnic table and a critter-proof metal box for food storage at each of the designated campsites along the creek. Cyd drops her bag, places her hands low on her spine, and arches her back.

"You okay there, Cyd-by-the-way?" Clint asks as Cyd digs her fingers into her neck, attempting to relieve some of the blistering tension, longing for one of Bobby's neck rubs.

"Did I mention I'm from Florida? The biggest hill we have is the bridge across the river."

"Oh, did you think you signed up for the beginner's hike? You must have hooked up with the wrong group."

"Hey, give a girl a break. This actually *is* my first rodeo." Cyd plops herself on a rock. "I'm not going to lie. I've run out of steam."

"It's not for wimps," Clint says, spreading out what looks like a weightless foam yoga mat that was rolled and clipped on his backpack. "Maybe that's why only 1 percent of visitors come all the way down here. Let me stake my claim here, then we'll go for a splash in the creek."

As if on cue, Kate and Megan come bounding up in bathing suits with wet hair.

"Hi, you guys! You have to go for a dip. It's fantastic. It feels soooo good!"

Cyd needs no convincing. She and Clint struggle out of boots, roll up pant legs, and are soon wading blissfully in the creek. The stream is as clear as any Cyd has ever seen. The shallow water glints under the late afternoon sun and the massive granite slabs tower in the distance. She splashes her face, the back of her neck, and the length of her arms, certain no spa ever felt more glorious.

"Excuse me, sir," Cyd inquires of Clint. She is wide-stanced in the cool stream. "Have we arrived at the heaven-on-earth auditorium, or is that down the way a bit?"

"Actually, Ma'am, this is the reception area. The real show starts when the sun goes down and the moon comes up. Every seat has a guaranteed view of the stage." Clint has taken off his Indiana Jones–style hat and is cupping water over his head and face.

Soon, the four kids are in the creek, all bright-eyed and smooth-skinned, like summer incarnate. Other campers are there, too, dragging in from the long trail at regular intervals. Cyd finds a flat rock on the opposite shoreline and situates herself on the broad, smooth surface, her sore feet cooling in the current. After a while, she lies back, shaded by a willow and her new sunglasses, and closes her eyes.

The sound of splashing water slowly registers, and Cyd opens her eyes to an endless blue dome. She is momentarily weightless, floating in the bright, glorious expanse and she resists the pull to wakefulness. When she groggily raises her head, she sees the slant of the sun has shifted and her friends are gone. She must have slept for some time.

It occurs to her then, with a nagging twinge of guilt, that she ought to check her phone. Holly or Bo might be concerned about her. She had actually, unbelievably, heard a phone ring earlier in the day along the trail, proving there was intermittent cell service, though how it was possible she couldn't fathom.

She pats down the sides of her yoga pants, feeling for the phone in one of the mid-thigh pockets. As she struggles to release it from between the slip of fabric, it is evident how little leeway there is in the snug material. She leans onto one elbow. A stone digs into her flesh and sends a shot up her arm. Winching involuntarily, she jerks forward. The phone, just barely in her grip, flies out of her hand as if in slow motion and lands in the stream with a resounding *plop*.

Her natural reflex—to instantly reach down and scoop up the phone—nearly sends her head-first into the water. Regaining her balance, she eases herself off the rock, creeps carefully on the uneven creek bed, and plucks the phone from its resting place. She searches the heavens as if a personalized message might be written there. If this is some sort of sign, it doesn't feel like a good one.

Her thoughts jump from her children to Helen to Bobby. Could she call him from another phone if she wanted to? She doesn't know his phone number. The days of knowing everyone's number by heart are long gone.

Cyd makes her way up the embankment to the thirty or so campsites that line the creek. She spots the girls lounging in fresh shorts and tank tops. Cyd pictures the numerous tiny outfits they likely have tucked into their backpacks—something

Holly would have done—and once again feels her age as she limps up the path.

"Hey, Cyd!" The girls wave her over. "We're all walking up to the ranch to have a few beers. Want to come?"

"Sure," Cyd says, not knowing what else she would do. "Let me squeeze these barking dogs back into my boots." Sitting, she examines her pink feet, grateful there are no blisters. "Where is it?" she asks, not knowing how much more she can ask of her legs for one day.

"It's only about half a mile," Kevin chimes in from a nearby log as he laces his boots. Cyd would swear she's seeing Baker in profile. Kevin pinches his fingers to his lips, then exhales smoke as he whips hair from his eyes.

"I guess I can handle that," Cyd says. "As long as it's not uphill."

"It's not, and you can." Matt stands and stamps his feet, offering a hand and pulling the girls up one by one, including Cyd. "The beer is the reward. But we have to get a move on. I'm not sure when they close."

Matt has naturally assumed the leadership role of their little group, though he seems more fun-loving instigator than responsible chief. He is the only one of the four who has done this hike before. He strikes Cyd as flawlessly polite and, unlike Kevin, has made her feel welcome the entire day.

In contrast, Kevin has been surly, his gloom accentuated by a slight Texan drawl. Though he physically resembles Baker at that age, his personality is distinctively opposite. It's as if Cyd is meeting the antithesis of Baker. She can't help but observe him. Throughout the afternoon, his interactions with Kate—his bending to whisper in her ear or her offering him a snack—all seemed upsetting to Kate, twisting her naturally pleasant expression into disappointment. There was something distinctly off. He glances up now as smoke dissipates around him and makes eye contact, having sensed Cyd's observance, the way a sneaky child might know a parent is watching from across the room.

"I'll give it my best shot. I could use a cold beer," Cyd says as the girls skip up, landing on either side of her.

The five of them head down the trail, leaving a note for Clint, who has not returned by the time they are ready to leave. Clint had told Cyd about Phantom Ranch during the walk from Havasupai Gardens. It was designed by Cyd's newfound favorite architect, Mary Colter, in the early 1920s, and the only way to get to the small group of cabins is on foot or by mule unless you come by way of the Colorado River on a raft. In fact, all supplies are still brought down by mules, just as they were a century earlier. Cyd finds it thrilling that such a place still exists, that someone had the foresight and fortitude a hundred years earlier to protect and maintain it.

The flat trail continues along the creek. They walk slowly and, without any gear, it is like a vacation compared to the earlier trek. The nap and the cooler evening temperature has left Cyd much improved. She somehow, impossibly, has tapped into a reservoir of energy. *Perhaps there* is *magic in the canyon*, she thinks. It has been twelve hours, ten miles, and nothing short of a miracle since she left her cabin in the village.

They find a picnic table outside the stone building that houses The Canteen and carry out beers and packaged snacks. Cyd also purchases four postcards and stamps—she is practically giddy when she spots the postcards and the special *Mailed by Mule* stamp available only from Phantom Ranch—another delightful holdover from the early days. She sips her beer and writes the first two cards as she half-listens to the kids joking and laughing around the table. She addresses one to Holly and one to Bo. She pauses. As she stares into the distance with the two blank cards in front of her on the table, she recognizes a sturdy profile coming toward her, backlit in the late-day light. She waves him over.

"Glad you could join us," Cyd says, striking a balance between teasing and sincerity, happy he is back, knowing the day would have unfolded so much differently without him. He has spent the day serving as her age-appropriate companion and her personal tour guide.

"Hey, Clint, my man!" Matt says, holding up an extra beer from the bucket on their table. "What's the good word?"

Cyd lets the conversation continue around her as she considers the remaining postcards. She wrote the first two cards easily, a few words describing the beauty of the place to her children. As she starts to write the third card, though, her sense of peace evaporates into the dry air. How can she send a card like this when there is so much suffering in Lola?

She sighs, writes a few words, and addresses the card to *My friends at The O.* Remembering the call she thought to make earlier, it suddenly seems urgent that she check on her friends.

She looks across the table. "Clint, may I borrow your phone?" Cyd asks. "I'd like to try to make a call."

He raises one questioning eyebrow. "A phone call? I don't think that's happening. Is something wrong?"

"Nothing's wrong, exactly. I just have a feeling . . . something came over me . . ." She struggles to explain her intuition without sounding like a nut. "I want to check on someone."

Clint pulls his phone from one of his cargo pants pockets and looks at it. "You might be able to send a text. I doubt a phone call will work."

"That's fine. I dropped my phone in the creek. Have I told you I'm a klutz? Don't ever give me anything breakable of value if you expect to get it back in one piece."

"I'll make a note. Here you go."

He hands her the phone, and she moves away from the table out of eyesight. She knows it is late in Florida, but she tries Helen's number anyway. There is a long silence as the call attempts to connect, then she hears a double beep, and the *call failed* message comes up on the screen.

She puts in Holly's number, then types: *Hi honey. It's Mom on my friend's phone. Mine got wet—ughhhh. Just want to make sure you're not worried. I've hiked into the Grand Canyon. So glad I took the plunge!!! It's beyond my wildest dreams! I'm safe and will call later tomorrow when I'm back at the hotel. Love you!! xxxooo*

She hits send and watches the blue bar move slowly across the screen. *Come on. You can do it.*

She relaxes when the *delivered* confirmation comes up. She deletes the message, then types Annie's number in the top bar.

Hey there. It's Cyd on a borrowed phone. Hopefully mine will dry out soon, don't ask. Just letting you know I'm fine. Made it to the Grand Canyon—amazing! Will tell all when we talk. How r u? Do you know anything?

This last question is code for a host of inquiries: *Do you have anything newsworthy to report? Has anything happened since we last spoke? Are you ok? Is everyone else ok? Do you need me for anything?* She waits again for the message to make its way up and out of the canyon.

She watches as the moving dots blip below the last bubble. Then a message appears: *OMG darling. I've been trying to get you. I hate to do this by text, but I think you would want to know straight away before you talk to Loren. My friend found out Mila is pregnant and it's not her husband's. I'm so sorry! I'm here for you. The Grand Canyon? Well done, darling. Call me asap. Kisses. Love you!*

Cyd stares at the phone as if struck dumb. She reads the words again. And then again before she types a response: *Don't even know what to say. Thx for telling me. I'll call u tomorrow. Love you too.*

She hits send. Waits. Delete.

A baby? Loren is going to have another child? Her children will have a half-sibling. *What does it matter? Your marriage is over.* Why does this feel like a gut punch? If she had decided she was moving on, if *she* had left *him* in Texas, why is this so devastating? Had she still been holding out hope? How long is she going to vacillate like this? *What is wrong with you? Get with the program!*

She bends at the waist and holds her knees. She feels light-headed, unable to breathe. *I am such an idiot.* Her mind continues, without her prompting, to compile a list of her most recent mistakes and regrets, a long, convoluted list: *I should have my head examined coming down here like this . . . What the hell am I doing? . . . I'm too old for this shit . . . I shouldn't have left home . . . I need to get back . . . a baby!?*

She straightens up and forces great gulps of air into her lungs. Once she feels somewhat composed, she walks unsteadily back around the building. When she approaches the table, Clint turns his attention wordlessly from the conversation to her. The other four, thankfully, continue their exchange. She sits opposite Clint and slides the phone across the table. She holds up her nearly full beer, tilts it into the receding sunlight, and pours most of it down her throat.

Clint's one eyebrow is raised again, but he doesn't say anything. Kate, who is next to Clint, makes eye contact.

"Hey, Cyd. Everything all right?" she inquires.

"Everything's fine," Cyd says, smiling wearily at Kate, not wanting to raise any concern. "I just wanted to check in with my kids. That hike is definitely catching up with me, though." She takes another swig from the bottle of beer for emphasis. "I hurt all over."

Never had four words held such truth.

The conversation continues around her, but Cyd is barely able to follow, much less participate. She smiles and nods politely, but the tightness in her jaw makes it feel as if her face is frozen in a grimace. She fiddles alternately with her third beer and the postcards, since those are the only items in front of her and she needs something to do with the energy coursing through her veins. She wants to scream. If she could run back up the trail and lock herself in the cabin, she would. She doesn't want to smile. She doesn't want to make small talk. She just wants to be alone and wallow in her misery.

The sensation of being watched causes Cyd to look up. Clint is studying her from across the table. An unmistakable sadness has settled behind his eyes. Heartbreak. Loss. Longing. Cyd recognizes that look. She knows the feelings behind it.

She looks away first, sliding the unwritten fourth postcard into her bag and finishing the last of her beer.

"Shall I do the honors and put those in the mail satchel for you?" Clint asks, standing, and motioning to the three completed postcards. "Can I get you another beer? Anyone else?"

"I'll go with you," Matt volunteers.

Cyd, still hungry after the chips and dried fruit, knows how she reacts to drinking on an empty stomach. "I should probably just have a lemonade," she says unconvincingly.

"I think starting a sentence with 'should' is a bad idea," Clint says, still studying her. "Nothing good ever comes after *I should* or *You should.*"

"He's right!" Kate says excitedly. "Like, *I should . . . start my diet tomorrow.*"

"Or, *You should . . . do it the way I want you to do it!*" adds Megan, sending the girls into one of their regularly occurring giggle fits.

"Exactly," says Clint as he and Matt head back to The Canteen.

"*You should* remember that next time you want to tell me what *I should* do," Kate says to Kevin good-naturedly. Kevin scowls and squirts liquid into his mouth from a pouch he'd been carrying with him.

After a few minutes, Clint and Matt return with bottles of beer laced between their fingers. Clint sets a bottle of lemonade in front of Cyd and the beers in the middle of the table.

"We can make it a fun lemonade," Kevin says, holding up the pouch. He grins at Cyd, his eyes glassy and pink.

"And I thought that was water you've been sipping on all afternoon," Cyd says, responding to his challenge by eyeing him directly.

"What are you, the drink police?" He sounds like a spoiled brat.

"Stop it, Kevin," Kate says, sharply but quietly.

"Oh, come on, babe. I'm just teasing with her. Ain't that right, Cindy?" Kevin puts a thin arm around Kate and pulls her toward him awkwardly.

"Her name is Cyd," Megan inserts.

"My apologies," he says, squirting more liquid into his open mouth. "I never can remember names."

"Maybe I will have one more beer," Cyd says. She stretches her neck from left to right to relieve the strain, suddenly irritated not just by Kevin's brattiness but also by her own unmanageable thoughts.

As the group carries on their conversation, Cyd mindfully takes in the scene before her—the towering canyon walls, the clear early-evening sky, the caress of warm air on her bare arms —and reminds herself how incredible it is that she is actually sitting here, in this spot, with these people. A week ago, she might have been killed. Two other people might also have been killed—one of them the father of her children. Four days ago, she had collapsed from despair and heartache in the middle of a park, without a clue what to do next, overrun with emotions, everything she thought to be dependable spiraling away from her like water down a drain. Now, here she is, at the bottom of the Grand Canyon, beyond anything she imagined, in the very place that her father so loved, the place he had vowed to return to with his beloved sister, that perhaps he might have returned to with his daughter if he had had the chance. If nothing else, she needs to appreciate where she is right now, this moment, because very soon she will be catapulted back into the disaster that is her life.

Tomorrow is guaranteed no one.

Cyd stops, her reverie broken. Inspired by her surroundings or the beer or both, she suddenly knows exactly what she wants to say and to whom. She reaches into her bag, retrieves the blank postcard, and writes without hesitation.

39

Before long, serious hunger overtakes them and, since dinner at The Canteen is only available to those with advance reservations, they walk back to the campsite. Cyd has willfully turned her attention back to the present. She is here, physically, in this incredible canyon; she might as well be here mentally as well.

After a meal featuring not-too-terrible MREs (Meals Ready to Eat) that Matt had left over from his time spent in the National Guard, Clint and Cyd make themselves comfortable, lounging contentedly against a log. "When I was little," she begins, "my dad, my brother, and I would lie on our lawn and look for the constellations. They would try to point them out to me, but I could never see what they were talking about. The big dipper, yes. Polaris—easy enough. But a guy with a sword and shield? Cassiopeia? Forget it. Either my eyes or my brain refused to participate. I felt like such a failure. My brother never stopped teasing me about it."

"You know, there's an app for that," Clint says dryly.

Cyd has come to appreciate his sense of humor. "You don't say," she prods.

"I've heard it's like magic."

"Hardly," Cyd chuckles. "My son put one on my phone. I look at the phone, I look at the sky, I still can't make out a damn thing. It's like I'm seven all over again."

As they wait in the crepuscular light for the first stars to emerge, Clint continues in his role as Cyd's private canyon tour guide. Over the course of the day, she has learned that Clint has a near-photographic memory as well as a knack for storytelling.

"It's hard to believe they've been able to keep it like this," he says as he studies the granite. "Did you know there was talk about building a huge gondola up at the rim so people could ride down by the thousands?"

"It's all so incredible," Cyd says, truly fascinated. "I wish I could go back in time. What I wouldn't give to spend just one night here back when Mary Colter was around. I would love to meet her."

"Ahhh, Mary Colter. I'm a big fan of hers, too. Did you know—"

Clint stops mid-sentence, and Cyd turns to see the distraction. Kevin is approaching them, holding out his hand, palm up. When he gets near, Cyd sees he is presenting them with two soft candies, the size of sugar cubes.

"Care to partake in this evening's festivities?" he asks, squinting through red-rimmed eyes.

Cyd looks at Kevin and then at Clint.

"I'm game if you are," Clint says, his playful tone tempting her.

"What is it exactly?" Cyd asks.

"It's a mix of CBD and THC. No big deal. Takes the edge off," Kevin says with a slight slur, still holding his palm open.

Clint takes one of the cubes and pops it into his mouth. "I

don't want to be a bad influence," he says as he chews. "I haven't smoked pot in years, but a gummy every now and again makes for a good night's sleep." He winks ever so slightly at Cyd.

Cyd is no novice. She has smoked her share of pot over the years but had stopped—for the most part—after meeting Loren. Helen and her fun-loving husband, Frank, have both taken to keeping their preferred stash of edibles handy. But it is Bobby who is the bad influence of late, occasionally pulling a joint out from behind his ear followed by his irresistibly mischievous grin. He makes everything so damn appealing. Usually, she likes how a little pot makes her feel—goofy, full of appreciation. But, she also knows she can become annoyingly paranoid. She ends up ruining the high by trying *not* to act stoned. And, her tolerance has definitely declined over the years.

Cyd sits forward. Her hips throb. The burning cord that has taken hold along the side of her neck continues its relentless sear. *Oh, what the hell.* Cyd plucks the sticky cube from Kevin's palm, holds it up momentarily, and offers a toast. "Yamas," she says, then chews quickly and swallows.

"Hey, what's going on?" Kate asks as she and Megan approach them, coming from the direction of the bathrooms.

"Just taking the party up a notch, babe," Kevin answers her triumphantly. He holds out another red cube. Kate and Megan share a glance.

"Are you girls not having any?" Cyd asks, their hesitation making her second-guess her decision.

"Maybe later. You didn't give her a whole one, did you, Kevin?" Megan looks seriously from Cyd to Kevin.

"Don't you worry about it, Meg," he slurs.

"Don't be an ass, Kevin," Kate interrupts. She turns to Cyd with big concerned eyes. "Do you ever eat gummies, Cyd?"

"I do, but it's been a while," Cyd says. Helen had invited her over for a movie night a few months ago and pulled out two candies as they settled on the sofa. "Here," she had said. "These are Frank's. I take no responsibility in the potency. But I'm warning you, you may need to sleep over." Cyd didn't realize the effect until, about an hour later, while in the midst of one of their laughing fits, she practically peed her pants, unable to walk a straight line to the bathroom.

"Those are super strong, Kevin, and you know it," Kate says, glaring.

"She's a big girl," Kevin says. "I'm sure she can take care of herself."

It isn't what Kevin says but how he says it that makes Cyd appeal to Clint with a look of her own. She really does *not* want to make an ass out of herself in front of these lovely people she barely knows. And she's already had, what, three beers? Four?

Clint's look betrays his amusement. "I won't let you out of my sight," he says. "You have my word."

The kids have settled in around the picnic table while Cyd and Clint, their backs protesting against the hard benches, situate themselves on Clint's sleeping mat. Cyd scootches herself to a comfortable angle and, leaning back, takes in the darkening sky. Clint sits next to her, resting his forearms on his knees. A short time passes in silence as he stares into the distance as if he's forgotton she is there. She has noticed this tendency throughout the day; a sadness overcomes him like a drifting haze, thickening then dissipating in irregular intervals. Instinctively, she reaches and touches his arm, stroking it lightly. He turns to look at her. A flinch of pain crosses his face, brief but clear as a flash of light. Clint collects himself immediately and launches into another story.

"Have I told you about the old pool at Phantom Ranch? They built it in the thirties."

"No, you have not," Cyd says, happy that the moment has lightened but concerned for her new friend. The edges of her consciousness are softening, and she easily switches gears, turning her attention to Clint's story.

"Apparently, they dug a giant hole, lined it with boulders, and filled it with diverted creek water. They even threw in a waterfall for effect. As you might guess, it was a smashing success. For years, the pool parties were all the rage. There are fantastic photographs of what look like movie stars—you know, the glamorous crowd, the kiss of death if you want to keep a good thing a secret—lounging around the water's edge, sunning themselves on boulders and standing in the chest-deep water. By the early seventies, it became too difficult and expensive to maintain, so the hole was unceremoniously filled in. They say they threw all kinds of stuff in there, stuff they wanted to get rid of, like old hand-carved doors, even a piano and a pool table. Hard to believe. Then they buried it all for good. So now, if we want to cool off, we have to use the creek."

"A pool?" Cyd asks, sitting up. "There was a pool down here?"

Just then, they are joined again by Kate and Megan, who emerge like mirages.

"Hi," Kate says, flopping down like a toddler.

"We're just checking on you," Megan adds.

"We're good," Cyd says, aware of her lips sticking to her teeth. "The stars are going to be beautiful. There's not a cloud in the sky."

"I know! It's going to be sooooo cool," Kate says, sounding adorably innocent for a grown woman. She exudes a genuineness rarely found in modern young women. Cyd can't fathom having to grow up in a world dominated by social media—app-swiping men, a soulless, superficial society, every move scrutinized under a constant barrage of suffocating, unsolicited analysis and criticism. She wonders how any of them maintain even an ounce of self-esteem. She knows she would have been emotionally crushed and likely scarred for life if she had had to deal with such things as a young person. Amazingly, Kate and Megan, like her own daughter, have managed to come through it emanating a strong sense of self and loving, generous hearts.

"I'm so glad you decided to stay with us, Cyd," Kate adds.

"Me, too," says Cyd. And she realizes she *is* happy she stayed. Somehow, she felt comfortable enough, especially with Clint, to do this. To take a chance.

"It's strange, really," Cyd continues. "When I met you kids, I felt like I was with my daughter and son and their friends. Then, this guy," she nods toward Clint, who is suddenly more interested in the conversation, "turns out to be the perfect tour guide. You are all *exactly* what I needed today. I can't tell you what it means to me."

Cyd meets Clint's eyes and smiles. He practically blushes. Right from the start, she felt as if she knew him and he knew her—an affirmation of her belief in past lives. There was an immediate ease between them, a rare familiarity.

Cyd reaches for her water bottle. As she lifts it, her arm moves in slow motion, and the bottle comes toward her face in an exaggerated movement. Her lips are slightly numb as they touch the metal rim. The girls continue chatting, but she has lost the thread of the conversation.

She turns to Clint and, speaking softly through uncooperative lips, says, "I definitely feel something."

"Welcome to the club," Clint says, his voice sounding distant.

"I hope I don't make an ass out of myself. I have a tendency to do that." Cyd leans toward him and catches herself just before she loses her balance. "I fancy myself quite a partier, but it's a sham. All talk. I'm a total lightweight."

"You're among friends. There's nowhere you need to go and nothing you need to do. You can sit back and enjoy the ride."

"I always tell my kids to be careful what you wish for. I wanted a memorable night." The crease between her eyebrows smooths, as if weeks of accumulated tension are being erased with one smile. "What did you girls call it?"

"YOLO!" the girls sing.

"Yes! You only live once. I'm going to work on that," Cyd says, trying to draw some saliva into her mouth.

"Actually," Clint says with a wink. "You live every day. You only die once."

The girls giggle in response, and Cyd lets the conversation meander around her without contributing. She observes the four young people, fascinated as much by their beauty and vitality as by the star-filled sky. Everyone has unfurled their sleeping mats, and they are gathered in a circle, laughing and rocking back and forth in the moonlight. All are golden-skinned and radiant. Cyd's face settles into a perpetual smile. Though she is unable to follow the storyline, no one seems to notice. They move with such ease—the girls, with their soft pink lips, and the boys, with their glossy muscles—all so strong, so alive. They are spellbinding and graceful. Cyd laughs along with them, unsure about what exactly, and realizes she is very high.

The night sky deepens and Cyd rubs her bare arms against the cool air with her hands. The skin is taut and slightly gritty.

She is suddenly hyper-aware of her body and how she feels in her skin. She is intrigued by the ridge of her tricep, its curved slant across her upper arm. Lower, on her wrist, the small knobs seem so smooth and accessible, as if she's touching the actual bone. She rests her hand on her belly, on the soft bulge below her navel, a remnant of her pregnancies and her twice huge belly. Those months had been the happiest of times. Whenever she told her children the stories of their first days—the descriptions that made them blush shyly—she told Holly that being pregnant with her, her first, was the most glorious time of her life. And she liked to tell Bo how much easier he had been, during both her pregnancy and delivery, so easy he'd nearly arrived in the passenger seat of his dad's truck. They had barely made it to the hospital. "Just keeping you two on your toes," Bo would add, never tiring of the story.

"How you doing there?" Clint gives her a shoulder nudge.

"I'm good," Cyd hears herself say. The strange sound of her voice makes her laugh. "I'm really thirsty."

"I'll get you more water. Sit tight." Clint picks up her water bottle as he rises.

Kate comes closer to Cyd and puts her arm around her shoulder.

"Are you having fun? You have this huge smile on your face. I'd feel terrible if you didn't have a good time. Kevin gets gummies that are way strong. He thinks it's funny or something to watch people get really stoned."

"Hey, I'm right here. I heard that."

"Mind your own business, Kevin. I'm just checking on Cyd. You're such an ass sometimes."

"I *am* having fun," Cyd says, aware of the grin glued on her face, over which she has no control.

"See, she's having fun," Kevin says. "She must be looking to have fun, coming all the way down here all by her lonesome. You must be the adventurous type, Cindy. I'm surprised your husband lets you stay out all night by yourself."

The words reach Cyd directly as if shot through a laser. Her focus shifts from Kate to Kevin, his near-white hair colorless in the moonlight. He looks ghostlike, almost translucent—a creepy sci-fi imitation of Baker.

"My husband," she begins with conviction, then instantly loses the next words. She feels four sets of eyes watching her. She laughs uncomfortably. "My husband . . ." She tries again. "I honestly don't know if my husband gives two shits where I'm spending the night."

The group goes silent.

"What'd I miss?" Clint's deep voice comes up from behind her, and the water bottle touches her shoulder as he hands it to her.

"The conversation is just getting good," Kevin continues with gleeful sarcasm. "Cindy was just trash-talking her husband. I think she came looking for a good time tonight. I think she came to the right place."

"Is that right?" Clint says slowly. He remains standing as Kate moves closer to Kevin.

"Come on, babe," Kate says softly, sounding equally frustrated and embarrassed. "You've had a lot to drink. Don't start anything."

"Yeah, dude," Matt adds. "Just chill out. And stop calling her Cindy."

"I'm fuckin' chilled out, dude," Kevin mocks. "And I don't need any stupid bitch telling me what to do. You are a total pain in my ass, Kate. A total fucking pain in my ass all day."

"That's enough," Clint says. "We're all having a nice evening here, a nice, friendly evening. Agreed?" Clint's voice is uncompromising. His eyes are locked on Kevin, who looks small and hunched under Clint's towering figure.

"Come on," Kate tries again, reaching for Kevin's hand. "Let's go sit down by the creek."

"Fuck off," he says under his breath, pulling his arm away sharply.

Cyd rises in one motion as if attached to a pulley. The ground is uneven under her feet, and she reaches for the tree to steady herself. If she had any doubt, the act of standing is irrefutable proof of how stoned she actually is.

"What is wrong with you?" she says shrilly. She looks in Kevin's general direction. Her focus refuses to hold. She immediately regrets having stood up. "Are you always this much of a jerk? Why do you want to be stoned and drunk all the time when you have this beautiful, sweet woman by your side? Don't you see how lucky you are? Don't you appreciate *anything*?"

All eyes are now fixed firmly on Cyd. Four youthful bodies glow in the moonlight, and Kevin's pale hair is illuminated like a halo. She knows she should stop, but still, she plows ahead. She sweeps her arm out as if encompassing some nearby group.

"What *is* it with you guys? Are you really that oblivious, or do you just not care about the pain you cause? You think you can treat us any way you want. You're like wrecking balls, bashing everything in your path. Everything is about *you*. You do what you want. You take what you want. It's always the same story. We give, and you take."

"I don't know what you're talking about, lady," Kevin grumbles. Then, leaning toward Kate, he adds, "If I knew you were bringing your mother on this trip, I would have left you behind."

"You did leave me behind!" Cyd hears herself as if from a distance, aware yet unaware of her confusion. "You left when I needed you most! I needed you, and you were too selfish, too busy getting fucked up to care!"

"Jeee-sus. Take it easy," Kevin moans.

"You were *not* a good brother! I thought I could count on you! What happened to you?"

"Come on now, Cyd," Clint interjects. "Let's just take a breath."

Cyd doesn't know what will come out of her mouth next. She is sliding down the slope, unable to stop the momentum.

"You want to know the truth of it? Shit happens! Awful shit. People die. When you least expect it, they up and die. Or they don't die, but they lie. Right to your face. And they cheat. They lie and they cheat and they . . . they . . ."

Her voice has risen in pitch. She is suddenly brutally aware of the absurdity of what she is saying. Deflated now, she continues, "One minute you have something, and the next it's gone. That's what life is. One loss after another. Don't you see how lucky you are? Don't you see what is right next to you, you foolish, stupid boy?" Her voice and her conviction trail off like smoke rings puffed into the night.

"Okay, let's all take it easy. We don't need to solve the world's problems tonight. Why don't you and me take a little walk, Cyd, and look at the stars?" Clint takes her gingerly by the elbow as if she might explode under his touch. "Let's just take it easy and enjoy this beautiful night."

"I'm . . . I'm sorry." Cyd struggles to put the words together. "I've had a rough few days. I'm really sorry," she repeats to no one and everyone, unsure of what she has actually said and what she has only thought.

"Come on, Kate," Megan says. "Walk with me to the bathroom."

As the girls leave the circle arm in arm, Cyd hears Megan
say, "She's right. You deserve better."

Cyd lets Clint lead her away from the group in the opposite
direction, her arm linked in his for support. She steps carefully,
unsure if her legs will hold. The drugs have hit her like a gut
punch, hard and swift, and have exacerbated the effects of the
alcohol. She tries to gather her thoughts, but it's like herding
cats. She has just met these people. *What must they think?* The
night is just getting underway, and already she is behaving like
a lunatic. She pushes away at the edge of paranoia.

"Why don't we sit down and relax? There's quite a show going
on above us."

Clint has led them some distance from the campsites and
they have found a patch of grass to sit on. Cyd is concentrating
on her breathing, trying to calm herself. She looks up and is
nearly flattened by the beauty.

"It's sad to think how many children don't even know what
a star-filled night sky looks like," he says thoughtfully.

Cyd has seen beautiful starlit skies over the marshland from
her dock, but never anything like this. This defies comprehension. Sometimes, after a long day of sitting with Baker at the
hospital during the height of his illness, she would come home
and lie on her back across the smooth wood boards and allow
herself to decompress. The release she experienced just lying
there, feeling her impossible smallness and, simultaneously, her
infinite potential, was like a tall glass of water for a woman dying
of thirst. She realizes she hasn't done it in a very long time.

She lies back on the warm ground. The starlight pulls her focus skyward and the memory takes hold like a dream.

40

July 4, 1979
Lola, Florida

The night began with an innocent excitement that, in hindsight, seems cruel. The Fourth of July fell on a Saturday that year, and the fireworks festival was held at the waterfront park near the small downtown. Cyd and Helen had been at the park most of the afternoon, watching as more and more families came, spreading blankets on the ground, lighting portable grills, playing frisbee. Her parents arrived with a picnic basket and lawn chairs, and found a spot near the water.

It was later—after the dazzling grand finale had faded and the sky had quieted, after the adults had dragged all the coolers and all the children back to houses or cars, and only a few stragglers remained—that someone pulled on Cyd's wrist. She and Helen were leaning against a tall pine, sharing a bag of strawberry licorice and feeling, at twelve, very grown up after finagling special permission to stay out extra late.

"What?" Cyd asked, in response to the tug.

They followed with their eyes at first, and then by walking behind the slightly older girl. She led them away from the park lawn. Cyd caught bits and pieces of what she said, something about Baker, that they really should come to see, that he might fall into the water at the rate he was going.

They walked along the water's edge, away from what was left of the crowd, past the block of old warehouses toward the marina and the stretch of dock slips. They went to the last dock. The lights faded behind them, and Cyd had trouble seeing into the darkness over the water. When she got closer, before she could make out what she was looking at, she heard her brother's voice. He was mumbling and laughing. Two guys were trying to help him stand but Baker seemed unable to put his feet in the right spot. There were several older kids around him, and more standing further back, watching.

Cyd froze, her peripheral vision gone, as if a tunnel had been slipped around her and everything was dark except for Baker at the end of the dock. She had seen him stumbling before, but never like this. She had known about his drinking for the past year, heard about it from other kids, and caught glimpses of it at school or under the bleachers at football games. He'd come home in such a condition more than once, but it was late, after their father was in bed, and their mother served as his coconspirator, helping him quietly down the hall, past Cyd's room to his own. Once she knew her brother drank, once she learned there was an entire other world directly under her nose that she knew nothing about, she felt a prolonged, underlying sadness for the loss of something she hadn't realized she possessed.

When they reached the last dock, an older boy approached Cyd. He slurred out his advice to take Baker home. *He's in bad shape, and they don't want to leave him, but they have to go and, man, he didn't know what happened.*

Cyd walked down the long, dark dock, aware of other kids

watching, until she was with Baker. He laughed when he saw her and draped a heavy arm around her shoulder. Cyd had never before smelled that mixture of cigarettes, pot, and cheap booze. He dragged her down with him and they landed hard on the wood planks, Baker losing his balance even once he sat, almost falling backward, laughing even more.

"Whoa," he mumbled. "Hey, Cyd! Hey, how's my sweet little sister? Where'd you come from anyway? Where'd my beer go? You got any beer, Cyd?" He found this very funny, and he squeezed her toward him with his heavy, loose arm and his stinking breath.

It seemed that Nick arrived immediately, appearing out of nowhere. Helen must have sent someone to find him.

"Baker, how's it goin'?" Nick said, squatting next to them.

"Hey, man," Baker said, his head loose on his neck. "Hey, Nick! You got any beer, Nicky? Let's have a beer. How ya been?"

"Yeah, let's walk. There's no beer here," Nick said, sliding his arm under Baker's.

Nick bent and lifted Baker to his feet. Cyd tried to help, letting his weight fall onto her, nearly knocking her over again. With Baker's arm around his neck, Nick began walking Baker back down the dock. Though two years younger, Nick was stockier and stronger than Baker. Baker was leaning on him, and Nick was saying something that sounded encouraging as they walked, slowly, leaning into each other, toward the street. She didn't know if she said it or just thought it, but Cyd knew it was a bad idea to take him home.

It wasn't a long walk from the docks to their house, but it was slow going. Baker was laughing and mumbling, saying he was okay, then thanking Nick profusely as his feet crisscrossed in front of him causing them both to zigzag.

"Thank you, man. Thank you, Nicky. Hey, where'd everyone go? Where's my car?"

The house was mostly dark as they started up the driveway. It had taken more than thirty minutes to make the walk, but Baker was in no better shape when they arrived. At one point, he made them stop as he fell to his knees and vomited in the grass. Cyd smelled the sour liquid from where she stood.

When they reached the house, Cyd saw the light on in the back room where she knew her mother would be sitting in front of the television. It was too early for Iris to be in bed, but Cyd was sure her father would have retired as soon as they got home from the fireworks display. His childhood on a farm and his life in the military still dictated his "early to bed, early to rise" sleep schedule.

She began to pray. *Please, God, please don't let Daddy wake up. Please just let us get Baker to bed. Please make him be quiet. Please, God, please.*

Baker was still mumbling to himself as the foursome made their way up the sandy driveway to the front door. Nick continued to talk softly, directing Baker up the two front steps, trying to steady him against his own body. The door was unlocked, and Cyd went in first, as quietly as she could. She heard the television. She motioned to Nick to head straight toward the hallway on the right, toward the two smaller bedrooms away from her parents' room. Maybe they could get there. Maybe her dad wouldn't wake up.

Her mother was on them immediately, panic across her face, trying to get up close to Baker, to either see him or to talk to him, Cyd wasn't sure. She wanted her mom to go away and let Nicky do it. Nicky was doing just fine. But Iris went on the other side of Baker and tried to put her arm around his waist, which was a ridiculous thing to do since their mother was small and couldn't begin to hold up a grown man.

Maybe Baker tripped, or maybe their feet got tangled, but before they reached the entrance to the hall, both Iris and Baker stumbled, falling away from Nick. The unbalance caused Nick to lose his hold. A lamp shattered against the wood floor. Cyd saw it was her grandmother's lamp, pretty porcelain with dark pink flowers painted on it. The small marble-top table went over too, and the thick glass ashtray, all hard and loud as they went crashing down. Then Baker was down, too, and his hands were bleeding from the glass as he tried to right himself, trying either to get up or crawl to his bedroom.

Her mother had slipped too, and when she stood up, her palm was pressed over her left eye. She'd hit it somehow, on the edge of the marble table perhaps. There was pain across her mother's bird-like face, and when her hand came down the skin above her eye was bluish, a gruesome lump forming along the bone under her thin eyebrow.

Suddenly, her father was there, in his pajama bottoms and T-shirt, momentarily confused, then enraged, his jaw set hard, his eyes fiery. He tried to grab Baker, to yank him up off the floor by his shirt. Nick tried to help saying, "Please, Mr. Williams, I'll get him to bed, sir. I can do it, sir. He'll be all right." All the while, her mother was pleading. There was blood running down the front of her bare shin, and her left eye was not quite open. She stood firm and small, one arm outstretched, the other reaching behind her, wedging herself between her husband and her son. Jesse tried to move her aside as he reached to grab Baker by the back of his shirt, telling Iris in a low voice that sounded so strange to Cyd, so unlike her father, to get out of his way.

Nick managed to get Baker up, his shirt twisted, his hair hanging over his face, and then he was down again. Cyd wasn't sure if Jesse had hit him or if Baker had slipped. Her father was holding her mother aside and saying things to Baker in a hoarse voice that wasn't his, and Baker was slurring and then seemed to notice that his hands were bleeding. Iris tried to get around Jesse to Baker, and Baker tried to get away from his father as Nick worked to keep Baker on his feet and moving toward the hallway.

When Cyd thinks back to that night, she sees herself standing in one place, just inside the front door, frozen. If she had moved or said anything, she cannot recall it. For years, when the memory rose up like a knife blade held over her head, it seemed like a scene from a movie. Cyd wanted to shout at the stupid girl to do something, *anything*! But she only stood there dumbfounded, useless.

At last, Nick and Iris, with Baker between them, disappeared around the corner. Jesse turned to the girls, pushing his hair back with one hand, his face anguished. It seemed he just realized they were there. Helen stood close, squeezing Cyd's hand.

"I'm sorry, darlin'," he said, his voice strained. "I'm sorry you had to see that. You too, Helen. You girls go on now, go to Helen's. Everything's all right now. It's over." He bent and kissed Cyd on the forehead.

The girls went outside and sat on the steps until Nick came out. They all walked to the Kondilises' house in silence. When they arrived at the end of the driveway, Nick stopped under a large oak and lit a cigarette. Helen continued toward the door.

"You okay?" Nick asked, turning to Cyd.

She nodded, unsure, afraid once the tears began there would be no end to them.

"Thank you, Nicky," she said softly.

He smiled wearily, then reached out and tussled her hair. "You're welcome, C."

Cyd had gone home late the next morning, Sunday, the fifth of July, after church, where she would learn the news that would change her life. She hadn't seen her mother at the ten thirty Mass. She had assumed Iris had gone earlier, as she often did, in spite of the events of the previous night, since nothing kept Iris from Sunday Mass. Not normally. Not until that Sunday.

Cyd had prayed extra hard. She prayed that Baker would stop drinking. She prayed that her parents would not fight. She prayed that her father would forgive her for bringing Baker home the night before when she knew it was a bad idea.

If she had known better, she would have prayed for something different. She would have prayed for her father's safety, or for the preservation of her happy childhood, or for the last of her own innocence. She would have prayed that her mother's discolored eye would be miraculously healed by the hand of God so that the neighbors would have nothing to gossip about. They couldn't know that she had bruised it when she fell against the table. Her mother would never clear up any misunderstanding that might have lingered in their minds about the integrity of Jesse Williams, who would no more hit a woman than he would set himself on fire. If Cyd had known what was to come, about the whispering and the speculation, she would have prayed for the black eye to be mercifully erased so that no one could possibly conclude that her father had struck her mother, something that Cyd knew was impossible *and* untrue, but that no one else could know for sure. She might have prayed for the strength not to hate her mother for that omission, or the wisdom not to blame herself *or* her mother for her father's death.

As they made their way over the course of the next week—with neighbors coming to the house offering food, through the wake and the service and the funeral—Cyd watched with dismay. All of it her mother attended with a black eye miserably covered with pancake makeup that no one dared inquire about. Of course, Iris could offer no reasonable explanation without shifting blame away from her husband and onto her son, and how could she do *that*? Iris would never say anything to make anyone think badly of Baker. That was a truth Cyd could take to her grave. No, her mother would not say a word about how she got the bruise. She would offer no explanation to anyone. And under the circumstances, as Iris Williams leaned in all her grief against her beloved teenage son while they buried her handsome young husband, under the bewildered scrutiny of her inconsolable twelve-year-old daughter, no one dared ask a thing.

In the end, it didn't matter what Cyd prayed for that morning. Not really. She realized that later. By the time Cyd knelt on the kneeler at the beginning of Mass and crossed herself, with the bright summer sun angled perfectly through the stained glass, it was already too late.

41

Friday, June 4, 2019
Bright Angel Campground,
Grand Canyon National Park

"Hey there. You still with me?"

Cyd jerks back to the present, breathless, shaken. She sits up.

She stammers, "I'm fine. I'm sorry. I was just remembering something."

"No pressure. Just checking on you. I thought I lost you there for a minute." He is teasing her, but she hears true concern.

"I had no idea how magnificent this would be," Cyd says quietly, inhaling deeply, reaching for her composure. "And no idea how much I needed it."

After a moment, she adds, "I'm sorry about what happened back there. I've been under some pressure lately."

"No need to be sorry. That kid's had it coming to him all day."

"Still, he's the kid. I'm the adult. I really don't know what is wrong with me. Clearly, I should not have taken an entire gummy, but it's more than being stoned. It's like I'm coming apart."

The sky is deep black behind the sparkling constellations. The entire display, though right above her, is incomprehensible in scope and majesty. She wants to take it in. Or rather, let *it* take *her.*

"Pretty damn incredible," Clint says after a pause, but the passage of time is warped now, out of reach.

She hears Clint's voice but it seems to travel a great distance to reach her. The earth is warm under her body, both familiar and alien. She hears the water gurgling across rocks, the volume fading to near silence, then growing louder as if someone is turning a knob slowly up and down. The stars dance and streak above her, expanding and contracting. The starlight seems to connect her to the heavens, and she feels a vibration running down her arms and into her fingertips.

Her sense of time has completely abandoned her. She tries to relax into the experience, to allow for the irrationality of what is happening. Clint speaks and she answers, though she's not sure she is linking her thoughts to the correct words. As soon as she arrives at a momentary understanding of the trail of the conversation or of her own line of thinking, the certainty is swept away like a feather in a stream. There is no paranoia, just recognition that she has no control.

Some time passes in silence, though how much she couldn't say.

"How you doin' over there?" Clint asks, his voice is once again deep and close.

"I'm good," she says, feeling the upward pull of her cheeks. She pauses, her thoughts coalescing, her confusion diminishing. She realizes the high is more pleasant now, less intense.

She continues, "I've been struggling lately. I thought coming down here might help somehow. I'm not sure what I should do next. I'm not sure about anything anymore."

"I think most of us know that feeling. It's the human condition."

"Is it?" She ponders something that has just occurred to her. "Do you think it would be helpful if we could stand outside ourselves and see what other people see, even for one day?"

"I think that would completely mess with my head."

"Lately, I find myself wondering how other people see me. I've lost touch with myself somehow. Maybe I could see things better from the outside, you know, figure out what I should do next. It's always easier to help other people fix their problems than it is to see what to do about your own."

"You think you need fixing?"

"Apparently. I feel like I've lost control of my life. Things are broken. I must have done something to cause it."

"I know that feeling," Clint says distantly.

"I tried to be a good daughter and a good mother. I thought I was a pretty good wife. Here I am, a middle-aged woman on the verge of divorce. No one really needs me anymore. I've got no discernible talent and no plan for the future. I have no idea what comes next."

"I gave up on that a while ago."

Cyd hears the defeat in his tone, a mirror image of her own. She thinks of Bobby's words in the car in Sedona. "Before I left on this trip, a friend told me I should let go of the oars. Go with the flow. It's much easier said than done."

"You know how I feel about sentences that start with *you should*," Clint reminds her.

She gives a little laugh. "Yes, I remember. Honestly, I think

I've lost my ability to imagine what I should do or can do. I need something or someone to believe in. I bet Mary Colter never questioned what she believed in."

Cyd has been intrigued by this woman and her accomplishments since she read about her at Hopi House the previous afternoon. There seems to be an important connection, something she needs to explore further.

"You're probably right about that," Clint agrees. "Colter was quite a trailblazer."

"What do you know about her?" Cyd straightens up like a child waiting for her older brother to begin a ghost story from beside a campfire in the backyard.

"I know she was in her fifties when she designed Phantom Ranch in the early twenties."

"My age," Cyd says wistfully.

"She was obviously quite brilliant. She graduated from high school when she was fourteen. She wanted to be an artist and was fascinated by Native American culture. You can see it in her work, especially here at the canyon. She loved nature. She wanted her buildings to blend in with the natural beauty of the surroundings. The Lookout Studio is a great example of that."

"Yes, The Lookout! I was admiring it yesterday. It looks like it's growing right out of the canyon wall."

"Mission accomplished," Clint says. "It was a few years later that she designed the cabins at Phantom Ranch. Everyone loved her plans, but when they wanted to name it *Roosevelt's Chalets,* she basically told them to shove it where the sun don't shine. She had already come up with the name *Phantom Ranch,* and obviously, she stuck to her guns. They say she was the consummate perfectionist."

"I had a perfectionist mother. My dad used to tell me," Cyd

begins, ready to explain how difficult it had been to please such an exacting woman when a thought hits her like a slap. She swivels to face Clint, the question so urgent she wants to grab him by the shoulders. "Wait! You said something earlier about a pool. Was there a pool here somewhere? Is it still here?"

"Yes and no," he says, clearly intrigued by her excitement. "They dug a pool at Phantom Ranch. Creek water flowed into it. It was there for about forty years, from the mid-thirties. Why do you ask?"

"I have a picture," she begins, turning and searching the ground around her for her backpack. "I brought it with me. It's in my bag."

"Here," Clint says, pulling the sack from the darkness like a magician. "I grabbed it for you."

"Oh my god, Clint! I love you!" Cyd digs frantically in the mouth of the bag, pulling out the small frame, practically shoving it at him. "Is this it? Do you think this picture was taken there?"

Clint squints at the image. "Absolutely," he says, tilting the frame to catch the moonlight. "I've seen old photographs taken there. This is definitely the pool. See here, in the background." He points to the edge of the frame. "That's one of the cabins."

"So we were there? I was right there?"

"Yes, we were right around the corner. If it was still there, you could have seen it when you left to make your phone call." Clint seems equal parts amused and confused by her outburst.

"This is fabulous, Clint! I can't begin to tell you what this means to me."

"You could try," he says teasingly.

"That's my dad." Cyd points to the man in the middle of the trio. "I've looked at this photograph almost every day for the past forty years. My dad died when I was young, and this picture captures him perfectly. I came here to try to find this spot. He looks so happy. I thought if I could stand in that very same place, it might help me make some decisions. I might feel the happiness he felt when he was here." Hearing the words spoken aloud, Cyd realizes how futile it all sounds. "I know, kind of silly, right?"

"I don't know how silly it is," Clint says, turning serious. "I told you, I come down here for a similar reason. To try to connect with someone I loved."

"Yes, I'm sorry to be insensitive," Cyd says, recalling Clint's explanation when they first met that he's been hiking the canyon since his wife died.

A wind blows, and Cyd shivers involuntarily. She wraps her bare arms around herself.

"You're chilled. I'll go back and get your jacket. I know where you left it."

"Thank you. That would be great. I swear, I go from hot flashes to freezing. There's no in-between."

"Don't move, understand? I'll be right back," Clint says as he disappears into the darkness.

Once again, the wondrous silence of the canyon engulfs her. She is aware of the quickness of her breath. In spite of the irrationality of her quest, she can't help but feel an excitement, a sense of accomplishment. She had stood right where her father had stood at Phantom Ranch. He may have sat right where she is sitting now. She lets the starlight draw her attention up and out. The tingling along her spine seems to connect her to the celestial scene above. *Are you there, Daddy?*

She hears it then, out of the sparse, low-lying brush, barely ten feet away, the faintest rustle and the glow of two greenish eyes. Instinctively, she freezes. The remaining drug-fog lifts as adrenaline pumps through her system. The moonlight reflects in the two small orbs. She stares directly into the creature's eyes, unblinking. She might have wondered what type of creature it was or calculated the level of danger the animal posed, but no thoughts enter her mind. She meets its unmoving gaze and waits. She cannot see its body, but her subconscious knows enough to cause her entire being to shift into high alert. This is an inbred reaction, as natural as breath itself. It is primal.

There is a thrumming in the center of her chest—the heart center in yoga-speak, where consciousness transitions from the earthly to the heavenly. In this heightened state of focus—part fear, part thrill—her awareness expands, encompassing what is right before her and, simultaneously, what is all around her. It is something she has only imagined from a spiritual perspective, but this thought does not enter her mind. There are no thoughts. It is as if she has been launched. She is suddenly capable of seeing 360 degrees at once, of sensing all there is to sense with unlimited capacity. Somehow, this creature, with its singularly focused attention, has drawn her into its realm or penetrated her in some magical way. She feels its ancient, survivalist energy as if it is her own. It is connecting her to its physical place in the world and also to the essence of this entire place, to a moment in time that might have occurred seconds ago or in a distant millennium—it makes no difference. As the glassy eyes radiate the harshness of the canyon like moonlit pools, Cyd knows this is a standoff as old as the canyon itself: two creatures, unsure and curious, assessing one another, evaluating, communicating through the silence, each determined in its own survival, each vibrantly alive, existing in a place where the visible meets the invisible. It is the very essence of what it means to be fully alive.

42

"Cyd?"

She flinches. For a fraction of a second, the connection with the creature remains intact. Then, with an almost imperceptible movement, it is gone. Cyd searches the darkness where the animal had stood. She is left with a palpable sensation that she has been handed a gift.

"Cyd?" The voice comes again.

Cyd realizes her arm is outstretched toward the brush. She turns to see Kate and Megan emerging from the trail.

"There you are. We came to check on you. We saw Clint at the campground. How are you?" Megan asks.

"Kevin can be such an a-hole," Kate adds. "I'm sorry about all that."

Cyd stammers, "Girls, hi. Don't be silly. It's not your fault, and I'm fine, really. I must confess, though. I feel like I've regressed about thirty-five years, back to when we used to smoke pot out at the quarry, only this stuff is unlike any pot I've ever smoked. Or maybe I'm just getting too old. Thank goodness it's starting to wear off a bit."

"I think you are a-may-zing," Kate says sweetly, bringing Cyd back to their first encounter that morning. "My mother would never in a million years have even *tried* to hike down here like you. I told you, those gummies are wicked strong. I never eat a whole one."

"Thanks, girls," Cyd says sincerely. These two young women have lifted her spirits all day and their concern for her is touching. She is again reminded of her own children and how fortunate she is to know they are safe when so many in Florida and elsewhere are not.

The girls sit next to Cyd and look up at the rich tapestry of light overhead. The effects of the THC have diminished, and her confusion is replaced by clarity. Her head pulses pleasantly to the rhythm of the starlight.

A sound breaks the silence. At first, Cyd thinks Kate has said something, but then she realizes it's a sniffle and that Kate is sobbing softly into her hands.

"What is it?" Cyd asks as Megan puts her arm around her friend. "What's happened?"

"Kate's having a hard time," Megan answers.

"I'm so sorry," Cyd says, concerned at the abrupt change in Kate's lighthearted demeanor. "Would you like to talk about it?"

This causes Kate to sob more intensely.

"Oh, sweetheart. I'm so sorry," Cyd says helplessly. "If it's any consolation, I can relate. I've had an awful time of it lately. Sometimes it helps just knowing you're not the only one who's struggling."

Kate lifts her head and wipes her nose with the bottom of her T-shirt. She looks to one side at Megan and then turns to Cyd. Cyd sees the change in her. Her face, only dimly lit, looks suddenly aged, hardened. After a few beats, she speaks quietly, without any of the lightness Cyd is accustomed to hearing in her voice.

"I'm pregnant. At least, I think I am. I'm late. My boobs hurt. I threw up this morning."

"Oh, sweetheart," Cyd repeats, unsure what she should say next.

"I don't think I can have a baby with him. I keep trying to picture myself being tied to him for the rest of my life."

Megan looks past Kate to Cyd. "This trip has been planned for a while. She thought she might talk to him before we left. When that didn't work, she was just going to try to enjoy these few days and then deal with it when we get back. You can see how *that's* working out."

"He doesn't want a baby. He's made that perfectly clear in past conversations," Kate says with an eerie calm. "I don't know what I'm hoping for."

"Do you love him?" Cyd asks, though as she says it she realizes the answer hardly matters. Loving him won't turn him into a good partner, much less a good father.

"I thought I loved him." Kate's voice is weak. "You've seen a very bad version of him today. He's not usually like this."

Megan makes a little huff under her breath but says nothing.

"Meg doesn't like him. She doesn't think he treats me very well."

"What do you think?" Cyd asks.

"I think I get on his nerves sometimes. I don't know. It does seem like he's mad a lot of the time. At me or at the world. He's had a hard life."

"That's no excuse," Megan says. "It's a cop-out. You're always making excuses for him. I wish you could see that."

"If I could say something," Cyd begins hesitantly.

"Yes, please," Kate says, turning to her, a neediness in her voice. Cyd is reminded of Holly, grown yet still in need of guidance. They are both young women trying to navigate the cruel adult world with remnants of their adolescence still very much a part of their personalities.

"I've only just met you, but I think I have a sense of who you are. I hope you don't let a man or anyone else extinguish that flame inside you. It makes you gracious and joyful and curious. You are lovely to be around. As women, at least in my generation, we tend to sacrifice a lot of ourselves for other people. I once heard from a very wise woman a good piece of advice, something I wish I was able to follow more often: *No* is a complete sentence. I think we need to set boundaries and hold people to them, especially the men in our lives. We need to believe we are entitled to be treated a certain way."

Kate sniffles and says, "I like that. Thank you, Cyd."

Megan reaches for her friend's hand. "You'll feel better in the morning. You'll figure out what to do."

The women fall silent for a few moments, listening to the sounds of the canyon. Cyd feels something touch her shoulder and looks up to find Clint with her jacket. He motions backward to let her know he is not going to disturb whatever is going on between the women. Then, leaving the right amount of distance between them, he sits out of earshot but within view of the threesome.

Finally, Kate shifts herself and leans back, taking in the fullness of the sky. "I keep vacillating between so many emotions. This feels like the most important decision I'll ever make."

Cyd feels her heart swell. She has the overwhelming sensation that her younger self is sitting right next to her. The time between then and now gone in an instant, the true brevity of a lifetime as concise as one single star.

"We come to many crossroads in life," Cyd offers into the

silence, as much to herself as to her friends. "It's usually only in hindsight that we recognize them for what they are. This is a very clear turning point in your life. It's an opportunity, a gift really, because you see it for what it is. You can choose what's right for you. Try your best to listen carefully to your heart. Sometimes you have to make a decision, and then make it the right decision."

Kate leans over and rests her head on Cyd's shoulder, something Holly has done many times.

"Thank you, Cyd. I'm so glad you've been with us today. It's really helped just talking to you. I hope I can be like you, you know, down the road when I'm older. I hope that doesn't sound bad."

They all laugh, and the moment lightens.

"Let's go find the guys, Meg. We can't hide from them all night," Kate says, sounding more like herself again, or at least like the version of herself she'd been putting forward throughout the day.

They stand, and the girls each hug Cyd. Cyd keeps hold of both of Kate's hands and looks at her directly. "Things will work out exactly as they are meant to. I believe that. You try to believe it, too."

Cyd hugs Kate again, holding her tightly, and feels the strength of her young friend come back to her through their embrace.

43

The girls walk back toward camp, leaving Clint and Cyd alone once again.

"I didn't want to intrude. Everything all right?" Clint asks. He has brought his sleeping mat with him, and he unfurls it for them to sit on.

"Hard to say. Sometimes everything will never be all right again. Then what do you do?"

"You get up and put one foot in front of the other."

"I suppose that's all you can do. I told you I've been going through a rough time. That's sort of why I'm here, although I'm not sure what I thought this whole detour would accomplish. I've found the place where my dad was, but . . ." Her voice trails off in defeat. "Now what? I guess I was hoping for some sort of miraculous clarity."

The resurfaced memory of Baker and her parents on the night before her father's car crash is still reverberating in her head. She doesn't like to think about it, but the anniversary, July 4th, exactly one month from today, is a date she can never accidentally overlook.

"You might be feeling the effects of the canyon," Clint suggests. "I told you, it has a way of working on you. This is all part of the process, this self-reflection. I wouldn't fight it if you can help it, but it's not easy."

"I'm sorry. I didn't mean to be insensitive," Cyd says apologetically, recalling the reason for Clint's visit to the canyon. "Tell me about your wife. You must miss her terribly."

"Yes and no." There is an abruptness in his voice.

"What is it, Clint?" Cyd is certain she has said something she shouldn't have. "I'm sorry if I've upset you."

He does not answer her. Instead, he gets up and steps away. For a moment, she thinks he is going to walk off into the darkness and leave her alone. He stops a short distance away and paces slowly in front of her, looking outward toward the creek and the towering granite beyond.

Cyd is reminded that this man, no matter how much she likes him, is a complete stranger. She knows nothing about him or the pain he is suffering. Five years, he told her. He has been coming down here for five years, trying to deal with the loss of his wife. He must have loved her very much.

Cyd stays seated, unsure what to do next. Clint turns to her, and she pats the space next to her. As he walks back over and sits down, she realizes she has tensed up, afraid she has said something else to ruin this beautiful night. She lets out a big sigh.

"My best friend, Helen, and I sometimes play this game. We call it Sucks/Doesn't Suck."

"I don't know that one," Clint says. His tone is full of something Cyd recognizes and relates to—a great, reluctant effort.

She continues, unsure. "My dad died when I was twelve. That sucks. He was a really great dad. Not just great, he was the best dad ever. That doesn't suck."

Clint is silent. Cyd's discomfort increases.

"I'll give you another example, but we both have to do it. Otherwise, it's just a boring, private pity party."

"Okay. We'll see."

"My older brother was an alcoholic since he was a teenager. He wasn't always easy to live with. He was selfish, truth be told. That little eruption back at the campfire . . . maybe . . . obviously, I've been suppressing a little anger. He died from cancer when he was forty-eight. I really miss him. I don't miss the drama that he brought, but I miss him. That sucks. I had a sweet, funny brother who never had a bad word to say about anyone. Not even me. That doesn't suck. My mother always liked him better, which kind of sucks. I've always thought everyone liked him better, except for my dad, who liked me better. That doesn't suck. Except he died when I was twelve."

"You're repeating yourself."

"I'm glad you're paying attention."

"I don't see where I have much choice," he says, his natural dry wit creeping back into his voice. "Go on."

"My mom was an invalid at the end of her life, and I had to take care of her. That sucks. But she got to live a good, long life, except for the fact that her husband and favorite child both died before she did. Wait. I did that wrong."

"Yes, you did."

"So, my parents and my only sibling are dead. That sucks. Helen, my best friend since kindergarten, and her family have always been my second family. That doesn't suck at all. But they're all back in Florida, and suddenly, I'm questioning where I belong."

They both take in the glorious night sky, leaning back, more relaxed once again. Cyd considers stopping, but something about being able to talk to this man, this near stranger, in this otherworldly place, encourages her to continue.

"My husband cheated on me," she says flatly. "That sucks."

She feels his eyes on her.

He says, "Yes, it does. That sucks."

"I just found out a week ago. I believed him when he told me it had just started. Then I found out it had been going on for a few months. And, like something out of a soap opera, I just found out today that the woman, his . . . girlfriend, mistress, whatever . . . she's pregnant. It's almost comical." The story sounds so strange now that she's spoken it aloud. "Only it's not comical. It sucks.

"On a brighter note, I just inherited a house in Sedona. *That* doesn't suck. And it turns out my brother is not actually my brother. He's my cousin. I just found that out—what's today?— like three or four days ago. I've lost track of the days. And, get this—my Aunt Mae, the one who left me the house, who I now know was really Baker's mother—my aunt, his mother, got pregnant with Baker by some older guy when she was a teenager. I'm guessing he was married. And, as if that's not bad enough, I found out she was in prison for a while, *while* she was pregnant. Imagine! I don't know why she was in prison, but she gave the baby, Baker, to my dad, her brother, and I never knew any of this until four days ago. I feel like my entire life—everything from my childhood up until my husband's most recent affair— has been reconfigured to the point I don't recognize any of it. I can't get my bearings. I don't know how to categorize all that. A little bit of sucks and a little bit of doesn't suck, I guess."

"Like most things in life," Clint says.

"Yes, true. I guess that's the point of the game, now that you mention it."

"That's what I picked up on," he says.

"You don't miss a trick."

"It's not easy keeping up with you, I'll give you that."

"Is that a compliment?" She nudges him with her knee.

"I suppose it could be."

After a pause, Cyd adds, "So, it's your turn."

"What?"

"It's your turn for Sucks/Doesn't Suck. I told you, it only works if both people do it."

"I don't think so. You did such a great job, I think we should leave it at that."

"You can't wimp out. That's cheating. I didn't take you for a cheater, Clint."

"No?"

"No."

"You don't know me very well, Cyd-by-the-way."

"Oh, I think I know you a little. I think we've got some past-life thing going on. Come on. It's good for you."

"Seriously. I don't want to play your little game," he snaps.

"I didn't mean . . . I'm sorry. See? There I go again. I never know when to shut my big, fat pie-hole. I'm sorry. I'll stop talking now."

Cyd is unsure what to do or say. She's sobered up enough to realize that coming down here, staying the night with complete strangers, might not have been the best idea she ever had. "Maybe we should go back to camp." She starts to get up.

"I lied to you," Clint says without emotion.

The words stop her.

"That's okay. I lie all the time. Don't worry about it."

"I told you my wife died."

Cyd waits.

"She's not dead," he says.

"Well, that doesn't suck. Does it?"

"No, that doesn't suck. She's alive and living in LA. We're divorced."

"That sucks."

"Yeah, it does."

Cyd senses he's not finished. Several beats pass.

"I come here every year because my son died, not my wife."

"Oh, Clint. I'm so sorry."

"Thank you."

"I'm so very sorry," she says, nearly choking on the words, unable to convey the depth of her sincerity. "What was his name?"

"Sam. His name was Sam."

"I am so sorry for your loss. I'm sure Sam was a wonderful person." They both sit up straighter and Cyd thinks to touch him, to offer some comfort, then stops, questioning her impulse.

"He committed suicide."

"Oh, Clint. Oh, my god."

Clint nods ever so slightly, looking straight ahead as if studying a painting.

"I don't know what to say. I can hardly imagine."

"It's okay. It's probably good for me to talk about it. I never do. That's why I come here. To spend two days and a night just thinking about him and trying to be close to him. We weren't that close while he was alive."

"I wish I knew what to say. I don't know how you keep breathing after that, after losing a child. Even a grown child. I watched my mom go through it. I still think about it sometimes in the dead of night."

"It was nice today, just being with you and those crazy kids.

It took my mind off of it. I just got to be here now, like Ram Dass says."

"Yes. It was like that for me, too. I've been thinking about shit nonstop for so many days, I'm surprised my head hasn't exploded."

There is a period of silence, then Cyd asks, "Is that why you got divorced? Because of Sam?"

"No, not really. That was the final nail in the coffin, though. I was a real son-of-a-bitch, believe me when I tell you. I was going through life like a pig-headed narcissist. It was all about me. You know what sucks? Me. As a father. That sucks."

"I'm sure you're exaggerating."

"Guess again."

Cyd thinks to debate, then stops herself and waits, letting his harsh words dissipate into the dry night air.

"In yoga, we learn that all you need to do to get all the benefits of the practice is make an honest effort. That's it. You just have to try. When I screw up, I tell myself, 'All you can do is get up in the morning and try to be a better person than you were the day before.' We simply have to try. What more can we do?"

After a moment, as if he's been pondering it, Clint says, "That's actually not the worst advice I've ever heard." There is another silence. "So what about your marriage? Have you decided what you're going to do?"

Cyd realizes it's best to let the subject change.

"Yes. At least, I think I have. I'm the one who has to live with me, and I know who I *don't* want to be after all this."

"That's something."

"It's all I've got." She sighs. "I know men cheat, Clint. I know *women* cheat. I know it's not the end of the world. But this new reality has flattened me. I feel like I've been run over by a bulldozer. I suppose I thought we were happy."

"I wouldn't know about that. I gave up on happy."

"Did you cheat on your wife? If you don't mind me asking."

"Yes, I did cheat on my wife."

Somehow, she knew that would be his answer. "Why?"

"I guess because I didn't like myself very much."

"What's not to like?"

"Easy for you to say."

"So, did cheating on your wife help your low self-esteem?"

"Nope. Quite the opposite."

Cyd considers this. "And it had nothing to do with your wife?"

"Not one thing."

"Did you love her?"

"I still love her," he says without hesitation. "I fucked it up. I was a selfish jackass. Still am, I suppose."

"Are you going to do anything about it?"

"I don't know."

They pause again. The night is deepening. The stars, beyond all comprehension, are increasing in brilliance.

"I've been flirting," she starts, then realizes how it sounds and tries to clarify. "I have a friend, a good friend. We've flirted with each other for years. Now I think there might be something more to it. Truth be told, I think I felt entitled. Entitled to flirt, I mean. I knew it wasn't what I should do, but I enjoyed doing it, so I let myself. I like how I feel when I'm with him— Bobby is his name. No one else has ever made me feel the way he does." She shivers, thinking of Bobby's hands on her hips pulling her to him. She remembers the look of pain on his face as they said their goodbyes. She wonders if he will wait for her or if he's already changed his mind.

Another thought comes to her. "They say girls marry their fathers. Maybe I married Loren in hopes he would replace the father I lost. It didn't take long to realize he wasn't anything like my father."

Clint is silent, but Cyd senses he wants her to continue.

"Loren cheated on me once before, years ago, when we were first married. I suppose that's why I felt entitled to my feelings toward Bobby. I thought about leaving him back then, but I decided to stay. I'm not unhappy with that decision. We have two beautiful children. But I suppose I've been angry all these years. Come to think of it, I've been really pissed off at a lot of people I love for a long time—Loren, Baker, even my mom. I didn't even realize I was doing it, hanging on to so much past hurt. What's the point?"

"It's like holding a hot coal so you can throw it at someone," Clint offers. "I do it, too."

Cyd's thoughts continue to swing wildly. "Maybe I need to be alone. I'm getting too old for all of it anyway—romance, that is. I've never been on my own, and the thought of it scares me. Maybe I need to force myself to do something that scares me."

"Maybe not force. Maybe just encourage," Clint offers. "And, you're not getting off the hook that easy. You're far from too old for romance or anything else you want in life. I may not know much, but I know *that* much."

"I feel too old to start over, Clint. Not just with a man, but with my life. I don't know how to do it. I'm terrified."

"I'm terrified, too." He nudges her again and gives her a slight smile.

"I knew I liked you right from the start," she teases.

"I guess we both need to make an honest effort. It's so simple, it might be brilliant."

"I don't feel brilliant. I feel pretty clueless, actually. I was hoping to find some answers down here. There's almost nothing worse than not knowing."

"Almost," he says, his voice barely audible.

Cyd knows what he is referring to: loss, regret, a desire to fix something he can't possibly fix. She knows all of it. She feels it, too. They both have a lot of letting go to do.

"I guess, in the end, I want to know why people do what they do," Cyd says. "Me, especially. I'm the biggest mystery of all. Why the hell do I do half the things I do? I have no idea. I don't even know what's going on inside of my own head. I just want some . . . peace."

They lie motionless, side by side, for a long time. Cyd is fixed on the glistening vastness, on everything and nothing. Instinctively, she knows she is seeing both the mystery and the answer. It is a primal sensation in which everything is stripped down to its very essence, to its truth, just as it had been with the animal in the brush. Each star represents a moment in her life, seemingly disconnected and random, but undeniably part of something complex, an interwoven perfection. It is right above her, right before her eyes, and she is part of it. She has been looking at it all night, but now she really *sees* it. It is all around her and inside of her, too. She is permeable. She touches the pendant at her throat, feeling the silver-etched wings. *It will keep you in close connection with the higher Spirit.*

A light flares across the sky, a streak that whizzes, then fades in the distance.

"Did you see it?" Clint asks.

Clint's voice is part of her, too. It is *her* voice. Somehow, it all makes perfect sense.

"It's a sign." Cyd knows this is true. "God sends me signs,

like little packages wrapped and set at my feet. Sometimes, if I'm not paying attention, I don't pick them up. From now on, I'm picking them up."

After a moment, she asks, "What time is it?"

Clint looks at his watch. "It's 12:23."

Cyd gets to her feet and stretches her arms wide, letting her head hang back, taking in the wholeness of the night sky.

"That's an angel number. I told you God sends me signs."

"An angel number?" Clint asks.

"In numerology, it's a sequence, three or four numbers, like 11:11 or 789. I can't help but notice when they pop into my day. They are said to hold little messages, maybe from an angel, telling you you're on the right path or making you pause and consider something that might have slipped by unnoticed. I know a lot of people think it's strange, but for me, it reminds me how much more there is to this world, how much lies beneath the surface. It's so much bigger than our daily experience. When I stop to think about it, I feel a certain . . . desperation. Like there's so much that I don't know and I'm running out of time. I have to believe I fit into a bigger cosmic picture. Maybe that's my spirituality—I don't know. But if I thought of my life in isolation—that I'm just a speck on this minuscule planet floating in some incomprehensible amount of space and time—I just can't think of my life like that. I have to believe there's more. That I'm more."

"I'm going to have to agree with you on this one, Cyd-by-the-way," Clint says, getting up, too. "The time is 12:23. My birthday is December 23. That *is* a little weird."

"Ha! I love it! Now, hang on to your hat, cowboy. I've got one better. *Today* is *my* birthday. Officially twenty-three minutes in."

"Well, damn. Happy birthday. If I didn't know better, I'd think you had this whole thing planned."

"Thanks. I didn't have to plan it. I think that's the takeaway. We shouldn't even *try* to plan. We should just let go of the oars."

"Maybe we should," Clint says, and she can hear the smile in his voice.

Cyd begins twirling, her head back, her arms flung wide. "We should!" she laughs.

"We should!" Clint repeats.

Clint is next to her, imitating her, his arms outstretched, slowly turning.

"We should!" they exclaim in unison.

As she turns, the starlight streaks and blurs. She turns round and round, watching the points of light soften into circular streaks in the dome of the clear night sky. It is a great dance hall and she is dancing with all of it. It is in her every cell, and she, in turn, is in every atomic particle that has ever existed since the beginning of time. And she always will be. It is as mysterious and as vital as a first breath. She knows this now. This is connection. The eternal. The glory. The hallelujah. This is the Divine. *She* is the Divine.

There is another shooting star. Cyd laughs out loud and stops, watching as the whirling continues without her, stumbling to regain her balance. The confusion of the day and the week and the decades evaporates along with the fading streak of light. Her mind quiets as the aftereffects of the twirling slowly subside, and her vision returns to normal. The surrounding rock walls grow skyward, glowing in the moonlight. The sorrow, the regret, the unending questions—all rise then, as if she has been given permission to hand off a heavy load. She feels the presence of her father and Baker above her, taking it from her, lifting it up and away. *You have carried it long enough.* She feels her mother, too, and she suddenly understands, as if by osmosis, more about her mother in this moment than she has in her entire life. Her mother loved her. Of course, she did. And she loved Baker, too, maybe more, because he needed her so much. Her mother loved the only way she knew how—flawed, imperfectly, as best she could. She made an honest effort.

Cyd is hyperaware of her physical body once again. It is fluid, softened, wrung clean. She is pain-free, almost youthful. The current running through her is strong, stronger than it has ever been. It is one cohesive flow of energy, circular, unending, running through her body, out, and back again. The answers come with clarity in a strange, silent language transmitted directly into her heart.

If nothing is true, then nothing is a lie.

The starlight glistens.

Everything is real and nothing is real.

The familiar, glorious vibration continues its celestial pulse.

You cannot hold on to anything. Ever. You can be free of the trying.

Her entire past floats up and out, drawn to the heavens from whence it came, like the granite to the sky.

There is no need to struggle. It is what it is. It is exactly as it should be.

It is a grand, all-knowing, voiceless voice. It is the voice of forgiveness. It is the voice of love.

You are a woman called Cyd. You are the great rocks and the magnificent sky and the celestial light. You are all of it. You are one beautiful harmony.

The sky pulsates with a great cosmic energy. She knows it then, as surely as if it were born into her: There is no one reality. Everything is her own creation—nothing more, nothing less.

Everything she thought she knew shifts in that instant. Suddenly and with great joy, she understands.

44

Saturday, June 5, 2019
South Rim,
Grand Canyon National Park

There is no sign of movement from their younger companions by the time Cyd and Clint are prepared to leave. Dawn is still a distant whisper, but there is enough light for Cyd to find a scrap of paper and write a short heartfelt note. Like any concerned mother, she leaves her phone number, as well as Clint's, and asks them to let her know once they've arrived safely back at the rim. It occurs to her, as she secures the note with a rock, that she might not ever see them again. She'll most likely never know how things turn out for Kate.

She looks skyward and takes a deep breath. The air holds a fragrance unique to the early morning in this place—shallow water and stone and vast open space. She stills herself and commits the fragrance to memory. She reminds herself—*people come into your life for a reason*—and she gives thanks for the gift of their brief but significant friendship. Silently, she wishes for each of them what she wishes for herself: a life filled with love and a heart filled with peace. She looks around once more. Her father's presence is with her, and she feels awash with emotion. There is fear and gratitude in equal measure. She is hesitant to return to her normal life, not knowing what awaits her, but she is ready to begin her ascent.

As the first hint of daylight engulfs the remaining stars, Cyd and Clint walk in comfortable silence. The canyon comes alive once more, layer by layer, emanating from the darkness in all its glory just as it had the day before, yet everything feels different. In spite of having stayed up half the night and then sleeping on the ground in her clothes, Cyd is filled with a youthful energy she hasn't felt for a very long time. The magic of the canyon seems to penetrate the space she created the night before as if an empty vessel is being filled. As she walks—up, up, up—she is saturated from the inside out.

Hour after hour they walk, stopping only briefly to rest, and even then in quiet contemplation. Her mind is as settled as the immense stone walls. She senses Clint's mind is mercifully still as well. There is a newfound ease in the way he smiles at her, like a man who has just come out of surgery and realizes, much to his surprise, that he's survived. Nothing has changed in twenty-four hours. Not really. Every challenge still awaits her at the top of the canyon: her broken marriage, her storm-damaged home, her uncertain future, the ghosts of her past. Every bit of it will still be there. All her problems are right where she left them, bundled neatly and waiting for her to pick them up.

Or not.

Where is it written that she has to pick up where she left off? She can—she *will*—maintain the state of understanding she grasped the night before. She is reminded of something she often said to her children when they were young: *If you think you can or you think you can't, you're right.*

I can, she tells herself as she walks. *I can and I will.*

As they approach the last leg of the hike, past Havasupai Gardens, back at the bottom of the last series of switchbacks, as the late morning sunlight drenches the towering slabs, Cyd finds the granite wall that had so moved her the day before, the spot where she had met the older couple, Dan and Ruth. She leans on Dan's walking stick and looks up. The wall is a good distance away, high up from where she stands, tiny in relation to the view she'd had on the way down. It is easy to find, creamy white set off from the surrounding reddish-brown. It stands in majestic salute as if wanting her to notice it. It is the same wall, but the difference in its appearance from this vantage point is nothing short of remarkable—and from nothing more than a shift in perspective. The same and different. Eternal and fleeting. Both equally magnificent.

The Lookout Studio sits miraculously on its precarious perch like a sentinel waiting to greet them when Cyd and Clint emerge from the trail. Once on the rim, they find a table in the café at the Bright Angel Lodge. As soon as she smells the aroma of hot food, she realizes she is as ravenous as she has ever been. She has to stop herself from devouring in an instant the plate of food that is set before her. At one point she does stop, a heaping forkful of mac-n-cheese balanced directly in front of her face, her mouth still full from the previous bite, to find Clint staring at her, one eyebrow raised. She bursts into laughter, practically choking herself, drops the fork onto her plate, and buries her face in her hands.

"I can't help it!" she squeals, elated that they are ending their time together as they started, over simple comfort food.

She knows she will never again eat either mac-n-cheese or Nutella without thinking of this man.

Clint shakes his head, his eyes bright with quiet amusement, and goes back to his sandwich.

Once they finish two bowls of ice cream—*Of course, we'll have dessert!*—she and Clint stand outside the lodge once more, looking over the canyon rim, the sun bright and full above them.

"Damn, it's hot," says Cyd, suddenly at a loss for words. She moves to stand in the shade of a pine tree on the opposite side of the walkway, out of the path of the stream of passersby. Clint stands to face her.

"I thought you were tougher than that by now," he says, giving her a crooked smile. He looks tired. They are both as gritty and dust-covered as the canyon trail.

"I hate to admit it, but I'm beat. If I don't get out of these clothes and into a shower . . ."

The look on Clint's face stops her mid-sentence. It is a confluence of emotions—sadness and joy, longing and contentment, trepidation and excitement. They are her emotions, too.

Before Cyd thinks to stop herself, she is hugging him. If it makes him uncomfortable, she doesn't care.

"Thank you for everything," she says into his shoulder. She hugs him tightly, knowing that once she lets go, it will all be over—the adventure, the quest, the entire magnificent, wonderful, exhausting, exhilarating experience. It will all officially end.

Or not.

She is momentarily terrified by the thought of what awaits her. Then, as sure and strong as the sun above, he squeezes her back.

"You got this," he says softly, just as he had as she took her first step onto the silver bridge.

"You got this," she repeats. And she knows it is true.

45

Once they have exchanged numbers and promises to keep in touch and said one more final goodbye, Cyd finds the correct path and heads toward the cabin. It is past the checkout time. She must shower and get on her way. It is time to leave.

As she walks, she thinks of the woman she had been, the one who had walked this same path the previous day. Her fingers find the small silver bird and she remembers once again the words from the artist's card: *It represents beginnings and endings, the natural passage of the cycles of life.* The perfection of the path that has led her to this moment is as clear as the stream she waded in the previous day. There is no room for regret. Regret is wasted energy. None of her past can be changed nor should it be. Only her mindset can change. The story can change.

Back in her cabin as she steps out of the shower, she stops to listen for a moment. She realizes what she is hearing is her cell phone ringing. Could it be that the phone actually *is* water-resistant? She is smiling at the miracle of modern technology as she hurries to dig the phone from her bag. The number is one she doesn't recognize.

"Hello," she says quickly.

She listens and responds, "Thank you! Thank you so much for calling. This is wonderful news."

As Cyd leaves the park, heading back toward Sedona, she listens to the voicemail messages that have accumulated over the past two days.

One is from Loren: *Cyd, look, I want to talk to you. I'm worried about you. Holly said you went to the Grand Canyon. I'm . . . uh . . . that's good. I'm happy you got to go there . . . finally. I've been at the house working. I really need to talk to you. Call me. Please.*

She frowns and hits the next message. It is from a remarkably enthusiastic Helen: *Sister! We finally have cell service! It's been a bitch trying to get things done around here without a phone. We're at The O. Where else? I may never leave here again. I've called you three times. Where the hell are you? Call me! Oh . . . and happy birthday! Love you! Call me!*

She is smiling now, relieved to finally hear Helen's voice. What would she do without Helen? What would she have *ever* done without Helen?

There is a message from Annie with her adorable accent: *Happy birthday, darling!* And from Bo and Holly, too, each wishing her a happy birthday and asking her to call as soon as possible, wanting answers: *What is she doing? Where has she been all this time? Why hasn't she called back?* They are thoughtful and loving. She knows she will give herself over to all of them shortly, but not just yet.

With only one bar lit at the top of her phone screen, Cyd knows there isn't enough cell service to return the phone calls now, anyway. Good. She wants to ease back into the world, take a few minutes to recalibrate. It's her birthday, after all. She's entitled. She is reminded of her mantra, the one she has repeated in earnest each birthday since she attained the age of forty-eight, the age Baker was when he celebrated his final birthday: *Every one's a gift.*

She decides to spend the three-hour car ride to Sedona in total silence. Her private birthday celebration. There will be time for returning phone calls soon enough.

Once back in the Adirondack chair on Mae's back patio, she greets her old friends, the red rocks, as they offer up their steady reassurance that miracles really do exist. *Just look at us if you have any doubt,* they seem to say. She talks with Holly and Bo together, on one phone call, as she loves to do. She gives them a brief summary of the past two days and promises she will tell them everything soon. She lets their love for her rush across the airwaves and fill her up. Instinctively, they do not talk about Loren, as if they have taken a pact to put that subject off for some other day.

Her next call is to Helen. After Helen tells her, succinctly, that The O is a disaster—the entire first floor was flooded, a fact which tells Cyd that most of the kitchen equipment and nearly all of the furnishings will need to be replaced, assuming the damage to the beautiful old building itself can be repaired—they move on to what she really wants to talk about. Helen had spoken to Annie. She knows that Bobby flew to Arizona, and she knows about Loren.

"I want to hear everything," Helen demands. "Do not leave out one detail. All I've done for five days is shovel shit. I want something good out of you!"

Cyd laughs and tells her friend everything—or almost

everything—about Bobby, including the fact that she doesn't yet know if he's still waiting for her or has thought better of it and flown back to his boat. She tells her what little she knows about Loren's impending fatherhood.

"I've been thinking a lot lately," Cyd says when she's finished giving Helen the update.

"The doctor told you not to think too much," Helen teases.

"I've never been good at following rules."

"So what have you come up with after all this prohibited thinking?"

"I've decided to let it all go."

"As in . . . ?" Helen prompts.

"As in, I'm not going to give up any energy to Loren or what he did or what he's going to do. I'm not going to think about it or wish things were some other way."

"You mean, you're not going to want something other than what is?" The sarcasm in Helen's voice is unmistakable. She's been preaching this to Cyd for longer than either of them can remember. And, yet, it feels to Cyd as if she's just now hearing it for the first time.

"Exactly, sister!" Cyd says definitively. "Aren't you glad I've figured it out all on my own?"

"Couldn't be happier," Helen retorts.

"I've decided I need to be more honest with myself. Honesty was everything to my dad. It was his north star. When I was young, I didn't think much of it, but now I know how important it is to be truly honest, to keep that promise to yourself every day. I thought I was being so strong, keeping everything inside, harnessing all that anger as if it was going to be useful one day. Now I realize I've just been holding it close to my heart, where it hurts the most and can do the most damage."

Cyd continues, "When my dad was taken from us so suddenly, I remember thinking—how is it possible that the planet is still spinning without him on it? I was in such a state of disbelief. First, I had to come to terms, in my adolescent mind, with the fact that Baker was a serious alcoholic. I didn't even know what the word meant. I was so angry with Baker, as if he didn't love me enough to stop. Then, I convinced myself that if I hadn't upset my dad that night, if I hadn't suggested we take Baker home in that condition, maybe Dad wouldn't have left so early the next morning, or maybe he wouldn't have been distracted behind the wheel. I actually blamed my mom, too. She let people think whatever they wanted about her black eye. She never told anyone she fell and hit it on the table. I've always wondered how many people thought my dad did it. I hated her for that."

"Cyd, listen to me," Helen tries to interrupt.

"Just wait. There's something else. A few years ago, I was in the car with Holly. We were coming home from a shopping trip in Tallahassee. We were on the highway, just laughing and talking, not paying attention. I started to change lanes to pass a big truck and there was a car in my blind spot. I had to swerve back into my lane and the truck was right there. It seemed I barely had room to get back over. It was a split second. Holly thought nothing of it, just called the guy an asshole for honking his horn so long. But I was so terrified that I might have hurt her. That's why I gave my car to Bo. That's why I never bought another one."

"Are you finished now?" Helen asks in her most authoritarian voice.

"I suppose."

"First of all, your memory is shit. The night before your dad died, you said you didn't want to go home. You said it several times. It was Nick's decision. He thought it was best to get him home. It wasn't your decision. So you can cross that one off your *I'm to blame* list. And your mom's eye was nothing. Literally, you could hardly see it. If anyone thought anything, they just thought she was crying a lot. No one could ever think your dad would do something like that. No one."

"But—"

"Stop! I'm not finished. About the car—it's okay to be scared, sister. Life is fucking scary. We're all on the verge of disaster all the time. That's why life is so damn precious. You make it sound like it's a weakness to want to protect the people you love. I think it's a superpower the way you take care of everyone."

Cyd is crying now. A full-blown, no holds barred, snotty breakdown.

"Oh, Helen," is all she can get out. "What would I do without you?"

"I don't want to know, and we're not about to find out. I know you think I'm indestructible, but *you* are my rock."

"No! You are *my* rock!" Cyd shrieks, still gulping down tears.

"So, now that that's settled, what's next?" Helen asks. It is just like Helen to move on without hesitation. There is no such thing as looking back.

"I'm going to find more answers. Stay tuned. You'll be the first to know the end of the story."

"I damn well better be."

They say their goodbyes, then Cyd blows her nose, lengthens her spine, and pushes the button to call Loren.

"Hi," he says almost seductively. She knows enough to know this is a conciliatory tone, an olive branch.

"Hi. How are things at the house?" As she asks this, she realizes the answer no longer matters. "How's Fern? I miss my dog. I want my dog back."

"I know you do. She misses you, too. And the house is coming along. I'll fill you in on the details later, but listen, Cyd. There's something I need to tell you. Not about the house."

She lets a few beats pass, then says, "If it's about the baby you're expecting, I already know."

There is silence on the other end of the line. She can practically see his jaw clenching. She decides to save him the trouble of asking.

"Annie found out through a friend. It's a small town, Loren. You know that."

"I wanted you to hear it from me," he says. She hears the exhaustion behind the words. The man she knows is deliberate and thoughtful. He would have agonized over making this announcement.

"We don't get everything we want, Loren. I'm beginning to see that as a blessing in disguise."

"It's not what I want." His voice cracks. "I'm sorry, Cyd. This is hard on me, too."

"Don't," she interrupts. "Just don't."

The silence rises up like a stone tower. Cyd waits, not sure for what. Absentmindedly, she fingers the silver bird at her breastbone.

"I want you to know that I know I blew it. I had it all, and I blew it," he says, finally.

"Yes, you did."

"Can you ever forgive me?"

She thinks about this.

"I forgave you all those years ago, Loren. I had no choice—

mentally, emotionally. I did what I needed to do. I'm not sorry I chose to forgive you back then, and I suppose one day, I will forgive you again. But right now, you can't ask that of me."

"I'm sorry, Cyd. I'm so sorry." He is crying now. There is no sound, but she can tell.

"I have no regrets about our life together, if that's what you want to hear. We have Holly and Bo. They are everything to me, and I wouldn't have them without you. And if you want to know the truth, in a lot of ways, I'm glad you ran into me the other day. It sounds strange, but I don't regret that, either. Everything is exactly as it should be."

Loren doesn't respond. She suspects he is unable to talk without completely breaking down.

"I'm going to hang up now, Loren. I have things to do."

She doesn't wait for his response. She hits the button to disconnect the call.

Immediately, she dials Bobby's number.

Part Four

Bottom of
the Breath

46

Monday, June 7, 2019
Phoenix, Arizona

Cyd Carr.

Cyd stands at the front desk of the Desert Garden Independent Living Facility, signing her name in the guest ledger. She concentrates as she writes, trying to quell her nervousness. The woman at the desk directs Cyd past a sitting room with a fireplace and bookshelves where three women sit at a table playing cards. As she waits at the elevator, a middle-aged woman pushing an older woman in a wheelchair stops beside her.

"Hello," Cyd says, offering a smile to the younger woman.

"Hello," she answers, wiping perspiration from her pink forehead. "It's too hot to sit outside. We tried, but we didn't last long."

"It is," Cyd agrees as the elevator door lumbers open. Cyd steps aside and holds the door with her arm.

"Here we go, Mom," the woman says, backing in the chair.

The mother's face is frozen in a faraway stare but she manages a small nod in Cyd's direction.

"I don't think I've seen you before," the woman says, once they are all settled inside. "Do you have family here?"

"Yes, actually." Cyd stumbles over her answer. "It's my first time here at the facility, though, and in Arizona. I live in Florida."

"Oh, Florida!" the woman says dreamily. "A beach would be awfully nice right about now. Doesn't that sound wonderful, Mom? A beach?"

The woman in the chair gives another little nod.

"It's pretty hot there, too, this time of year," Cyd offers.

The elevator bounces to a stop, and there is a stillness before the heavy door slides slowly open. Cyd holds the door again as the woman maneuvers the chair over the lip, tilting it up slightly by stepping on the back. Cyd recognizes the technique. The memory is like a pinch. Her mother's face flashes in her mind, and she realizes, perhaps for the first time, how much she misses her.

It is coming up on the third anniversary of her mother's death. She had been living alone in the family house, not far from Cyd and Loren, when the falls first started. Once the diagnosis was made—progressive supranuclear palsy, *what the hell?*—and the inevitability of her impending decline was undeniable, Cyd and her mom braced themselves for the bleak future described in the medical pamphlets.

"Thank you. Enjoy your visit," the woman calls back as they start off down the hallway.

Cyd reads the sign and turns the opposite way. The corridor is windowless, long, and dim but not unpleasant. Along either side, a series of small shelves protrudes into the otherwise bland hallway, each displaying something of assumed significance chosen by the owner: a statue of Saint Francis of Assisi, a stuffed bear holding an American flag, a piece of pottery. A few of the residents have hung wreaths on their doors in addition to the carefully chosen knick-knacks, all providing a glimpse into the life being concluded on the other side of the wall. There is a sad defiance to it all.

At the end of the hallway next to the last door on the right, there is a tasteful basket overflowing with silk ivy. Cyd uses the small knocker that hangs on the door.

A young man wearing blue scrubs answers. He steps back and waves Cyd in.

"Hello," says Cyd, queasy with anticipation.

"Hello. I'm Lawrence," the man says with a welcoming smile. "Come on in. I was just leaving. She's expecting you."

The apartment is small and tidy, with a bright red sofa as a focal point. The blinds are closed halfway, but the bright morning light still hinders Cyd's vision as she peers toward the windows to a large recliner. A small figure sits as if in a hammock, her legs elevated.

"I'm off," the man says kindly. "Just ring if you need anything else. Otherwise, I'll be back to get you for lunch, Mrs. McFann. Bye, ladies."

"Goodbye," says Cyd to his back. "Thank you." Her voice trails off. She turns to face the figure in the chair, unsure what to do next.

"Well," says the woman. "If it isn't like looking into the past . . . my, my. Come on, now. Sit down. I had Lawrence pour us some nice sweet tea." The woman gestures by lifting a delicate hand toward the sofa. Two tall glasses drip condensation onto coasters on the coffee table.

"Thank you," Cyd repeats. "Your home is lovely. I know we've met, but I'm sorry, I really don't remember."

"Well, of course not. How could you? It's been such a long time, and you were only a little girl," the woman says. "You sure do look like your aunt. And your daddy, too. They sure were handsome, those two."

Cyd moves to the sofa with her back now to the windows. From this angle, the woman is perfectly lit by the filtered light as if sitting for a portrait. The face is covered in wrinkles, like crinkled tissue paper, and the eyes are narrow and pale, resembling blue-green river stones. She is very thin, dressed in pressed slacks and a cotton blouse. Iris, too, insisted on being impeccably dressed, right up until the end. The old woman's face, like her voice, is vaguely familiar.

"I understand you've been out to the cabin," the woman says.

"Yes, I have. I got here a week ago. I saw the lawyer and then drove out to the house the same day. It's so beautiful."

"Oh, that it is. We had a lot of good times there." She smiles as if returning to a long-ago place. "I'm so glad you're enjoyin' it." The remnants of a Southern accent sweeten her words.

"I am," Cyd says. She notices herself sitting rail-straight on the edge of the sofa, cords of suspense holding her rigid.

"Well," the woman says, drawing out the word. "I know you probably have a lot on your mind. Why don't you make yourself comfortable."

Cyd forces herself to sit back.

"Now then. Where shall we start?"

Cyd isn't at all sure where to start.

"I've learned a lot this past week, things I never knew about my family . . . about *our* family, Aunt Lucy. It's been overwhelming, really. Looking back, some things make more sense now, knowing what I know. But with every answer comes another question. I thought, with everyone gone—dead—I would be left with these questions. Then, I found out about you."

Cyd has a desire to reach out and touch the old woman's hand—her aunt's hand. They are seeing each other for the first time since visiting Mae in Atlanta so many years ago. This woman is her family.

Aunt Lucy nods her head as if she's been expecting to hear these exact words. Lucy had been living in Phoenix all along, and Jonathan Walker intended to tell Cyd as much during their meeting, but in the midst of Cyd's emotional reaction in his office, he had forgotten. Once her water-logged phone dried out and Cyd was able to answer his call, Jonathan explained and apologized and passed along Lucy's contact information. Cyd drove back to Sedona, then the next morning, *this* morning, to Phoenix and Aunt Lucy's apartment.

"I found a letter my dad wrote to Mae," Cyd says. "It was mixed in with a box of letters Mae left me. It was addressed to her at a women's correctional facility. A prison."

"Yes," Lucy replies knowingly. "I thought that's what might be on your mind."

Lucy reaches a veined hand toward Cyd, offering her niece a folded paper. Cyd takes the yellowed paper and quickly realizes it's a newspaper article.

"Go ahead. Read it. Take your time."

Cyd reads the headline: "Local Woman Convicted of Manslaughter."

Below the headline is a square headshot of a young woman. Cyd gapes at the small faded photograph. Mae's youthful, flawless face stares back, expressionless. The photo is cropped so tight that the frame contains nothing but her face ringed with wavy, chin-length hair. She is stunningly beautiful.

Under the headline in a slightly smaller font, it reads:

"Miss Mary Jane (Mae) Williams, eighteen, sentenced to three years in prison for the killing of Mr. Newell P. Hudson."

Cyd feels lightheaded as if the air in the room has thinned. The article appeared in *The Virginian-Pilot*, dated August 31, 1959. Cyd continues reading.

The article explains that Miss Williams had gotten into the back of a cab outside her apartment in downtown Norfolk where Mr. Hudson was waiting. She was wearing a string of pearls and carrying a small brown suitcase.

According to the cab driver, a valuable eyewitness, the couple started arguing. The driver testified that "Miss Williams became extremely distraught."

After a few minutes, the man, Mr. Hudson, asked the driver to pull over. It was then, the driver said, that Miss Williams pulled a handgun from her purse and shot Mr. Hudson in the chest, killing him. She then turned the gun on herself.

The seasoned cab driver, able to keep his wits about him, saw what was about to happen and grabbed the woman's arm as she pulled the trigger. The gun discharged a second time but the young lady was unharmed, as was the cab driver.

Shortly after her arrest, it was learned that Miss Williams was in a family way, nearly five months along. It would come out during the trial, the article went on, that Mr. Hudson was thirty-one years old and married, with two young children. Miss Williams's sister, Lucille Williams McFann, testified that her sister did not know the man was married and certainly did not know that he was a father. She believed that her sister, known as Mae, had believed Mr. Hudson was divorced and learned of his family only after the relationship had been underway for some time and further complicated by the condition in which Miss Williams found herself.

Furthermore, Mrs. McFann told the court, Mr. Hudson had promised Miss Williams some months earlier that he planned to marry her. The day of the murder was to be their wedding day. Apparently, Miss Williams had been prepared for her fiancé to have a change of heart, since she came to the meeting equipped with a firearm that she had taken from her brother-in-law's gun case some weeks prior.

The trial was brief and concluded without testimony from Miss Williams herself, who, it was noted, sat still and pale in a gray prison dress. By that time, her condition was apparently quite evident. After a short deliberation, the empathetic jury took pity on the frail Miss Williams, who stared blankly throughout the proceeding, and the judge gave her the most lenient sentence allowed under the law.

It was also noted that her older brother, an officer in the United States Navy living in Florida, was in the courtroom every day, along with her sister, Mrs. McFann, a Baltimore resident. After the verdict was read, Miss Williams was led out of the courtroom. She showed no sign of emotion.

The article concluded by saying Miss Williams would give birth to her child in prison and that her family had agreed to take responsibility for the baby. Mrs. Hudson, the widow, was not available for comment.

Cyd looks up at Lucy, who has closed her eyes. A jumble of thoughts race through her mind. She studies her aunt's wrinkled, peaceful face, seeing herself reflected back, then looks again at the yellowed paper in her hand.

This is not the first time in my life I wanted to die.

Cyd recalls the haunting words from Mae's letter as Mae stares out from the grainy photograph. Her expression offers nothing. The newspaper printed a second headshot lower on the page, one of the man Mae had killed, also young and handsome, in the prime of his life. Clearly, Mae had been out of her mind. There was no other explanation.

Mae was Baker's mother. She had shot and killed Baker's father. She had tried to kill herself, which implied she had also tried to kill the baby—*Baker*. Cyd tries to fit these newfound facts into the narrative she has known her whole life. Her parents would have been married for three years at the time of the trial. Her mother had already had three miscarriages by then. Cyd remembers another sentence Mae had written: *Iris went a bit mad herself.* Was Mae referring to the miscarriages?

Her father had been at the trial. He was at Mae's side all along. Had her mother been there, too? Had the whole awful affair caused a rift between her parents? Her dad would have been terrified, knowing his beloved little sister had been taken advantage of by this older man and faced the possibility of spending much of her life in prison. Her mom, certainly, would have hated the publicity. She would not have sat in the courtroom. Could she have been at all understanding about Mae's predicament? They might have started out as friends—his glamour gals, her father had called them—but after cold-blooded murder? Not a chance. Cyd is sure of it. Her mother was not a sympathetic person. She was devout and strong-willed. She did not condone weakness, and Mae, it could be argued, had tried to take the easy way out.

What Mae had done went against every Catholic bone in her mother's body. Not only had Mae had sex out of wedlock, but she had also had an affair with a married father of two. She had actually murdered a man. She had tried—it was unimaginable—to kill herself while she was five months pregnant. That would have been the final blow as far as Cyd's mother was concerned. *That* would have been more than she was capable of forgiving. Even years later, even though it was undeniable that Mae had been distraught to the point of insanity, her mother kept her distance. Cyd glimpses her mother's feelings: Baker was, rightfully and in the eyes of God, her own son. Mae had attempted to kill herself to get out of becoming his mother. What more justification did she need to claim him as her own?

Lucy opens her eyes. "I'm sorry, dear. I have a tendency to doze off these days."

"No, it's fine. I'm sorry to barge in on you like this with such short notice. When I learned you were here, I wanted to see you right away. When Jonathan, the lawyer, told me you were so close, I was so surprised and happy. To think I didn't know you were still alive until two days ago." Cyd knows she is babbling, repeating things she had told her aunt on the phone when she called to arrange the visit. "This is so much to take in. It's hard to comprehend."

"Sometimes there's a big ol' gap between how it is," Aunt Lucy says, "and how we thought it would be. Mae was always a wild one, that's for sure. Like a racehorse in a stall, prancin' like the devil until the gate swings open. She dreamed of things I never understood. Your daddy, too, the both of them. They wanted off that damn farm. They looked around, saw our mama, saw the life that was waitin' for them there, and they just wanted to be gone. Your daddy joined the Navy, of course. That was his ticket out. Even lied about his age by one year to get in early. After Jesse was gone, Mae got real antsy. She had her nose buried in those magazines, wantin' to be like those models, I guess. As soon as she could, she moved to Norfolk. That was a big city to us, back then. She was such a pretty thing. And a hoot, too. Sassy. Full of spunk."

Lucy reaches for her tea, and Cyd lifts it for her, unsure her frail hand can manage it.

"Dad and you were there, with Mae, at the trial."

"Oh, yes. Mama couldn't go. It would have killed her, too, I suppose. And no one else in the family would go. No, it was me and your daddy. We tried to talk some sense into her, but she was almost dead herself, all the life drained out of her. She never did try to defend herself. She would hardly speak. We just thanked the good Lord that those jurors and that nice judge took pity on her. They saw that belly of hers and I guess they figured there was no sense in ruining that young life on top of everything else."

"Did my mother ever go?"

"Oh, no. Not Iris. No. But she came up with the idea right away about takin' the baby. She talked your daddy into it. He had been so frantic about your mama those past few years, losing all those babies like she did. He just wanted to do something for her, I suppose. And Mae agreed right away. Didn't hesitate for a moment. Never looked back, neither. She handed that baby over and that was that."

"But how? How did she handle it all those years?"

"Oh, honey-bunch," Lucy says as if addressing a child. "How does anyone handle anything? You just do. Either that, or you just give it up and walk into the lake with rocks in your pockets. We were used to not having things. That helps, I suppose. Our daddy was a drinker, and any little money he got was like water through his fingers. Goin' without made us tough, I suppose. And Mae didn't want a baby, not then anyway. She wanted so much more."

"I never knew," Cyd says. "About the adoption. Not until last week. I never suspected."

"Your mama made your daddy swear on his life he would never tell you kids. Iris never spoke one word of it. Both she and Mae were the same in that way. I suppose they had to be. They made up their minds that it never happened, that Baker belonged to Iris, and the rest was between Mae and the good Lord and no one else."

Cyd looks down at Mae's young face and up at Lucy's ancient one, the time between the two moments as brief as a shooting star across the night sky.

"Thank you for this."

Cyd reaches to give the paper back to her aunt.

"No, you keep that. I've got no use for it. It was a long time ago."

Cyd is lost in her thoughts when Lucy continues unexpectedly.

"Jesse told me a story once. Pa had taken Jesse with him to the corner store. It was about a two-mile walk. It was hot as blue blazes. Pa was always broke, of course, but always managed money for cigarettes and whiskey, which really burned Jesse. When they got to the store, Pa got whatever it was he needed, and he also got an ice cream cone. And you know what that son-of-a-gun did? He ate that whole ice cream himself walking back home. He didn't give Jesse, his own boy, even one bite. Jesse never forgot that. It said everything there was to say about that man, our pa.

"Jesse didn't mourn him when he died. Good riddance, he said. He joined the Navy the minute he could, even though it meant leaving Mae behind. Then, she had to go, too, of course. I was already married then, living in Baltimore. Mae got a job in a department store in downtown Norfolk. Made her own money and was able to buy some nice clothes. She was a real beauty. That's when she met that man."

"Did she really intend to kill herself? It's so unbelievable."

"Oh, I suppose she did. Mae was as headstrong as they come. She wanted her life to go a certain way, and being left like that, well, I guess she saw that man fixin' to take every bit of hope with him when he tried to walk away. She just snapped. That last morning, she had packed a suitcase for her honeymoon. She was all dressed up, ready to get married. But some little voice had been whisperin' to her, I suppose. You know that little voice. It always tells the truth. She took that gun with her because she knew something wasn't right."

Lucy continues, "When Iris got the idea to take the baby, she put a lot of pressure on Jesse. Mae was barely able to take care of herself, and in prison no less, well, we just thought it was the best thing to do. Slowly, she came back to herself, Mae did. She met Peter soon after she got out, and he wanted to marry her. Mae told him everything, and he didn't care. He worshipped her. So did Jesse. She was very lucky to have him for a brother. We all were. Very lucky, indeed."

"Baker . . . his name. Why did they name him Baker?" It suddenly seems like an important detail.

"Oh, that I can tell you. It was your daddy. He insisted upon it. He was named after our brother, Buddy. Baker was his given name, Buddy was a nickname. An accident took him. A tractor accident. Terrible. He was only fourteen." Lucy pauses as if unable to continue. Her focus is no longer in the room. "Your father named him Baker to remind Mae she had something to live for."

Lucy turns back to Cyd, and Cyd reaches to touch her hand. It is a small pile of bones.

"Thank you, Aunt Lucy. It means the world to me that I got to see you. I'm sorry I was never in touch. It makes me sad that I missed knowing you and Mae."

"No sense cryin' over spilled milk, dear. You'll come back again, I hope. I'll be right here until I'm not."

Cyd laughs. "I will definitely come back, Aunt Lucy. You may be tired of me before it's over."

There is very little certainty in her future, but Cyd knows this much is true—*I will be back.*

"Good. That's settled then," Lucy says, a sudden weariness in her voice.

Seeing the fatigue on her aunt's face, Cyd stands to go. "I'll let you rest. You did a lot of talking. I appreciate it very much."

"Nonsense. I'll sleep when I'm dead. I'm so glad you came and that we had a chance to talk."

Cyd bends and kisses her on the cheek. Lucy pats her hand.

"You take care of yourself now, dear. Don't let all that ancient history get you down." Lucy smiles up at Cyd, her blue-green eyes glistening. "Somehow, it was all meant to be, I suppose. The good Lord does work in mysterious ways."

"Yes, He does," Cyd says. "He certainly does."

Cyd starts to leave, then stops.

"There's one more thing. There was a rabbit's foot in with Mae's things. Do you know anything about that?"

"Oh my, yes. She carried that thing around for years. Your father gave it to her. Said it would bring her luck. She said she thought it was hogwash, but she carried it around, nevertheless."

"Baker had one just like it. Dad must have given them each one. I can't help but wonder if Baker knew about any of this. I wish he would have told me if he did. Maybe I could have helped him somehow. Does that sound silly?"

"It's never silly to want to save someone you love from hurting. It's just not always possible. Mama always said, 'You never get it right, and you never get it done.' That's just how life is. That's the beauty of it, isn't it?"

"That *is* the beauty of it, Aunt Lucy. That, and so much more."

47

Two Weeks (and a Lifetime) Later
Lola, Florida

Cyd parks in the sandy lot in front of the restaurant. Her high heels dig into the soft earth as she walks toward the building at the end of the pier. A single bulb lights the stylish sign above the door. She stops to look out over the water. The lavender sky blends so perfectly with the bay that the end of one and the start of the other seems almost mythical.

Inside, the recently refurbished room has an urban-rustic feel with dimmed lights and teak furniture. She is directed to a small table by the window.

"You look beautiful," Bobby says, standing as she approaches, kissing her with some formality on the cheek. His eyes reflect the purple hues of the sunset.

"You're making me blush," she says, surprised by her nervousness. "It doesn't suit me."

"It suits you just fine," he says, eyeing her up and down with exaggeration. "You can relax, you know. We're just having dinner."

"You're a regular comedian," she says, looking down at the drink menu, her cheeks undeniably flushed.

"I've missed you," he says.

"I've missed you, too." It is all she can do not to leap over the table and into his arms.

They haven't seen each other in two weeks, not since the day she saw her aunt for the first time in Phoenix. As promised, Bobby had been waiting for her when she called. He drove to the cabin that evening. When Cyd invited him to spend the night, he said he thought she'd never ask, then swooped her up and carried her upstairs, not unlike Rhett Butler with Scarlett O'Hara.

"Damn you, Swanson," she had said. "Do you have to be so fucking good at this?"

He laughed and practically threw her on the bed, his face buried in her neck, and she knew she was a goner. So much for swimming slow.

They order two tequilas: Bobby's neat, Cyd's with soda and lime. Bobby settles back in his chair as only a truly confident man can. "To the birthday girl," he says, holding up his glass but otherwise not moving. His fingers, long and tan, wrap perfectly around his glass. Cyd consciously stops herself from reaching for them.

"My birthday was two weeks ago," she argues with a downward tilt of her chin. "And so was yours. Happy birthday, Bobby."

"Happy birthday, Sunshine."

Cyd had returned to Lola earlier that day. She made a point to see Nick and Helen at The O, then came straight here to meet Bobby, somewhat secretively, at a restaurant outside of town.

After their first and only night together, he had driven her from Sedona to Phoenix and waited while she visited with Aunt Lucy. Then she dropped him at the airport. He had to get back. He needed to move his boat and help at the marina. Cyd spent the next two weeks getting situated at the cabin, then paid another visit to Aunt Lucy before flying back to Lola.

Bo had picked her up at the airport that afternoon. Upon seeing her son, Cyd nearly broke down with relief. It had been months since she'd seen him, and she'd been worrying about him for weeks. She hugged him with a fierceness she had forgotten she possessed.

"I'm okay, Mom." Bo laughed, returning her embrace. "I'm not a little kid anymore."

"I know, Lorenzo, but you're still my baby. I'm just so happy you're safe, and I'm so happy you're home."

When Bo had first informed his mother of his abrupt decision to leave Miami for good, she questioned his motives. "Too many fake people down there, Mom. It's not for me. I miss home."

Bo had driven to Holly's right after the storm, and they came home together to check on the state of the house and their father. Holly hadn't stayed long, just long enough to help Loren pack his things and leave the house for good. Both Bo and Cyd knew how hard Holly was taking things. "She'll come around," Cyd assured Bo when he conveyed his concern for his sister. "She has to. We all have to."

Bo's plan is to run fishing charters in the mornings and work on his paintings in the afternoons. Annie has insisted that she sell them in her store. "Annie's been a big help, Mom," Bo told Cyd on the drive home. "She's got a great eye for display. Between her shop and the gallery in Miami and the income from the fishing charters, I can make a good living doing the things I love. I'll take care of the house, and you can spend as much time in Sedona as you want. Fern and I will be fine."

"It sounds like the stars are aligning," Cyd said as Bo relayed his plans. His excitement was contagious. Once he assured her he was doing it all for himself and for Fern, and not for her, Cyd agreed.

"Only if you're sure. And I have to admit, I like that I won't be coming home to an empty house."

Cyd had told her children of her plans, too, as they took shape over the days since her hike, such as spending time in Sedona and visiting Aunt Lucy as much as possible. "No one's getting any younger," Cyd told them both over the phone after her first visit with Lucy. "I can't wait for you to meet her. She's an amazing lady. I'm sure she's got lots of good stories about your grandfather."

She hadn't yet told them about Bobby. There was time for that. And she hadn't forgotten her promise to herself to spend time alone. That, too, was important. Scary or not, she knew she needed to be by herself. "The old me needs to get to know the new me," she told Helen.

"Well, if one of them wants to pick up a few shifts around here, tell them both to feel free to give me a call," Helen quipped in response.

"So, has Nick started putting your money to good use?" Bobby asks, after the waitress has taken their order. "I haven't been in there since before the storm."

Cyd is aware of his eyes on her bare thighs, and she pulls self-consciously at the hem of her dress. He breaks into one of his dimple-framed grins.

"Stop it," she hisses, aware of how hopelessly charmed she is by his every move.

He continues smiling. "What? I'm listening. Go on."

"Things are moving along," she says, trying to ignore his penetrating gaze. "But only the upstairs dining room is usable. They think they can save the downstairs floors, which is great news. Nick's still trying to argue with me, of course. But he has to admit the insurance company is not moving nearly fast enough. He had no choice but to agree. And I have to admit, it feels pretty good to be able to contribute."

It was clear the entire town had benefited from Nick's ability to get The Osprey Cafe's kitchen up and running so soon after the storm. He had spent all his cash just to get the basics done as quickly as possible, piecemealing things together as best he could to have takeout available for all those in need. Many families went weeks without power. Nick started serving hot meals almost immediately, donating many of them. Even now, The O is one of the few restaurants for miles that is fully operational, paying the staff and serving the community.

Cyd had called Nick within days of returning from her hike. She had seen Jonathan Walker again in Phoenix and arranged to get access to the inheritance. Nick was at The O when she reached him, exactly where he had been for the previous six days, the minute the water and the muck receded enough to allow him through the streets. Cyd heard him take a deep breath on the other end of the line as soon as he answered.

She got right to the point, not even asking how he was doing; she knew how he was doing.

"I know you're going to want to argue with me, Nicky, but

there's no time for that. You're just going to have to set that masculine Kondilis family pride aside for now. We need to get on with it."

"Okay," Nick said, obviously confused. "Need to get on with what?"

She knew he had no idea what she would say next. She wasn't sure herself. What she did know is that she had to do something. She knew Nick was bone-tired and probably as fearful as he had ever been. The work that needed doing—first in preparation, then the cleanup and repair—was all-consuming. According to Helen, the storm and its aftermath had nearly brought him to his knees. How they would put the pieces back together, no one knew. She hadn't figured out her finances yet, but she would, she told herself. Yes, she had always let Loren handle their money, but that didn't mean she couldn't learn to do it now. She could rent the cabin or sell it if she had to. She could have Mae's Navajo rug collection appraised. According to Aunt Lucy and confirmed by her internet searches, they were worth more than she would have ever guessed. She had choices. She had people who were offering to help. Somehow, she believed she would find her way. All she knew for certain—the truth she felt in her heart and her gut—was that all the cash that Mae had given her was meant for this one purpose. She knew it as clearly as she had ever known anything.

"C? What do we need to get on with?" Nick repeated.

She realized Nick was waiting for her to continue, seemingly as grateful to be hearing her voice as she was to hear his. He seemed to have a level of patience reserved only for her. She searched for the right words.

"I'm going to transfer money into the business account. Use what you need to get things back to normal."

It obviously took a moment for Nick to understand. She felt like a different woman from the one who had left some twelve days prior. She supposed she sounded different, too. As soon as her words penetrated, he launched into his objections. Surely Cyd knew he had never taken a handout from anyone in his life, nor had his father or grandfather, and surely she didn't think he intended to start now.

"No way, C. I appreciate what you're trying to do, but it's out of the question."

She let him ramble. She let him vent. She pictured him looking around at the disastrous state of his kitchen, squeezing his rubber ball, and remained silent. When he finished, she went on to explain that she wanted to use the money Mae left her to help him, Helen, and Sophia with The O. It was her home, too, Cyd insisted. It symbolized the strength and resilience of the residents of Lola.

"It's the least I can do," she said, refusing to listen to any more of his pushback. "I will wire the money immediately. You'll pay me back when you're able—if you insist—and, if you're never able, that's fine, too. I want to do it, Nicky. It's important to me. Please."

"Okay," he said, finally. "But you're becoming a partner. That's the deal. Take it or leave it."

A smile hijacked her entire face. She was glad he couldn't see it.

"I'll take it," she said.

She heard a sigh of relief come across the airwaves.

"Thank you, Nicky," she said.

"You're welcome, C," he answered.

෬ࡉට

It is everything Cyd can do to extricate herself from Bobby's embrace and open the door of his Jeep. He has been kissing her for more than a few minutes as they sit in front of her house. She knows if she doesn't get out of his truck soon, every one of her good intentions will vanish into the balmy summer night.

"I have to go," she groans, placing her palms on his chest. "I'll see you tomorrow. I'll ride my bike over to the boat in the morning. Bo's home. You know I can't." Her voice is muffled as he kisses her one final time.

"Okay, go, quick, before I take you in the back and have my way with you," he says, letting go of her face.

"Geez, Swanson. Do you have to make everything sound so appealing?"

She walks up the driveway. Even though there is no other car, Bo has parked his truck off to the side the way his father always did. Bo's bedroom light is on, but the rest of the house is dark. She goes in through the unlocked front door, stepping on the brown paper taped down to protect the freshly sanded floors. Fern greets her with wiggly hysteria, and Cyd bends to give her a belly rub.

She walks into the kitchen and goes to the refrigerator. She stops when she sees the card Bo has stuck to the stainless steel. She had come and gone so quickly earlier, she hadn't noticed it there.

It is one of the postcards she had bought at Phantom Ranch with a photograph of the Grand Canyon on the front. The picture was taken at sunset, the great chasm aflame beneath a brilliant sky. She releases it from the magnet and turns it over. She sees her handwriting and the *Mailed by Mule, Phantom Ranch* stamp at the bottom. It is dated June 4, 2019, one day before her birthday, and it is addressed to Cyd Williams Carr.

Cyd walks to the back patio and sits, inhaling the familiar fragrance of the marshland. A large golden moon hangs over the bay, perfectly full. She stares at the sky, then down at the card, reading the words by the light of the moon. When she looks up again, a cloud has moved across. She waits, enjoying the stillness. She is tired. She is peaceful. She has no plan. The one thing she knows for sure is that she has made an honest effort today. And that everything, really, is exactly as it should be.

The cloud drifts past, allowing the moonlight to embrace her once again. She angles the card to the light and reads the words once more:

Dear Cyd,

Never stop exploring.

Trust a stranger.

Accept the invitation.

Get dusty and bathe in a creek.

Look up at the stars.

Always watch for signs.

Listen for the stillness at the bottom of the breath.

Love,
Cyd

THE END

Bottom of the Breath
Reflection Questions

How do you think Cyd managed to forgive Loren for his earlier infidelity? Do you think he was deserving of forgiveness? Do you think she was right to forgive him?

What do you think about the power of forgiveness in general? Are women too quick to forgive?

When we have to make hard choices in life, as we all do, is it possible to forget about the path not taken? Should we try to forget about those unlived lives completely, or is there some value to imagining what might have been? Is there a choice you made that you can't stop thinking about? Do you find the memories become more haunting with age?

Cyd has found a breathing and meditation method that helps calm her when she gets upset, as she did at the rim of the canyon. Do you have a helpful practice to calm yourself in times of personal crisis?

Do you think Cyd is wrong to jump into a new relationship so soon after her breakup with Loren? Have you ever regretted acting impetuously in love? Do you feel that Cyd and Bobby will stay together? If they do, do you think it is the best path for Cyd at this point in her life?

What do you think about the decisions made about Baker by Mae, Jesse, and Iris? Do you think family secrets can play an important role in a healthy family?

Why do you think Jesse went along with Iris' idea to keep the baby permanently rather than temporarily? Do you think Iris' Catholic beliefs were the reason she was so judgemental about Mae, or do you think she wanted a baby so badly she needed a way to justify her behavior?

Mae was obviously in a mental health crisis during her pregnancy. Did Mae deserve to keep her baby after what she tried to do? Did she deserve forgiveness? Did she deserve more time to decide?

Do you think Mae ever regretted her decision to give up her baby? How do you deal with big decisions you later regret?

Do you think Baker knew or suspected the truth about his parentage? Have you ever learned about a family secret and kept it to yourself?

Do you think Clint began to fall in love with Cyd? Can you maintain a friendship if one person is secretly in love with the other person?

Do you think Cyd's enlightenment in the canyon will stay with her? What do you think she'll need to do to keep the experience fresh in her mind?

Have you ever had such a life-changing experience? If you did, were drugs involved? Were you able to hang onto the feeling and the knowledge you gained during the experience? For how long?

Is it important for Americans to visit, support, and preserve our national parks? How does being in nature help you physically, emotionally, and spiritually?

Acknowledgments

I acknowledge with utmost appreciation the generosity of my earliest readers. Your input was invaluable. I took something from each of you and brought it forth into these final pages. I am grateful I didn't know any better than to ask you to endure the awfulness of those early drafts: Deborah Sharp, Carol Grisanti, Thea Sommer, Jennifer Grace, Ruth Anderson Coggeshall, Kim Allum, Valerie Burton, Joy Eritreo, John Eritreo, Donna Jenson, Betty Vandenbosch, and Janie Caragher. (Jeannie Calaverne, who has supported and encouraged everything I have done or attempted to do personally and professionally for the past thirty years, offered to read the early drafts, too, but I made her wait for the finished product.)

A special note of gratitude to Ruth Anderson Coggeshall, Elaine Blattner, and Pat DuMont whose wisdom, encouragement, and practical ideas helped spread the word about this book.

I want to acknowledge the support of my sister, Eileen Palmer, my niece, Erin Fettner, and my remarkable and loyal friends: Gayle Metcalf, Viola Yeotes, Jane Smith, Susan Weeks Holt, Camilla Matthews Miller, Christine Mills, Michelle Sabbia, Ragnhild Greve-Isdahl, Debbie Sheme, and Karen Gavrilov. I cannot adequately express my gratitude for your presence in my life. This book is dedicated to all of you. A special shout-out to Sev Sanders, who designed my perfect logo and is the living embodiment of my target reader, and to my technical assistants, aka those who answered my cries for help at all hours and without complaint: Connor Warren, Eric Fettner, Claire Fisch, and Tina Jordan.

Thank you, Greg, for all the quiet time, without which I couldn't have written any of this, and for showing me you cared about what I was doing long before anyone else even knew.

Thank you, Meteorologist Valerie Mills, for being my official expert on all things hurricane related. You make me proud every day.

Many thanks to my three talented editors. Rebecca Heyman's invaluable insight helped to shape and reshape this story. Pamela Grath dropped everything at the height of the summer rush at her Michigan bookstore to read for me. And nothing got past Anne Durette's sharp eye as we neared the end of this process. I am forever grateful to you all.

Many thanks to Brooke Warner, Lauren Wise, Shannon Green, and all the women at She Writes Press, where every day is a quest for excellence. I appreciate you all!

Thank you to my new friends, Tanya Farrell and Elena Stokes, at Wunderkind PR. Not only are they talented and energetic, but they share my fascination with astrology—a good sign that they were the right people to help me promote this work.

Thank you to the Grand Canyon Conservancy and to Joelle Baird at the National Park Service for helping to ensure the accuracy of my descriptions.

Last but certainly not least, I want to thank my children:

Bradford, my most valued editor, I am certain you, too, will write a book someday. Thank you for always being interested and making time to read whenever I needed you.

Valerie, you were in my heart throughout this process for many reasons, but primarily because I wanted to write a book that you would love. We both inherited our love of reading from

Gramma Honey, and I know she is smiling down on us.

Jackson, you read this book early on with an enthusiasm that inspired me to keep going (and to keep the sex scenes G-rated.) You reminded me not to take things too seriously.

Finally, to my granddaughter, Harvey, who already loves books in a way most young children do not. You, too, were in my heart every time I sat down to write. This story is sprinkled with life lessons passed down to me. May they guide you as you face, with grace and courage, whatever challenges life has in store. Give thanks each day, my darling, for tomorrow is guaranteed no one.

Author's Note

If you are interested in the work being done to protect and preserve Grand Canyon National Park for future generations, I urge you to contact Grand Canyon Conservancy @ grandcanyon.org.

Since I began writing this book in 2019, Indian Garden has been renamed to Havasupai Gardens out of respect for the Havasupai Tribe and Native Americans. Even though the story takes place before the name change, I refer to that area of the canyon as it is known now for sensitivity reasons.

The dates, the hurricane, and the town of Lola, Florida, are all fictional.

Regarding hurricane evacuation orders: For the purposes of this story, the plot required that the characters remain in their homes during a major hurricane. This should not be taken as an endorsement of ignoring evacuation orders. Having lived in Florida since 1981, I have personally evacuated many times to ensure my family's safety. I strongly urge everyone to follow the guidance of local officials and evacuate whenever instructed.

About the Author

Jayne Mills was born in Chicago and graduated from Florida Atlantic University. She is a Certified Investment Management Analyst and has written and taught about the relationship between wealth and wellness. An avid yoga practitioner since the 1980s, Jayne is a registered yoga teacher who has taught yoga and breathwork. She currently resides in St. Augustine, Florida.

Looking for your next great read?

We can help!

Visit www.shewritespress.com/next-read
or scan the QR code below for a list
of our recommended titles.

She Writes Press is an award-winning
independent publishing company founded to
serve women writers everywhere.